WHERE
THE HEART
LEADS

WHERE THE HEART LEADS

Susan Evans McCloud

Bookcraft
Salt Lake City, Utah

Library of Congress Catalog Card Number: 79-54208
ISBN 0-88494-381-X

First Printing, 1979

Lithographed in the United States of America
PUBLISHERS PRESS
Salt Lake City, Utah

To James Wylie

through whom I have become myself

and realized the vision . . .

ACKNOWLEDGMENTS

The author wishes to extend special thanks to the staff of the LDS Genealogical Library; to Gregory L. Seal for counsel on legalities and his concise, creative handling of the Buchanan wills; to Dr. and Mrs. Jack Johnson, both for medical advice and for the gracious use of their St. George home as a family retreat near the time of the completion of the book; to Brian and Tayva Patch for their sensitive, valuable advice and criticism in reading the manuscript as it was written; to James Russell, the "Scottish connection"; to George Bickerstaff, the "Sassenach" in the project; and most especially to James, Heather, Jennie, Jared, Rebeccah and Morag McCloud, without whose willing and patient sacrifice this book would never have come to fruition.

O Time, thou must untangle this, not I;
It is too hard a knot for me t' untie!

—Shakespeare, TWELFTH NIGHT

1

And, by that destiny, to perform an act
Whereof what's past is prologue; what to come,
In . . . my discharge.

THE TEMPEST

I t's something you must do, Andrew, and you know it. The plans are all laid. In the morning you leave, and that's that."

"If it were only as simple as you make it sound." Andrew squinted at Edwin against the sun. In the distance he could see the long silver streak that was Loch Lomond and, further yet, the uneven greens and grays of the hills. Ben Lomond stood grandly above them all, and Andrew noticed, with unusual clarity, the stray fragments of clouds that shifted and stirred along its green flanks. He realized, suddenly, that in all his twenty-four years he had never been very far from home. Was that part, then, of the uneasiness inside him?

"She's confined herself to her rooms," Andrew said to his cousin, "and refuses to come out."

"Your mother? You know her reasons well, Andrew. Actually, I think the sooner you're off, the better. Once it's really over it will be easier for her to accept."

"Without you I wouldn't be leaving them at all. You know that, don't you, Edwin?"

"It'll be my charm you're meaning, Andrew." Edwin's dark eyes lit with just a twinge of the mischief Andrew knew so well. "I've always had a way with the lassies."

"Especially Mother."

"Aye, but only because I'm so like yourself."

1

"Well, she loves you and trusts you, and—"

"And there's no call for fancy speech-making between us, Andrew. I'm off to the house to see Janet. If there's any appreciation to be shown, I'd far rather it come from her than from you."

Andrew couldn't help smiling as he watched Edwin stride off across the grass. He *was* charming! He had always had an easy, natural charm that he seemed able to manipulate at will. He turned now and spoke over his shoulder, his merriment spreading from his eyes into his voice.

"It's a rare opportunity to be able to step into your shoes, Andrew —a rare opportunity."

"Off with you! Tell Janet I'll be in for dinner."

Edwin whistled as he walked away, and Andrew was struck with the amazing likeness between himself and this younger cousin. Edwin was a little lighter of frame, more lean of build, but he had the same blue eyes, so dark that at times they seemed black in their intensity, and the mane of thick, black hair, a definite Buchanan legacy.

But there was more. Something about the arrangement of his face —the fine, narrow nose, the line of the chin, the deepset eyes beneath a jutting forehead. It was uncanny. How often had schoolteachers mistaken them for brothers when they were boys? How often had he looked at Edwin and seen mirrored the same expressions he felt on his own face: the set of his jaw, the lift of an eyebrow, the smile that began, almost reluctantly, at the corners of his mouth? He'd never enjoyed the dubious honor of being Edwin's look-alike before. But maybe now it would serve some good purpose at last.

He turned, and walked down to the pond, away from the house. Bieldmor House, named by the original Andrew from the Gaelic, meaning *great shelter*—which, indeed, it was: warm and massive and secure, sheltered by the little valley in which it sat and by the winding line of trees which further screened it from wind and storm and intrusion.

As Andrew walked, the acres spread around him, seeming to enfold him with a sense of strength and security. Six miles down the road in Paisley stood his father's mills. There were five mills if one counted the water works further up on the River Clyde. How many was it now? Four hundred and seventy-nine employees who turned out some of the finest thread and woven goods that were shipped all over the continent, and to Canada and America as well. And he mustn't forget the holdings in Lancashire, and the interest in the Glasgow National Bank. Wealth and influence Andrew was to inherit; and because of this he was boarding a plane in the morning to begin an incredible search in obedience to a decree whose iron hand could thus control his actions down the span of six generations.

Andrew Buchanan. *The* Andrew Buchanan, who founded the Canonaich Mills and Cotton Works in 1823. A weaver, himself, since the age of thirteen, he had shown amazing thrift and determination. Bit by bit he had saved enough to begin to employ others and establish himself as a manufacturer.

With a loan from his wife's father, the original Andrew became a large-scale dealer in fine cotton cloths and in what were called "fancy goods" as well: muslins and silk gauzes, cambric and lawn. The industry was then at its height, with 177 cotton factories in the Clyde Valley alone, success just begging to be purchased with a little industry and skill. Andrew possessed both qualities in abundance, and within ten years his three factories boasted 350 men and women operating 17,000 spindles and 264 steam-powered looms.

An image of this great-great-great-grandfather came easily to Andrew's mind. He had stood as a boy gazing up at the old man's portrait in the great hall many long hours, for then the legend of the missing son had held a sense of sweet and tragic romance to his impressionable mind. He had never looked far enough into the future to consider the part he, himself, would have to play when his turn came. He had merely loved to listen to how Andrew Buchanan, who had desired a long line of sons to perpetuate what he had created, had been granted only two sons—scant compared to the store he had anticipated. But bonny lads they were, and it was well known how Andrew had doted on them both. He educated them well and brought them up in habits of honesty and hard work.

The elder son, Andrew, was his namesake; but the younger, Charles, was his father's favorite. The boy possessed a certain spirit and warmth that the crusty, hard-disciplined man responded to. It was a story too good to be true: everybody happy and loving each other, with prosperity and security clacking away with each fly of the weavers' shuttles, thousands of times each minute, clack-clacking the promise of the future.

Then, as swiftly and as quietly as the waters of Loch Lomond pull away from the shore, Charles disappeared. No reason, no warning— just suddenly he was gone, leaving emptiness in all the places his presence had made warm and bright. The father would allow no ill to be spoken of his son. His faith seemed absolute. He knew something evil had befallen the lad, and each day he awoke with the determination that word would come concerning his lost son. But although his determination had worked so many miracles before, in this it failed.

He did not, however, sit idle. He notified his large network of friends and associates to keep watch for even the slightest clue to his son's whereabouts. He placed advertisements in every newspaper throughout Great Britain, describing the boy and offering rewards for news of him. But the days dragged into weeks and the weeks crawled by, until at last the months could be counted. And each day as it passed tore with jagged fingers of pain at the old man's heart. He was not one to lie down and lick his wounds; he was already acquainted with courage and her ways. But she exacted her terrible price, and the strain could be seen—in the lines around his mouth and the anguish in his eyes.

Several months had already passed when a stranger appeared at the door. He had spotted one of the advertisements in a London paper; he told that he had sailed with Charles Buchanan on board the vessel *Enterprise*, sailed for the New York harbor on that vast continent of America.

Where had Charles been going? The young stranger could not tell. From the conversations they had shared he could only divulge the fact that Charles had been excited concerning his purposes in America and that he had held high hopes that things would go well for him there. Did he mention his family, his home? Only to say that he had a brother he loved and a father whose good opinion he valued above all else.

What mystery did the stranger's information unravel or reveal? It served only to intensify the feeling of hopeless wonderment which possessed them all. But the stranger identified Charles so well there was no doubt in Andrew's heart that this had, indeed, been his son who had sailed so mysteriously for a far and foreign land.

4

After the stranger left, Andrew confided to his disappointed wife and elder son that the relationship between himself and Charles had been strained for the few months preceding the boy's disappearance. Charles had taken to wandering off for long hours at a time, no one really knowing where he was or exactly what he was doing. His interest in the mills had seemed to lag. The boy appeared less keen, less involved in things which had been life and breath to him before. Even some of the foremen at the mills had remarked that Charles seemed a wee bit strange and preoccupied, as though the lad wasn't quite aware of where he was or what was going on around him; and this behavior of his son bore heavily on the old man's jealous pride.

Concerned, his father had confronted Charles at last, but the boy would not confess his secret doings. This was one of Andrew's favorite parts of the old tale, for the story had it that the young son had looked his father square in the eye, bold in spite of the accusations which had been hurled at him in anger and dismay.

"I would never do aught to shame you, Father," he had answered, "nor to sully my own name. But what I am involved in I'm afraid ye'll no understand. Give me time, Father, and trust me yet a while."

But his father had responded in anger and hurt and, for the first time he could remember, he had parted with his son on unhappy terms. The subject had never been brought up between them again, but Charles had seemed more attentive and enthusiastic at his work, and his unexplained absences were less frequent than before. And so his father had convinced himself that his hard, firm attitude had brought Charles to his senses and had been good for the boy. Then suddenly, with no warning, the lad had disappeared.

So now, after the anxious months that had already passed, Charles's mother and brother understood that the old man had been bearing an additional burden of guilt and shame, feeling in his heart that his own hardness and lack of understanding had driven his son away. But what could have been so important to Charles that it could drive a wedge between them? Where had the lad gone off to, and why?

After that his mother watched the mails eagerly, knowing her boy's soft heart, certain that he would write to alleviate their suffering and fears. Week after week no letter came, but she reminded herself

5

that miles of land and ocean lay between them, and anything could happen to a letter which attempted to traverse that awful space; she struggled not to think of all the perils which could befall a man in that great unknown wilderness on the other side of the world.

Rather than sinking into despair and admitting failure, Andrew Buchanan only intensified his efforts to discover and communicate with his lost son. He spared no means, overlooked no vague possibility as he extended his search across the ocean. Advertisements were placed in all the major newspapers throughout the United States; several men in Andrew's employ spent months traveling the long expanses in search of a name, a face. But the months wore ruthlessly into years, and nothing substantial concerning Charles Buchanan was ever found. The older brother, Andrew, married and settled into the business. Did the father reconcile himself to the loss of his son? Who could say? He spoke of Charles only briefly, painfully, as the years stretched away, separating him even from his memories of the bright and handsome youth.

That had been more than a century ago, Andrew reflected, as he sat down on the low rock wall that bordered the pond on two sides. His thoughts were a turmoil within him. He pressed his hands against the rough stones, and their warmth seemed to flow into and through him. The old man's wall. He could look around him and name so many things, tangible things, that went back to the original Andrew Buchanan. The double row of oak trees that bordered the long drive; the tidy network of brick walkways that wandered in such subtle order through the gardens; the huge, gnarled rowan tree in the south meadow; the carriage house; the sturdy rock byre—and the great house itself: the entire west wing, as well as the main building, the mammoth highboard in the dining room, the delicate French chairs, the Chinese pottery, the silks and gauzes turned out by his own hand. Andrew could have gone on and on—things the old man had left his mark on, things that had survived him and would continue to survive. Why hadn't that been enough?

When the old man had died and his will and estates had been settled, an unusual legal clause came to light. Andrew Buchanan had left his lands, holdings, and business to his elder son, but had stipulated that 20 percent of all the profits be carefully figured yearly and set aside in a trust, a fund to be reserved for the descendants of his lost son,

Charles. And the one condition upon which the elder son's possession of his inheritance rested was the unusual stipulation that, upon the death of his father, he make a full, exhaustive search for those descendants. Certain conditions of the search were outlined, with a time requirement of no less than three months spent within the United States by the son himself, assuming he was an adult. At the end of twelve months after the father's death, if no discovery had been made, then the search might be abandoned—until the next generation! The clause required that the inheritance be perpetually reserved, and that the son following repeat the search for descendants, for heirs to the fortune of Charles Buchanan.

So the fruitless search had been carried on by son after son, while the money in the trust grew and compounded, sitting uselessly in darkened vaults, lost to life and use and joy, just as the unknown men and women for whom it existed seemed undiscoverable and lost. Now, since his father's death, Andrew had for the first time some real idea of just what sums of money this idiotic trust represented.

With a sudden, aching loneliness Andrew missed his father; Alexander Buchanan, who had always been both his teacher and his friend. Whoever would have thought that a man like his father—so healthy and vigorous, so vital, so alive—could suffer from such a senseless thing as a heart attack and be instantly, irrevocably dead? Andrew shivered, in spite of the pulsing warmth of the May sun on his head and shoulders. Why had he taken his father's closeness so for granted? Why had he assumed that there would be time—time to do all they wanted to do, to say all they wanted to say?

This line of thinking was senseless; it was getting him nowhere. He had gone over and over it so many times already. And now, the months since November and his father's death had slipped too quickly away, and Andrew could no longer avoid the inevitable responsibility —this journey into the unknown which loomed in such dark uncertainty before him.

He rose from the wall, brushing the crumbled bits of loose cement from his clothes. Looking up he saw Janet coming out of the garden and across the lawns. He was late, then! How long had he been sitting here, mulling over his troubles, feeling sorry for himself?

He started toward her with long strides. She waved her hand to

7

him and broke into a gentle run. Her long hair seemed to float around her face, and Andrew realized how graceful the girl was. Even Janet didn't want him to leave. Their father's death had been very difficult for her; she seemed more sensitive now, more easily hurt.

Andrew shuddered, thinking momentarily of those awful days following his father's death. Janet had made a brave effort to immerse herself in her usual holiday preparations for Christmas and the even bigger celebration of the New Year, but only a very thin pretense covered the aching despair which wore away her bright spirit. Janet was used to being pampered by her father; she had lost the first joy of her life in losing him.

As she drew nearer Andrew stopped and watched her coming. She looked so much like a woman that it frightened him. Seventeen. He guessed that was more woman than he wanted to admit. What a delicate blue her eyes were! Fragile and pale, like the sky washed clear after a summer storm. She possessed none of the dark Buchanan looks. Her skin was fair and her hair a warm blend of gold and brown and red.

"Stop frowning so, Andrew. It makes you look fearsome." She laughed lightly as she took his arm and headed him back toward the house.

"I'm sorry you had to come for me, Janet."

"I'm not. I wanted some time alone with you."

"Something special?" Andrew hoped his concern didn't show itself in his voice.

"Not really. I just wanted you to myself for a little while. I just wanted—well, I wanted to make sure I didn't send you off unhappy."

"Unhappy?" Andrew couldn't help sounding surprised.

"Yes, unhappy. Well, you know Mother's making a fuss—"

"Do you think she'll relent?" Andrew interrupted.

"Mother never relents. You know that, Andrew. You'll just have to leave her to Edwin and me. But I know you've been afraid I'll do the same thing—make a fuss. I want you to know I'll be just fine now that Edwin's here. I don't want you to worry. You have enough to think about right now."

As she finished speaking she smiled at him, the same soft, elfin little smile she had used with him since she was a mere infant. Andrew had a difficult time replying. He slipped his arm around her waist and gave her a brief hug. He wanted to be able to say, "I'm not really concerned about leaving Mother to Edwin. I know he can handle her—more easily almost than I can myself. If I could only be that certain of him in other ways. . . ."

Leaving business matters in his cousin's hands was somewhat of a risk, Andrew knew. Edwin was brilliant and capable; of that he had no doubts. But would his old weakness get in the way?

It was three, perhaps four months now since the last time Andrew had given in and covered Edwin's debts for him. He couldn't keep away from the betting shops, and sometimes the sums he lost were staggering. But what bothered Andrew even more than the gambling itself was Edwin's complete lack of contrition. He seemed to feel he was entitled, somehow, to live this way, and Andrew knew that he resented the fate which had not provided him with the means he felt he deserved.

Ever since Andrew could remember, anything with the element of risk or chance had held an almost mesmeric fascination for Edwin. Perhaps Andrew shouldn't encourage the lad by bailing him out as he did. But he couldn't help it; Edwin was nearly impossible to refuse. He had never told Janet or his mother of Edwin's gambling, so he couldn't appeal to them for help now. He kicked at the gravel beneath his feet. Well, he would just have to trust the safeguards he had set up, and hope that what sense of honor Edwin possessed would work in his favor.

He wondered, with a surge of curiosity, if Edwin had had a similar arrangement with Andrew's father when he was alive? How would his father have handled it? He wished he knew. He felt suddenly very young and inexperienced, and it bothered him.

He pushed his hair back from his forehead impatiently. He would stop worrying over all these things he could not control and enjoy his last few hours at home. He took Janet's hand and asked her a question, listening to the soft, pleasant sound of her voice as they walked the last few yards to the house.

2

The leaves were still dripping, as if they had soaked up all of yesterday's rain they could hold, and the moisture gods of the cornlands were still not satisfied. The July air was too heavy to admit the sun; a weak, murky light did the best it could to brighten the humid day.

Hannah knew she should go home. The interview for her article on the Hamilton Fair and Horse Show had gone well. But there had been so much information that her notes were sloppy and disjointed. If she didn't recopy them now, while everything was fresh in her mind. . . . She couldn't help it. She just could not face sitting down to her typewriter in that cheerless house. So she turned the car off Highway 96, down Parley, into the old city. She would only stop at a spot or two, then her father ought to be back from his summer classes at the high school and her grandma home from Ladies' Aid, and it would be time for lunch.

At the corner of Parley and Bain she stopped. Parley became a gravel road here, leading down to the river, and Bain was little more than a dirt path heading off through the field to her left. She parked in front of the Seventies Hall. There were no other cars. Good! To the left of the building, loosely enclosed within a log fence, four horses grazed quietly, switching only occasionally at the pockets of flies and mosquitoes that hummed around them. The heavy peace made Hannah sleepy. She slipped into the building and sat down on one of the long benches. The cool wood against her back relaxed her even more. She settled against the smooth wood and closed her eyes.

Some would have thought this an unusual pastime for a girl of twenty, but Hannah thought nothing of it. She had lived in Nauvoo her whole life—that is, in what might be called the new city of Nauvoo, which consisted of eleven hundred people and boasted one main street with a bank, a post office, a make-shift library, a few cafes, and a nickel-and-dime store. It was a quiet, sleepy little Illinois town.

But the old city of Nauvoo had been something different altogether. Settled by the Mormons in 1839, Nauvoo quickly grew into the largest, loveliest city in the state of Illinois, with a population at times totalling twenty thousand. More than 250 brick homes were built, as well as hundreds of frame houses. And every business and industry conceivable flourished under the hands of these intelligent, industrious people.

But in June of 1844 Joseph Smith, the prophet leader, was killed by a mob in nearby Carthage. And in February of 1846, under conditions of severe persecution, the main body of Mormons crossed the Mississippi in wagons and began the long, tortuous trek to a remote desert spot in the midst of the Rocky Mountains.

The stories had always seemed so real to Hannah. Even as a child she could picture the women, huddled in the Iowa wilderness under tents and makeshift shelters to avoid the freezing, drizzling rain. She recalled reading that on the second night out nine women gave birth to babies under these pathetically primitive conditions; gentle women, accustomed to the graces and comforts of their own homes. Hannah had always tried to imagine how they felt as they thought, perhaps, of their clean, warm houses across the river, knowing that the future held fear, danger, and hardship—how much hardship before they would again know the beauty and peace they longed for?

Hannah's sensitive heart thrilled to the spirit of Nauvoo and its past. Something about the Mormons—their history, their character, their beliefs—had always fascinated her, capturing her sense of romance and wonder. So, almost unknowingly, Hannah had made herself acquainted with as many of the old stories and legends as she could. She kept abreast, too, of all the changes as the deserted parts of the city had become transformed and restored. Something in her felt at home here, and there wasn't an inch of the old city she didn't appreciate and love.

Hannah realized suddenly that the room was filling up with people. The guide had come down to show them through, and was explaining how the building had been constructed and the dedicatory services held in December of 1844, six months after the death of Joseph Smith. Someone coughed; a baby was fussing near the back of the group. Hannah turned around to look. There were two families, an older couple—and a young man, tall and dark. He asked a question, but she wasn't close enough to hear. The group began moving out, filtering up the two quarter-turn staircases in the vestibule. Hannah rose and followed them quietly.

At the top of the stairs Hannah stopped. The young man was talking. She found herself completely enthralled by the sound of his voice. At first she thought the accent was English. But as she listened she caught certain elements that made it more difficult to identify. What a lilting, musical rhythm his words possessed! And he was certainly full of questions, one right after another. Hannah tried not to stare at him as she wandered among the glass cases of "curiosities" that had been brought back to Nauvoo from distant lands by the early Mormon missionaries.

All at once the man was right beside her! Hannah stared straight ahead with all her might, not focusing on any of the items in front of her, but struggling to resist the impulse to look up at the stranger. It was silly, she knew. Why was she acting so strangely? Then, right at her elbow, his soft voice asked another question. She hazarded a glance, and realized that the guide had just turned to address another tourist and hadn't seemed to hear him. She noticed that he knit his brow in frustration, as though the answer to his question really mattered somehow. Incredibly she heard her own voice saying, "Nauvoo is a Hebrew word meaning 'lovely spot' or 'beautiful place'."

He turned and looked at her, and it was all Hannah could do not to look away. His blue eyes were piercing and bright, but they seemed to hold a gentleness, like his voice.

"Thank you, miss. That's right. They told us that at the first spot —what do they call it, visitors' center, or something? But I'd forgotten. It's a lovely name, isn't it?"

"Yes. I love to say it. Joseph Smith chose the name. He must have known no other name could fit the city he was going to create."

The stranger raised his eyebrows and looked at Hannah appraisingly. "You're an assistant here, then?"

Hannah couldn't help smiling. She didn't realize just what a beguiling mixture of shyness, pride, and warmth the little smile betrayed.

"Oh, no. But I live here. And I suppose I know as much about the old city as anyone does."

"Good!" The stranger returned her smile with one that hesitated mischievously at the corners of his mouth before breaking out into a warm grin. "I've been making a nuisance of myself, I know. No one else seems to ask any questions! Would you, well . . . might you be able to . . ."

"Give you a private kind of tour, and answer all your questions? I'd love to."

It was that simple. It was that simple! Hannah couldn't believe it! Her heart was racing, but she smiled to herself. He was taking her at her word. She had answered three questions and was working on the fourth by the time they reached the bottom of the winding stair.

At the landing the stranger paused. "Forgive me for not introducing myself up there. I got rather carried away with that book collection. My name is Andrew Buchanan."

"And you're from—"

"Scotland. Not far from Glasgow. Loch Lomond country."

So that was the accent. Scottish!

"Loch Lomond country," Hannah breathed. "How—"

"Romantic? Yes, it is. It really is. I love it."

Hannah could feel the increasing warmth, the sincerity in his voice. He was homesick.

"And yourself?" he prompted softly. Hannah blushed.

"Hannah Martin. But I feel more comfortable with Nan."

"Hannah. Is that a common American name?"

She laughed. "A hundred years ago, yes. It's quite old-fashioned."

"I like it. And Nan as well. Where to now, then, Miss Martin? What do you suggest?"

On a sudden impulse Nan decided she would take him to the burr oak. It was one of her favorite spots, but she ought to keep it as something special, till the very last. Did she feel she had to impress him right from the start? Or did she realize that, since the burr oak stood off the beaten track, she would be able to have Andrew Buchanan all to herself?

"Follow me," she said, and he held the door for her as they walked outside. "Would you like to walk? It's a little way."

"I'd love to."

Hannah turned right, heading down Parley to the west, away from the city, toward the river. She was acutely aware of everything. The crunch of the gravel under their feet, an angry bumblebee that brushed her arm, a wet leaf that pasted itself against Andrew's dusty shoe.

"They call you Andrew, don't they?"

"Andrew, and 'lad', and 'you there'—and a lot of other things."

"I mean—well, I somehow couldn't see you as an Andy."

They walked on a few moments in silence.

"You're a Mormon, then?" he asked her suddenly.

Hannah was startled; almost embarrassed. No one had ever taken her for a Mormon before!

"Heavens, no! I mean, no, but I can see where you might think so."

"Yes, you seem to know so much."

"And to love it so well? I know it shows. I do love Nauvoo. I have since I can remember."

They talked now, and Hannah ceased to notice anything, save the sound of his voice and the things he was saying, and the feeling of really talking to someone, saying things that mattered, and being listened to and understood.

As they neared the site Hannah slowed down. The oak was easy to spot, and as soon as Andrew caught sight of it he whistled appreciatively under his breath.

"It's a grand tree, that."

"Would you like to know the story? Long before the Mormons came, this land belonged to the Indians. These were noble forest Indians who had lived here for hundreds of years. They called their settlement Quashquema. Captain James White, the first permanent white

14

settler here, made a treaty with the Sac and Fox tribes that they would leave Quashquema and go west.''

"Just like that?"

"Just like that."

"What were the terms of the treaty? What did they receive in exchange for their lands?"

Hannah said the words carefully, watching for his reaction. "Two hundred bags of corn."

"Ach!" he turned aside, indignant. "I'm thinking Captain James White and his kind were much like the Sassenachs who ravaged the Scottish highlands, robbing the clans of their ancestral homes."

"It was a pity. I've always thought so. Over there stood the ferry landing, and right here is the spot where Captain White built his large stone house."

"And the tree?"

"This is the very tree under which the treaty was supposedly signed."

"An unhappy spot." He leaned against the scarred trunk, his fine black eyebrows knit in concentration. Did it really upset him that much to think back on the tragedy of the Indians? Or was there something else as well?

"What are you thinking?" Nan asked the question as softly as she could, her voice warm with concern.

The sparkle returned to his eyes, but he didn't smile. "Oh, you've made me think of something I've been happily forgetting these last few hours."

"I'm sorry."

He moved then and came near to her. "No, lass, you don't understand. Let me explain."

He took her arm and they walked, down by the river among the logs and rotting stumps, under the full willow where there was some protection from the insects and the sun. Andrew told her of the death of his father and the devastation it had caused; the awesome loss that nothing else could fill. Expressed in his beautiful, melodic voice the story held even more pathos for Nan than it otherwise would have. He told of his sister and his mother, and Nan found herself saying something she had never said to anyone before.

"At least you had your father this long, with a lot of memories to fall back on. And I think you really love your mother, as well. You're actually quite lucky, Andrew."

As soon as she had spoken, Nan was sorry. Andrew simply gazed at her. Was the sympathy she read in the depths of his blue eyes for himself, or for her?

"You're right on both counts. But you aren't all that lucky yourself, are you?"

Nan opened her mouth, but it was difficult to form the words, and she was afraid the sound of her voice would betray the depths of her feelings.

"How did you know? I mean, how did you guess? I was seven when my mother died. The oldest. Mama's little darling. We were really very close."

"I'm sorry, Nan. I'm so sorry. What a beastly thing for a little girl to suffer!"

Andrew was dismayed by the strength of his response to this girl. Was he merely playing the part of a concerned big brother? Was she a substitute for Janet and his feelings about her? How else could he feel so much, so soon—toward a perfect stranger?

"But you still have your father, haven't you? What about him?"

Nan hesitated before answering him, and a slight, wistful smile played around the corners of her mouth, giving her face an almost childlike appeal which wasn't lost on Andrew as he stood watching her carefully.

"He's a very stern man, my father. And since Mother's death he hasn't given much of anything to anybody."

"He's afraid of getting hurt again."

"I know that. I've figured it out. But it doesn't make it any easier."

Nan was appalled at herself. She had said far too much. She was the most private person she knew. And here she was, crying on the shoulder of a stranger! How could he possibly have any respect for her now?

"You've never actually said that to anyone else before, have you?"

Hannah shook her head.

"Well, then, it's about time. And I'm glad I was here to listen."

He meant it. As he said the words, Andrew knew that he really meant it. Nan sensed his sincerity and relaxed. He understood, somehow; she could tell that he did. It was going to be all right.

"Let's start back, Andrew. The mosquitoes are getting awfully thick down here."

"Yes, it's 4:30, and I must have kept you from your lunch."

"Four-thirty! I don't believe it!"

Nan laughed, although a little feeling of panic began to rise inside her. *Whatever will they say when I get home?* she thought.

In spite of her hurry, the walk back to town passed too quickly for Nan. As she got into her car and turned the key in the ignition, the thought came, *I'm not even the same person who last got out of this car.*

Andrew was leaning on the open window frame. "What is the very nicest eating place in town?"

"The Nauvoo Hotel."

"What time shall I come for you?"

Hannah laughed, and the merriment in her voice was deep and real. "You're hopeless, Andrew, hopeless."

"An hour—an hour and a half?" Andrew persisted.

"No! I'm afraid I'll need longer than that." Hannah thought of her jumbled notes that needed retyping.

"Kindly write your address for me, Miss Martin, and I shall come to collect you at 7:30 sharp."

Hannah handed him the paper, glad that her handwriting was pretty and would make a good impression. She was aware that he stood watching her drive away. And she realized, as she steered the car the familiar route home, that with all the things they had talked about, she hadn't even told Andrew she was a writer. How strange. That was the thing she was the most proud of, the first thing she usually made certain to bring up, if possible. And although Andrew had told her of his father's business and the textile mills, he hadn't mentioned what he was doing in America. There was still a lot to talk about!

3

Is it possible
That love should of a sudden
take such hold?

TAMING OF THE SHREW

The sultry day had melted itself away. A cool little breeze blew up from the river, and the summer evening spun its gentle spell. Nan felt in total harmony with the beauty around her. Things at home had gone much more smoothly than she had dared to hope; her father wasn't even home when she arrived, and her grandmother was lying down with a headache. Julie, Nan's younger sister, thought she had a date with Tom, and Nan hadn't corrected her. Tomorrow would be soon enough for explanations.

As Hannah and Andrew wandered around the lawns and gardens waiting for their reservation to be called, Hannah was acutely aware that she was with the best-looking man there. The guests ranged from wealthy, well-dressed tourists to teenagers in sleeveless knit tops and jeans; and all of the women noticed Andrew.

As he seated her at their table, Andrew placed his hand over hers for a brief moment.

"You're a 'nut-brown maiden' if I ever saw one."

She looked confused, and he smiled warmly, lights leaping into the blue eyes.

"A 'nut-brown maiden'—there's a song by that title. Nut-brown hair and nut-brown eyes; it's a lovely combination. They write songs about girls like yourself in Scotland."

If anyone had asked Nan about that night—what they ate, what they drank, where they walked after dinner—she would not have been

18

able to reply. The entire evening blended into nothing but a backdrop against which her eager mind enacted the fascinating, implausible tales Andrew wove for her: the ancient grandfather who founded the family fortune, the lost son, the amazing will with the power to control men's lives long after the hand that wrote it was dead and cold.

"It's as far-fetched a tale as I've ever heard," she told him, her eyes on fire. "So it must be true; no one could possibly have contrived it. And you know what Lord Byron said."

"What did Byron say?"

"For truth is oft'times strange," she quoted, "stranger than fiction."

He took her home at last, but she couldn't sleep. How could she, with so much singing and surging inside her? Too much to really sort out and understand. Nan lay awake long hours, because she was too much alive for the safe forgetfulness of sleep to claim her without a struggle.

When Nan awoke the next morning the wonder was still there. She felt as though her life were just beginning, as though a mist had been removed from before her eyes, and she could see with pure clarity into her own heart, and into the heart of life, itself. Her time spent with Andrew was not only wonderful and romantic, it was real. She felt as if all that was good and of value within her was being released, given the breath of reality for the first time.

They toured every building in Nauvoo, even the ones Andrew had already seen. They sampled gingerbread cookies baked in the bustle oven at Scovill Bakery; admired the blacksmith as he operated the old-fashioned forge; ate a lunch of hard salami, Nauvoo bread, and cheese in the park. Time kindly turned her back, allowing them to wander those regions which exist, if but briefly, in a sphere all their own, outside her binding power. It didn't matter what they did—a night on the town in Keokuk, or a quiet stroll by the river, with the lightning bugs tracing patterns of golden light, blinking pinpricks of brilliance among the trees and far out across the dark water. Everything they did together had the feel of happiness about it.

Only when she returned home, at such times as she could no longer avoid it, did the hard facts of daily existence press down upon Nan.

"The newspaper called today. They have an assignment they want you to take."

"Tom came over. What should I tell him? That you simply dropped out of existence?"

Her father made it clear that he thought the stranger must be "out for what he could get"; what other interest could possibly exist in a relationship of such short duration? Her grandmother thought she was playing the fool and would get her heart broken. But then she deserved to, if she wouldn't listen to good advice when it was offered. No one seemed to really care, much less to try to understand. It was as if they expressed their opinions, and then left her to her fate, her doom. Nan ignored them all, just as she ignored the one little spot inside her that would ache whenever she counted too many tomorrows ahead, and wondered what next month would be like, and the following month, and the month after that. . . .

For Andrew it was a time of renewal. His wanderings, his hopeless searchings from one strange place to another, had exhausted him body and spirit. He had worked methodically across the country, but the country was so vast! He had traveled the space of a dozen Scotlands when he found himself in Chicago. Here the immensity of the country hit him full force, and when he inadvertently mentioned that Mark Twain was one of his favorite writers, and someone said—with more enthusiasm than he had heard in weeks—that he ought to run down to Hannibal, the author's home, site of the Tom Sawyer stories, Andrew jumped at the opportunity.

Hannibal had enchanted him, and the Mississippi had captured his heart. For the first time during the weeks in America he was enjoying himself. And he hated for it to end. Several people in Hannibal had suggested that he cross the river and tour the old Mormon city of Nauvoo. And so, against all likelihood, he was here. And he was staying! Long past the most generous allotment he had given himself in his mind. And the longer he stayed, the harder it was to leave. Nothing like this had ever happened to Andrew before, and he knew it. And he didn't know what to do about it.

The river road that winds between Nauvoo and Hamilton on the way to Carthage is one of the most picturesque stretches in Illinois. Andrew took it with Hannah one afternoon, then toured the jail where

Joseph Smith was shot. Charming in its restoration, the jail still held traces of the hatred and horror that possessed it that night.

"I'm very impressed with Joseph Smith," Andrew told Nan. "There's a spirit about him that's hard to deny."

Nan was sympathetic. How could she be anything else? It would be impossible to love Nauvoo without holding at least a warm respect for the man who was its creator.

"What he accomplished in the space of so short a life was more than impressive. He reminds me of William Wallace, the great hero who prepared Scotland for King Robert the Bruce. A man strong in every way, but without guile, who suffered a martyr's death with dignity."

On the drive back to Nauvoo Nan listened to tales of the Scottish heroes—first Wallace and Bruce, then all the lesser yet still colorful men: the Black Douglas, Bonnie Dundee, even the daring Rob Roy. She loved it. As Andrew spoke of his homeland he came to life, and seemed to Nan the very embodiment of those virtues he spoke of with such love.

Nan suggested, for the second time, that Andrew look into the vast genealogical library the Mormons had in Salt Lake City. She felt that, if his answers existed anywhere, it would be within the extensive archives of the Mormon Church. Andrew promised he would go to the visitors' center in Nauvoo the next morning and ask for more details. Then, after a little silence, they spoke of other things. For what could perusal of that course bring, even in their talk, but the inevitable?

North on Partridge Street, a little over a mile along the main graveled road, they stood on Lookout Point. Here they gazed down upon the wide sweep of the Mississippi, graceful even in her lazy summer murkiness. Beyond the river lay Iowa, and the blendings of water and land were lovely to see. Here one could get an idea of what Nauvoo must have looked like when the Mormons first claimed it in 1839. Andrew and Nan sat long hours, talking, wondering, and admiring.

Somehow they both knew when the time had come. They met down by the river, under the willow where they first had talked. Nan expected to feel angry and depressed; hurt inside. She hadn't expected this strange, accepting calm which enveloped her.

"I'd be glad to drive you to the airport, Andrew."

"No, I couldn't bear that kind of parting, lass. It's better here, like this."

He took her into his arms and kissed her; so softly, so gently, but with a power that surged through her being. He kissed her once more, then stood back to survey her. His eyes were so warm and deep that Nan felt entranced by them, powerless to look away.

"I shall write you often, Nan. Let you know how things develop."

"Salt Lake is thirteen hundred miles away."

"I'll keep in touch." He spoke it with such firm purpose that Nan's heart thrilled. "You take care of yourself, Hannah Martin, with me not here to look after you."

How will you ever be here to look after me again? her heart suddenly cried out. *Ever?*

"It's time to be going, then." He turned, as if to leave, then came back and took her hands in his.

"Please don't look so miserable, Nan. We'll work something out. You must believe it—you must." He kissed her mouth, her forehead, her eyes that were trembling with tears. Then he was gone; with only the faintest whisper of movement in the long arms of the willow to show where he had passed.

4

*I will go lose myself
And wander up and down to view
the city.*

THE COMEDY OF ERRORS

The crisp, tidy pages were closely covered with names; Richards and Allens and Andersons dating back to the 1800s, the 1700s—one as far as 1433. His name stood there, too, neatly typed with the rest. Bradley Richards, son of Stephen Richards, son of Joseph Richards . . . but it wasn't really him, and the names were not really his own. Why did it have to matter so much? Still, after all these years?

His ten-year-old daughter came in with a book and cuddled in the corner of the sofa. Four children he had now. It seemed with the coming of each one, he loved the whole lot of them more. Whose children were they? Where did they really belong? Was he going to have to tell them the same tale he had been told, the story that had shattered his security and self-image when first he heard it?

Brad had always known that his great-grandfather came west with the Saints from Nauvoo when he was little more than an infant, and survived the many hazards of the journey to carve out a place for himself in the valleys of the mountains as a man. Brad had always been proud of his pioneer heritage; most Mormons were.

But when he was nineteen years old Brad's father took him aside and told him that this great-grandfather, the youngest of the thirteen Richards children, was not really a Richards at all. He was an adopted son, given to Sister Richards to rear with her own. Given? By whom? Perhaps by a mother who didn't survive long enough to care for her infant herself? Certainly not by parents who didn't care!

23

Perhaps his father waited too long to tell him. At twelve—even at sixteen—he might have easily accepted the little incongruity, the question mark in his past. But now, launching into manhood, struggling for *his* future, establishing *his* name, he felt suddenly as though all the moorings that had secured him so long were wrenched away, setting him namelessly adrift in a vast sea of humanity, where everyone else but himself seemed to know who they were—seemed to belong.

His father was kind enough to answer the unspoken question in Brad's heart. No records had survived that bore the names of the real parents; things were often confused as the early Saints left Nauvoo. Perhaps a record had existed and had been lost, somehow. There was no way to know, no way to possibly find out.

Brad still remembered vividly how heavy, how warm his father's hand had felt as he laid it on his son's shoulder. They talked for a while, and by then some of the initial pain had subsided. But for months—for years—Brad would create fantastic dreams and stories concerning the lost ancestors; pathetic stories, really, thickly laced with romance, kept alive with the fierce strength of his desire.

He tried to comfort himself with his own religious convictions: he knew that after this life it would be worked out; he would know and be known, and all would fit into its proper place. And it wasn't as if he didn't love the Richards line; it was a noble family to be part of. But sometimes he needed more. Sometimes he felt he needed to know now.

So the old wound was troubling him again; irritated by something the stake president had said two weeks ago in conference. He had issued a challenge to the members of his stake to tackle their deep genealogical problems with faith and spiritual strength, using fasting and prayer to create some of the breakthroughs they desired.

Brad couldn't forget the impression those words had created within him. In his logical mind he knew that nothing short of an actual miracle could uncover his lost ancestry. But in his heart he knew he had to put the stake president's challenge to the test. He began a private program of fasting and prayer. He knew it would not be easy, working toward such an elusive goal. But he had confided in Jenny, and she had given him the sweet support he knew he would need to continue.

Brad was determined not to grow weary, but to carry on, month after month, if necessary, trusting the Lord, proving his promises to the faithful. Maybe others had tried in the past. But he had never tried. He knew, in order to live with himself in peace, that he had to make at least one real effort to uncover for himself the answers he was seeking.

The clouds began to clear. The immensity of white through which Andrew was being carried, with little sense of substance or proportion, diffused and spread, and beneath him lay a prehistoric wilderness. In the distance the violet-blue mountains, laced with snow, still merged into the blues and whites of the sky, but directly below him, tossed and scattered at random, Andrew gazed upon a mass of brown, wrinkled ridges; bits and pieces chewed up by some mighty force, then flung forth in breathless disorder. Some were ruffled in smooth, curving sweeps, others monstrously withered, dull and dry.

He had little time to savor the sight, for the plane was preparing for descent and already the city of Salt Lake was rushing to meet them —a city set in a valley, surrounded by mountains. Andrew could see the jagged line of houses creeping up the slopes, extending their claim higher and yet higher. His view of the city pleased him. And the mountains; how he had missed the sight and the feel of mountains! And these were so mammoth, standing rocky and stark against the sky.

Out beyond the city sat the lake from which it had derived its name. The Great Salt Lake. A desert kingdom. City of the Saints. All the lovely, romantic nonsense Nan had expressed so beautifully was nothing but a jumble of facts and feelings inside his head. What kind of people would he find these modern-day Mormons to be? He still had a picture of men in beards and high boots, women in worn, mud-spattered calico. But for the first time the search was something he looked forward to. He was anxious to begin, to get going. Why should there be this sense of excitement here, that he had never felt before?

Nan. Her image came so easily to his mind. Nan was the only new factor. Her spirit, her enthusiasm had influenced him, he knew. But he didn't want to think about it, examine it too closely. If he did, he was afraid it might explode into a force he couldn't handle or control. Now he needed all his energies and attentions trained upon the problem at hand. He needed a mind sharp, perceptive, uncluttered.

So he held his feelings at arms' length, dangling there, just inside the sphere of his awareness. He held them in reserve, regarding them as a treat, a reward he had promised himself at the completion of his search, upon fulfillment of his promise—the "coming home" from the journey to which he was bound. With a cushiony bump the plane touched ground and glided down the runway. Andrew was the first person on his feet and waiting at the door.

He rented a car at the airport and drove straight for the heart of the city. There were several nice hotels and motels, including a new-looking Hilton. But once Andrew discovered Temple Square and drove around a little to get his bearings, he realized that the stately old Hotel Utah was best situated for his purposes, being only steps away from the Church Office Building, which he counted as twenty-eight stories high, the tallest building in the city.

The city looked clean and friendly in the late afternoon sun. Several people smiled at Andrew as they passed on the street. He couldn't help noticing how cheerful everyone seemed, and that more of the women he saw wore dresses than in any of the other cities he had visited. He liked the elegant hotel and immediately felt at home there. By the time he got settled it was too late to begin any work. Tomorrow first thing he would locate the genealogical library. But now, since the mountains had swallowed the scorching desert sun, there was a cool, releasing freshness to the air. Andrew was eager to explore. Any direction he might pick as he stepped outside the hotel looked promising. He would wander, a willing guest, and let the city take him where it would.

Before the evening was over Andrew wore himself out with walking. He explored the little avenues above the hotel, discovering to his delight the small, fenced graveyard, unpretentious, hardly marked, where Brigham Young and some of his family were buried.

At first it puzzled him that this great leader, whom the Mormons were supposed to have so highly revered, should rest in such humble, almost obscure conditions. But as he thought about it he realized that monuments to Brigham Young stood all around him: the statue of Brigham, himself, that towered at the intersection of Main Street and South Temple, the temple and the tabernacle, Young's graceful houses which still stood, the schools, the industries—the state, itself, and the people who filled it—all were a tribute to the man and the work he had done.

Andrew walked back down State Street toward the inner city. It seemed wherever he looked he captured a different, breathtaking view of the many-spired temple, silver-gray and graceful against the evening sky. As he walked Andrew passed the Beehive House where Brigham Young had lived. The softly-lit windows revealed lace curtains edged with panels of heavy velvet drapes and, here and there, glimpses of the elegant paintings and statues and furnishings within. There was something charming here—a sense of warmth and peace which Andrew found beguiling.

Hungry after all the walking, Andrew headed down Main Street past the rich, elegant store front with the curious name he must ask about—Zion's Cooperative Mercantile Institution. Further down the street he discovered a little restaurant called the Shakespeare Dinner House where he ate a hot English sandwich, reminiscent of the food at home.

He had indulged himself all evening, and he was paying for it now. A sad, creeping loneliness overtook his spirit and he began to feel sorry for himself. He had brought it on, he knew, by thinking of Nan all evening, picturing her beside him, trying to imagine what she would say, how she would react, which places would give her the greatest delight. It was wretched. He not only had his homesickness to contend with, but this Pandora's box of new emotions unleashed within him.

He stepped out of the restaurant and was instantly aware of the transformation around him. Some hand in the heavens had lit the stars, but what mystic powers they might possess were rivaled by the jewels of man's creation—mile after mile of glittering lights, scattered generously about, tossed far up the mountains to meet the lowering stars. Andrew beheld a far-flung kingdom of throbbing, dancing, living light. Each prick of light was a gem of its own warmth and intensity. Strung together, massed together, they spun a magnificent spell, touching every corner, each shadow with their splendor.

The spell of lethargic loneliness began to dissolve. As he walked, Andrew's natural spirit and confidence revived themselves. He sensed that he was facing some of the most important choices and decisions of his life, and a wave of excitement swept over him. He was young, strong, and capable, and the sweetness of life was something he was only beginning to taste. All that was fine within him hungered for the challenge of grappling with fate on its own ground, wresting every dream and desire he had out of the hands of possibility into a singing, certain reality.

The next morning there was still a breath of coolness, a tinge of fresh canyon air in the city as Andrew crossed the plaza of the L.D.S. Church Office Building. There were few people about, but he noticed a pleasant, friendly-looking man approaching, and decided to question him for directions.

Brad Richards didn't at first notice the stranger, or the clean freshness of the morning air, or the colorful summer flowers along the walks, set so carefully to please the eye. It was four weeks now since he had begun his secret attempts, his spiritual probing into the darkness of the past. He had prayed more consistently than ever before, fasted, studied the scriptures, tried more than ever to live worthily in all respects. He wasn't discouraged, really, but he wondered if his efforts were in the realm of the ridiculous, beyond what intervention God can make in the affairs of man. When the young man spoke to him it took a moment for the question to register.

"The genealogical library? Right on the main floor," he explained. "Just go through those doors straight ahead, and walk inside the building to your left. You can't miss it."

The stranger thanked him and walked away. What a lovely accent he had, Brad thought. Not English. Irish, possibly, or Scottish. He walked on, wondering why he was torturing himself so. He thought about it a moment and decided that, despite the frustration and doubt concerning the outcome of his pursuit, this kind of spiritual discipline felt good. He didn't want to give up, not yet. Nevertheless, the thought kept teasing at the back of his mind with fluttering unrest: *What is it you expect? What can possibly pierce the mute silence of generations?*

5

*Therefore, out of thy
long-experienced time,
Give me some present counsel.*

ROMEO AND JULIET

It was no use. No matter where she went or what she did, Andrew was there. Every spot held memories of him, and the emptiness was even worse than Nan had expected. As soon as he was gone, he simply ceased to exist as far as everyone else was concerned. His name was never mentioned around the house. What Nan thought and what she was feeling were her own business. As if with a sigh of relief, everyone settled back into the old routine of things, before Nan's "unpleasant interruption." And "everyone" included Tom Briggs.

He had casually dropped by the house the day after Andrew left. Just sat and talked for a while. Quiet. Pleasant. Nothing pushy. But it was there. The subtle pressure; the expectation. How Tom had made the transition from being just "one of the boys who likes Hannah," to "the suitor most likely to succeed," Nan was never quite sure. Perhaps because there were so few boys around in the first place. And although Tom was quiet and unassuming, he was ambitious in his own way.

He had known what he wanted since he was six years old: to play with motors. And surely he had the skill, both in his head and in his hands. Straight out of high school he had worked a year as apprentice in the best shop in town. Mr. Ives swore his business had increased 200 percent since Tom had put those new ideas of his to work.

Tom did have a certain knack; Nan couldn't deny that he was successful within his own field. And she couldn't forget her own enthusiastic gratitude when she had been looking for her first car and he had hunted out the creamy little '66 Mustang, repairing and restoring it to beautiful condition. By local standards Tom was making good money by now. As far as her father and grandmother were concerned there was a long list of positives—every reason in the world why Nan should be interested, even flattered by Tom's attention. And, to top it all, as Grandma would say, he adored the ground Nan walked on. What else could she possibly want?

Nan knew what else she wanted. She looked at Tom now as he walked beside her. Everything about him—his mannerisms, the things he said, the way he assumed certain rights with her, assumed she was attracted to him in turn—all this annoyed her, angered her. And she couldn't help comparing Tom to Andrew; in every way Tom fell short. For, though she had always cared for Tom and appreciated his good, gentle qualities, she had never come near to loving him. There was no real communication between them; no speaking of spirit to spirit.

Nan, in spite of being somewhat shy during her growing-up years, had always held a certain disdain for boys. At first it had been for the gangly boys of thirteen and fourteen who had interrupted her romantic reveries to show her their rock collections, or ramble on about their prowess on the baseball field.

And it didn't get better with time. Many of the boys Nan dated offended her with that same assumptiveness Tom was guilty of: assuming they were showing her a good time, when they were boring her to death talking only of themselves, then assuming, because they had shown her a good time, that she would be willing and rewarding in return. They discovered with Nan it didn't work that way. She was kind, but she was firm. And, if she thought it once, she had thought it a dozen times as a boy tried to kiss her: *Just who do you think you are?*

There had been a few boys Nan had really cared for, whose company she had genuinely enjoyed. They stood out like welcome oases in the desert of her teenage years. Through it all she had hugged to herself her secret desires, nurtured her dreams about what real love would be like.

"Nan, that's the second question I've asked you, and you haven't said a word. What's the matter?"

Nan had never been more grateful for the darkness, as she felt her cheeks go hot and flushed. "I'm sorry, Tom. I've been such miserable company tonight."

"That's all right. I think you're tired. I'd better get you home, I guess."

Kind. Solicitous. Why didn't he ask her what she was thinking? What she felt? Didn't he want to know?

"I need to talk to you, Nan. It's time you and I had a good long talk. But it's waited this long. I guess it can wait a little longer."

So it was coming. It was coming to that at last. Nan felt herself tremble as Tom helped her into the car.

"Thank you, Tom. For some reason I don't think I could talk about anything serious tonight."

He said goodnight at the door. Thank heaven no one else was there to invite him inside. Gratefully Nan slipped into her bedroom and flung herself onto the bed. Why was she feeling so sorry for herself? She had known all along that this time would come, sooner or later. Andrew's presence had probably acted as a catalyst, though—opened Tom's eyes, made his sleepy mind realize that perhaps he had better do something. Nan hated to feel manipulated! She sensed her father and grandmother were aware of Tom's intentions; that everyone was waiting to get the awkward moment over with, waiting for everything to be settled.

It had always been easy for Nan to put Tom off before; not that she had wanted to "keep him dangling," wanted to dishonestly encourage his attentions. But it seemed no matter what she did, no matter how carefully she tried to explain herself, Tom always kept coming back for more; quiet, patient—assuming again—assuming that someday Nan would come around, see it his way, accept things as he wanted them to be. Nan knew she could no longer put him off. And she was afraid of what would happen—with Tom, with her father, with her grandmother—when she told him *no*.

It took her a long time to get to sleep, and when she finally slept her mind swam in and out of a series of strange, disjointed dreams, where she would be with Andrew, but he would suddenly change before her eyes, and it would be Tom whom she was walking with and smiling at. The dream man never smiled at her; whether he was Andrew, or whether he was Tom, the man in the dream never said a word. He just walked beside her, and wherever they went, willow trees grew. Tall graceful willows, that quivered and whispered and sighed.

When Nan awoke, she wasn't rested. She felt drained of all energy, and lonely inside. As soon as she had finished the work that her grandmother required around the house and had set her own room in order, she got into the Mustang and drove down to the old city. It was Saturday, and her poor car was covered with layers of dust from a week's driving on dry country roads. Normally, before doing anything else, she would have run it through the carwash in town. But Tom would be bound to spot her there. And she couldn't face him now. Not before she had every little detail resolved and worked out in her mind. And for that she needed Grant.

She found him working in the basement of the Masonic Temple. There had been some flooding there in the spring, and one of the sump pumps needed repairing. He was dressed in a pair of old blue coveralls, faded and grease-stained, surrounded by an assortment of pipes, wrenches, bolts and sockets, and pieces and ends of dirty hoses and pipe fittings. It was total chaos, as far as Nan was concerned, but she knew he loved this kind of work, and could sort and identify the pieces easily in his mind. She watched him for a moment or two, his white hair nearly brushing the greasy cement floor as he bent over his task. He was getting old, Nan knew that. Closer to eighty than she wanted to think. A little stab of fear shot through her. What if she were to lose him?

He had been her only confidant since she was ten years old. It never really occurred to her that Grant Morgan was a Mormon, and that her family had never trusted the Mormons much. She had trusted Grant and his wife, Ellen, ever since that rainy day when they had discovered her pushing her bicycle through the mud, fighting the weight and drag of a flat front tire, nursing a scraped, gravel-infested knee. Ellen had bandaged her leg and had fed her hot chocolate and warm buttered banana bread. Grant meanwhile had repaired the offending bicycle, and they had sent her on her way.

Somehow, on her many bicycle excursions through Nauvoo, the trail she mapped out for herself would lead past the Morgan home, and it seemed each time that either Grant or Ellen was there to pass the time of day or to offer some little treat. It soon became a ritual they all three looked forward to. Nan often ran errands on her bike for Ellen, or helped Grant work around the various gardens and buildings it was his responsibility to maintain.

Already retired when Nan met them, Grant and Ellen had sold their home in Chicago and come to Nauvoo to work for the Mormon Church. They loved it. They had a charming little home on Mulholland, and they used their diverse talents in doing everything from conducting guided tours to painting rooms and planting gardens, and preaching sermons, as the men did in the Mormon Church. Nan loved Ellen and felt completely at ease with her; but, somehow, Grant was the easier to talk to; and even as a child she would jabber to him for hours, sharing every thought and impression that popped into her head.

The old man was grasping for a wrench that was just beyond his reach. Quickly Nan bent down and slipped it beneath his fingers. He grunted in surprise, and twisted around to see who it was. His eyes lit up as he recognized Nan, and he looked ten years younger than he had a moment earlier.

"I should have known it was you." He bent again to his work, and she knelt down beside him. "You've always been able to sneak up on me like that."

"How was the trip?" She handed him a length of pipe.

"Good. Good. But I'm getting too old to gallivant around like that."

Grant's second daughter lived in Missouri. He was devoted to his children, Nan knew. But he hated traveling.

"Did you see the new baby? Is she pretty? Who does she look like?"

Grant paused in his work a moment and looked right at Nan, his eyes warm and deep.

"She looks just like Ellen. She really does. I told Laura after twenty-three grandchildren it's about time I got one that looked like my Ellen."

"She'll be a beauty, then. I'm glad." Hannah paused a moment, playing with one of the tools at her feet. "I certainly could have used you the last couple of weeks," she said, trying to keep the excitement out of her voice.

"Huh?" He bent again to his work. "What's been going on? Can't you ever take care of yourself while I'm gone without getting into some kind of trouble?"

Nan loved his gentle teasing. She grinned at the back bent before her. "This time you really won't believe it."

And that was that. She began to jabber, just as she had done when she was ten years old. She didn't plan what to say, or agonize over how to say it. She just let her thoughts and feelings flow in their natural way from her heart into the heart of the old man who knew how to listen so well. Nor did she realize that in this relationship alone she lost her natural shyness of speech, her self-protecting privacy, and bloomed in the atmosphere of safe acceptance and love. Grant Morgan realized it, and granted this rare friendship the value it deserved.

Finished with his work, he wiped his hands on an old rag, but didn't move or disturb the girl. So Nan completed her story, through Andrew's departure and the frustration and loneliness that followed, to this last, impending crisis, and the fears that centered around the resolve she had already made. When it seemed she had finished, he still took his time in replying.

"There are a lot of would be's and might be's and may be's here, Nan. Nobody else, as much as they'd like to think so, knows what will make you happy. You're the only person who can decide that."

"I'm afraid."

"I don't blame you. The future's not an easy fish to catch. But don't be afraid of what has to be done. Even Tom Briggs will thank you someday. You'd be doing him no favor, Nan, to marry him without love."

"But me! What will become of me, then?"

He smiled at her drawn and tense little face. "Oh, you just keep your heart in the right place, Nan, and try to be patient. The Lord will take care of you."

A dead-end answer. Comfort for a child who couldn't understand any deeper explanations. Nan didn't even know what it meant, actually. Her family was totally unreligious. Jesus and God were only names for very vague images in her mind. But she had come to trust Grant's "the Lord will take care of you." Whenever he promised that, it seemed as though things did, somehow, work out entirely for the best.

They walked out into the bright sunlight together.

"I'd better run. I've got a newspaper interview in half an hour. You take care, now, and I'll see you tomorrow."

He watched her as she walked to the car. He had seen her outgrow her awkward, little-girl ways and emerge into the graceful young woman she was. *The girl doesn't realize how beautiful she is*, he thought to himself. Not only physical beauty, but the strength and sensitivity of her spirit.

More than ever it hurt him—this enforced silence, this holding back, when he knew how much he had to give her! How he would enjoy turning the keys of his knowledge in her behalf, unlocking her real self and opening wide the eyes of her understanding. *Follow your own advice*, he said to himself, as he bent to pick up his box of tools. *You've felt it before. Have faith and be patient. The Lord will take care of her.* He walked to his car and pushed out of his mind the thought that for an old man, with time running out of his grasp, patience was a cruel taskmaster, indeed.

On the way to her appointment Hannah didn't think about Tom, or even about Andrew. She thought about Grant Morgan, and about the lonely pain she had seen in his eyes. Perhaps it was because she had never really talked to him before about love and marriage. Romance, yes, and girlish dreams, but not "the future" in terms of marriage and the right one and being happy ever after.

It was seven years now since Ellen died. Nan had been thirteen. She remembered vividly her own pain. She also remembered the fear, the helplessness she felt when she looked into Grant's eyes and saw the burning anguish there. She knew the Mormons believed in life after death, and were married in their temples for what they called "time and eternity." As she grew older she decided that that was what sustained Grant against the great loss he had suffered. If ever two people had been one—in qualities, in sympathy, in unity and purpose of heart —it had been Grant and Ellen.

Grant went on after Ellen's death with strength and kindness, and a gracious kind of happiness, but part of him was gone, like a puzzle that would be incomplete until the missing part was fit smoothly back into place again.

That's how it ought to be. That's how it had to be with her. She wondered, with a slight chill, how many people were lucky enough to make that kind of a marriage. An image of Andrew came into her mind, but she forced it away. It was too soon to tell. Too soon to commit her heart and have it broken. Too many ifs and maybes. She had to keep telling herself that. She flipped open her notebook to check the address of her interview, and forced herself to think about the article she would be writing.

That evening as she typed her notes, Julie came into the room. She needed to borrow Nan's blow dryer, and could she please use some of that new perfume, and Nan's blue heart earrings would go perfectly with the color in her blouse. Julie at sixteen was in most ways very unlike Nan. Her hair—a warm, light brown—could almost pass for blonde. She had a sprinkling of freckles across her nose, and gray eyes. Everything about her was warm, cute, and vivacious. Nan thought she was a little shallow, but maybe that was because they had never been interested in the same things, and she couldn't understand the things that Julie liked. Julie never picked up a book if she didn't have to, and Nan was seldom without one. Julie liked to play tennis and swim and waterski—Hannah did, too. But Julie didn't have the patience for a walk along the river or through the fields and wooded meadows Hannah loved. Julie always had to be doing something exciting; she always had to be on the go. They really had very little in common, even though they were sisters. She was glaring at Hannah now, and she tossed her head in exaggerated exasperation.

"You told him you had to type up your articles! I don't believe it!"

"It's the truth."

"Not really, Nan—admit it! If you wanted to go out with him badly enough you could get up early and finish them in the morning. You don't have to turn them in until ten o'clock, and you know it."

"I need some time to think; is that all right, Julie? I just don't feel like going out tonight."

"Well, I don't understand you. How anybody could stand to sit home when they've got a chance to go somewhere! And I don't think you're very fair to Tom, besides."

Nan bit her tongue. Fair to Tom! Well, she couldn't expect much else from Julie. Her very best girlfriend dated Tom's little brother,

36

Fred. In fact, Julie and her date were doubling with them tonight. *I wonder what they'll have to say about me,* Nan thought fleetingly.

"Have a nice time, Julie, and be back by—"

"I know," Julie interrupted her impatiently. "Be back by midnight. Grandma already reminded me."

Nan was grateful to hear the honk of the horn and see Julie disappear out the door. She went back to her typewriter, but the words wouldn't come. *Boys never honked for me,* she thought idly. *They always came to the door and knocked. I'm different,* she thought. *I always have been. Not quite a part of the crowd, not silly and happy-go-lucky like the other kids.*

She felt tired—as if she had been fighting a battle, but had forgotten what for. She had always known what she wanted. But deep down inside, little doubts tugged away at her confidence. Was what she wanted unrealistic, impossible to achieve? She tore the sheet of paper out of the machine and slipped in a new, clean one. *I have to be true to myself,* she thought, as she typed the heading and title. *Even if I lose. Even if I don't make it. For me there's no other way.* What was it Grant had said? She smiled, in spite of herself, as she remembered the simple, loving words.

"Just keep your heart in the right place, Nan, and try to be patient." Patience when you were young and life was tugging at your sleeve, she decided, was as difficult to grasp as the slick, singing wind that laughed with the summer rain through the wet and slippery corn.

This was Andrew's fifth day in Salt Lake and he was loving every minute of it. That first day at the genealogical library had been one of the most fascinating in his life. The twenty-minute introductory tour revealed so many staggering facts: the library housed an impressive amount of books with an even greater number preserved on over a million rolls of microfilm. Andrew couldn't recall the amazing figures, but the Computer File Index listed literally millions of names. More than six hundred employees, including those at the vaults and in the labs, staffed the library, along with a large corps of volunteers. Andrew was impressed. Nan had been right to send him here.

His first step had been to search on the fourth floor through the family group sheets and computer file indexes. On the third floor where records from the British Isles were kept, a reference consultant helped

Andrew continue his search. For three days. At that time he decided to consult a professional genealogist from the large list the library furnished him with.

And he found one to his liking: Heber Shumway, a man in his early fifties, tall, graying at the temples, robust and energetic, with an optimistic gleam in his eye that sent Andrew's spirits soaring. As soon as he had confirmed their arrangements Andrew telegraphed his mother, explaining how hopeful he was concerning this new lead, how necessary it was for him to extend his time for a few weeks longer. He hated to do it. It was August already, and he had been away from home long enough as it was. He could see the withdrawn and distant look that would come into her eyes as she read it. Janet would be soothing; she would try to smooth things over. Could Edwin, with all his gaiety, work her out of her angry fears? He didn't like to cause her pain, conjure up those wild, unrealistic fears that galloped into reality at even the mention of America. Well, he must let his confidence in Janet and Edwin support him.

And there was so much work to do that, hopefully, there would be little time left for him to think or fret about how Edwin was handling the family business at home. If Edwin was intent on any mischief, he had time for only a very small-scale caper, anyway.

Actually there was a lot more than work going on. Andrew was finding the Mormons to be very intelligent and thorough businessmen, yet warm and personable as well. Heber Shumway was taking care of him far and beyond what was required, or the charge of the modest sum which he exacted as a fee. Twice he and his wife, Lucille, had invited Andrew to dinner at their home. A home-cooked meal was nothing short of manna from heaven after months of impersonal meals on the road. Andrew was impressed by their graciousness and the easy, close relationship they held with their seven children, even though most of them had been reared and had established homes of their own. They showed him Memory Grove and Gravity Hill, the This Is the Place Monument, the salt flats and expansive wastes of the Great Salt Lake. They picnicked in the canyons and caught trout in the cold mountain creeks. Their attention was lavish and sincere, and Andrew blossomed under the touch of their friendship.

With them he toured every inch of Temple Square, enchanted by the gardens and trees, shrubbery and vines; touched by the graceful

Seagull Monument in tribute to the bird who saved the Mormon pioneers from starvation; characteristically amazed at the domed tabernacle, constructed of wood alone, the vast elliptical dome resting on forty-four buttresses, many of the beams and trusses held together originally with wooden pegs and cowhide thongs. They didn't miss one display, film, or diorama at the visitors' center.

Andrew found it difficult to comprehend why the Mormons would spend such staggering sums on missionary efforts. Their sincerity, the depth of their own beliefs, was impossible to ignore. Yet how beautifully they achieved that delicate balance of sharing their own strong feelings and convictions without infringing on the beliefs and privacy of the person they were trying to influence. Andrew's admiration grew, and so did his efforts to suppress his own inner reactions to the things he was seeing and hearing daily. Everything he heard sounded right; reasonable, orderly, beautiful. But he didn't want to become interested in religion, especially right now, especially in anything as unusual and demanding as this religion seemed. An American religion, Mormonism. Impossible for him. So he filed it away with all the things he wasn't going to think about right now.

Tonight was going to be a little different. Alan Shumway, Heber's son who was Andrew's age, had invited Andrew to be part of a foursome: Alan and his wife Diana, and Alan's younger sister Rebecca. Andrew had only met the girl once, briefly, at her parents' home. She was a pretty girl with bouncy black hair. But he wasn't really interested. It was crazy—he couldn't believe it was happening—but all he could think about was Nan.

He had been in Salt Lake City a week now, and had determined the first day there that he would call Nan at the end of one week. He was showered and dressed and ready for the Shumways, with over half an hour to spare, but he couldn't make himself pick up the phone. He felt suddenly awkward, shy.

He paced his room, which seemed, at times like this, unbearably confining. He stood at the window and gazed out at the mountains that edged the city. He had discovered as a boy that mountains never look the same. They change with the light and the atmosphere; there are moods upon a mountain that not everyone can interpret or even discern.

Andrew was already beginning to love these rugged, rocky hills.

They stood now etched against the sky, every jagged edge distinct and clear, green and gray and black against the startling blue, the last triumph of the sky before evening saps its color and spreads her own scarlets and roses and golds in brilliant display. He marveled how there could be such a feeling of peace, and at the same time a sense of intensity; an aching sort of hunger, a beauty too outrageous to bear. He turned and reached for the phone, itching suddenly to hear the sound of Nan's voice.

When Nan picked up the receiver and heard Andrew speak her name, a wave of pain, or gladness—she couldn't tell which—swept over her, and left her weak.

"Nan? It's yourself, then. I'm glad no one else answered. If you only knew how good it is just to hear your voice."

"I know," she replied softly, and she meant it as deeply as she had ever meant anything in her life.

There was a moment of silence, then they both began to talk, and it was all right, as if there were no time, no distance between them.

"It's you who should be here," Andrew told her excitedly. "You would appreciate it ever so much more than I." It was incredible to him that Nan had never set eyes on a mountain. "I wish you could see the last sun on the mountains. It's a sight I can't begin to describe, though I'd love to show it to you. What's it like there?"

"Raining," Nan replied, struggling to keep her voice even. "A magnificent Illinois storm. There's an angry wind, branches down all over. And the sky's so black we've had to turn the lights on indoors."

Good heavens, this isn't working, Andrew thought to himself. I'm only missing her all the more. I want to see her face and touch her hair . . . it isn't working at all.

"Andrew? Are you there?"

"Yes. Can you wait just a moment, Nan? There's someone at the blasted door!"

The door! Whoever could be pounding on the door like that? Andrew was angry at the interruption, and startled when he opened the door to find Alan Shumway grinning at him. He stared back, stupidly, he knew.

"Ready to go, I see." Alan just kept grinning.

"Well, no, not actually . . . you're twenty minutes early, Alan, and I'm on a long-distance call."

Then there was a flurry of apologies and everyone tramping in good-naturedly to wait, laughing and hushing each other in an embarrassed confusion of voices. Nan heard on the other end and picked up the sound of both male and female voices. Somewhere inside the little point of pain flared into life, fed from some independent source over which Nan found she had a frustrating lack of control.

When he returned to the phone she tried to sound natural, but he could tell, and she knew that he could, without being able to do anything about it. She was angry at herself, angry that her feelings could so easily show. Andrew explained his connection with the Shumway family, their kindness and generosity. He made it sound as casual as he could, knowing that his very protestations gave him an aura of suspicion, of guilt.

"Oh, Nan," he said at last, "I'm wretchedly sorry for the interruption. I canna say how much I miss you, lass."

He was lapsing, lapsing into the speech that best expressed strong feelings for him. They said goodbye—an awkward, unsatisfactory goodbye—and she was gone, and he must face these people—kind, well-meaning. He mustn't disappoint them. It wasn't their fault, surely. He would do justice to their friendship, go out and have a good time, as he knew he could in their company.

He just couldn't bear the thought of hurting Nan, of leaving her so abruptly, so unsatisfied. There were a dozen ways he could make it up to her, and he would use them all. He smiled and held the door for the pretty girl, but his mind was busy, planning surprises—lovely things to wipe away the little furrowed frown on Nan's brow, the frown he knew was there, the frown he had caused, when all he had wanted to do was to brighten her day, to somehow let her know how much he cared.

Nan sat holding the silent phone long after it had gone dead. She felt numb and empty inside. Andrew was gone; as if the greedy, grasping storm had swallowed his voice, his very being, and hurled him on a whirlwind away. Nan sat beneath the weight of the storm, not quite knowing if the sobbing was the wind, or the voice of her own heart; feeling the streaks of water that wept against the glass wet upon her own eyes, running chill against her cheeks.

6

*A finder of occasions that hath an eye
can stamp and counterfeit advantages,
though true advantage never present itself.*

OTHELLO

Janet awoke trembling and cold. She shut her eyes tightly, but the image of her father's face was still vividly clear. She switched on the light beside her bed and propped up the pillows behind her. If anything, this dream had been even more startling, more real than the others. And yet the same. She marveled how every time the details were exactly the same. And each time the dream repeated itself her own sadness and loneliness and frustration increased. What did it mean? And what could she do about it?

She didn't want to close her eyes and risk seeing her father's face again, but she hated the quiet loneliness around her that was almost fear. Oh, things had been going miserably since Andrew left, she admitted. Even though everyone was trying so hard. Edwin's presence was doing miracles for her mother, she knew, and although Janet loved Edwin and appreciated his kindness and flattering attentions, he was by no means a satisfactory replacement for Andrew. It was to Andrew alone that she had confided her disturbing dreams. He was the only one who understood how hard it was for her to accept her father's death. He had been more gentle and sensitive than ever, trying to fill the awesome gap, but realizing, at the same time, that no one can fill another's place, and time is the only hand that can heal.

For a moment Janet wished, wished fervently, that she could turn to her mother and find comfort and security within her arms. But the thought didn't stay. She had learned years ago, as a little girl, that no comfort waited there. She didn't resent it. She knew that, in her own

42

way, her mother loved her. But she knew, too, that Jessie wasn't capable of the gentle, giving love she needed, the love all children need.

She had been lucky, she knew, to have someone else to turn to. Her father—her blustering, busy father who charged through life with a will and determination that was staggering—had never been too busy for her. With him she had found the warmth and acceptance she needed, encouragement at each new step to discover, dream, and dare. He was the light and the force of her existence. Now he was gone. And what can you fashion from emptiness and pain? But much as she felt the loss, she would not shame him. So she didn't give up, and she didn't give in. Only her wet pillow and her silent room knew how often the battle was waged, and how shaky, how insecure each victory was.

The sun rose to a dull and dripping sky, drawing out the hours in a sameness that was like a trance on Janet's spirits. Edwin was in Paisley, keeping busier with Andrew's work than she had ever expected him to. The household ran smoothly under her mother's capable hands. For even though Jessie Buchanan spent long hours in her rooms, she ran a tight house and held a firm hand, and the gardener, the cook, the serving girl, and the cleaning girl knew it well.

School was in recess for the summer, so Janet's hours spun empty and unfilled before her. She watered the plants, fed the dogs, and spent an hour on the loveseat in the library searching for something to read that would hold her interest. She even talked the cook into letting her put together the trifle for the evening's dessert. Not all her days were so narrow, so drear. But the dull ones came more often than she desired, and she longed for the kind of activity which would engage her total commitment, allowing her no time for despondency and doubt.

Dinner over at last, Janet slipped away. In the drawing room with his after-dinner cordial, Edwin shared with his aunt the pleasant chit-chat of his day's affairs, knowing it would be useless, even harmful, to mention his many frustrations, the awkward mistakes he made, the aspects of the Buchanan business that he still, after two months and more, couldn't quite follow.

It was a new world for Edwin; he wasn't accustomed to making decisions that influenced the lives of dozens, sometimes hundreds, of men, or that consigned and controlled thousands upon thousands of pounds on the basis of his word alone. It was an awesome power, and Edwin loved it.

His own world had always been too narrow for him. At the age of ten his parents separated and his father was never heard from again until Edwin received word, through a solicitor, that he had been killed in an auto accident near Worcester in England. His mother, frail and frightened of life, had died when Edwin was fourteen, leaving him in the care of a maiden aunt. His mother had left enough money so that he could get by—there was even enough to indulge a few of his wayward habits. But the kind of life he longed for seemed always just a little beyond his grasp.

Edwin lived in a flat in Glasgow when there was a temporary shortage of places to go and people to take him in. He owned part interest in a sporting goods store there, but it had never held his attention, although he had a brilliant mind for detail, a smooth, easy manner, and enough personal experience in most of the sports he promoted that, as his partners would have agreed, he was the greatest asset the business had. Edwin didn't realize this, nor would he have admitted it if he did. All he knew was that after a time the business bored him. That's how it was with most things he set his hand to: after a while there was no more incentive, no more stimulation: they became flat and boring, and the challenge was gone.

This work of Andrew's was a different matter. There was enough here to occupy the energies and enthusiasm and creative impulse of any man. Edwin hadn't realized the Buchanan business held as many exciting facets and dimensions as it did.

He snickered slightly as he watched his aunt over his glass. Ever since he had been old enough to know what a name meant, Edwin had wished that his own was Buchanan. Edwin Bain. A pleasant-sounding name. But not quite the right one. His grandmother, Sarah, had been a Buchanan, sister to Andrew's grandfather, so the line was there. But all the money, the influence, the prestige, and the success seemed swallowed up by this one direct branch of the line—by this family that was not quite his own.

Edwin resented it. He had for years. It didn't keep him from caring more about Andrew and Janet than about any other people he knew, nor did it prevent his honest admiration of his kindly uncle and high-strung aunt. But it fostered a kind of "chip on the shoulder" attitude. Edwin, with his charm, had a gift for working things his way, and he loved the challenge of getting something for nothing. It seemed incongruous, unjust to him, that Andrew, who had everything a man could want and more, should work like a common Highland crofter, with no need to whatsoever, while Edwin, who possessed the gracious art of knowing how to enjoy his leisure, was often prevented the opportunity by his own more meager circumstances.

Except for the killing work, he was enjoying his position in Andrew's place. Unlike many men, Edwin felt comfortable in the company of women, and these two women possessed every quality necessary to hold a man's interest. He remembered vividly how, as a boy, he had been madly in love with Janet, bitterly rueing the fate that had linked them as cousins in a family where, no matter how distant the connection, intermarriage would never be countenanced.

"Where is the girl, anyway?" the harsh question startled him.

"It's Janet you're meaning?" He knew that a slow answer and a soft smile could easily divert Jessie when her ire was up. "Out walking. I saw her leave with the collie."

"Can't she ever keep to the house? She shouldn't be so much alone. Not at her age."

"All the more at her age. With so many things to sort out in her head." Edwin refilled his aunt's glass and as he handed it to her he laid his hand briefly over hers.

"You speak with the wisdom of age and experience, I presume?" She couldn't help smiling at Edwin's expression, wonderfully intermingling innocence with impish delight. At times his resemblance to her Andrew was so overwhelming that it was painful for her. Yet what was her alternative? She much preferred the pain of his presence to the desolation of total loneliness. She knew a brief, unsettling concern as she thought of Janet, out there alone somewhere, struggling with her own loneliness and fears. She rose, restless.

"I must go to the MacRaes'. Will you drive me, Edwin?"

"Gladly, madam." He rose and gave her the slightest bow. The prospect pleased him. Young David MacRae had a fine collection of old dueling pistols. There would be good company, lively conversation, and the promise of a glass or two of the best whisky the county could boast. He walked over and held out his hand to his aunt.

Janet was already past the gardens and the low-walled pond. The little burn sang at her feet, lulling, musical and low. She had sent

Tybalt back to the house. The dog's company was a nuisance, for he found something to bark at or chase after constantly, and she needed solitude. The rowan tree shone silver, the light from the moon splintering through the leaves in delicate patterns that danced and shimmered in constant motion. She pulled loose a heavy spray of berries off a low branch and, sitting on the thick, cool grass, plucked at them absently as she thought.

The rowan tree had stood for hundreds of years, and the solidarity of its presence alone was a comfort to her. The rowan had been planted anciently as protection against witches and evil spirits, and the berries of the tree were supposed to bring good fortune. Janet smiled into the dark. Good fortune and protection from evil. She had believed that so firmly as a child that the superstition still had power to allay her fears.

She sat there watching the clouds ride over the moon until she had pulled and discarded all the berries and had made up her mind. She would go with Mary in the morning. Twice already she had attended meetings with the missionaries at Mary's house. She was interested. She wouldn't deny that. And she had so many questions she wanted to ask! Mary's entire family was going together. Surely it wouldn't hurt for her to go along. She felt she needed to find out for herself, to discover what her own reactions and feelings would be. Her mother would never approve, and Edwin needn't know. If Andrew were here she might have told him, but he wasn't, and she was nearly eighteen, and it was time she make up her own mind about something without worrying too much about what everyone else would think. She rose to walk back to the house, but not without breaking off a little spray of leaves and berries which she wound into the thick strands of her hair as she walked.

By Wednesday evening Janet was thoroughly excited. She had told her mother she would be spending the entire day the previous Sunday with the Camerons, so she had been able to attend both of the meetings that the Mormons held; Sunday School in the morning and—what was it?—sacrament or something in the evening. It had all been very strange to Janet, so foreign from anything of a religious nature she had ever experienced before. But it wasn't weird, something repulsive as she had feared it might be. In fact, she experienced a good feeling there, especially during the singing. The people were all very friendly, though it made her feel awkward to shake so many hands, the women's as well as the men's. She liked the way everyone participated; there was a more personal atmosphere than she had expected to find. Actually, she hadn't known what to expect. All she knew now was that she was becoming more interested as she found out more.

Sunday evening the missionaries had spent an hour at the Cameron home, and some of Janet's questions had been answered. It was then that Janet brought home a copy of the Book of Mormon and half a dozen little pamphlets the missionaries had given her. She stuffed them inside her purse, and she spent all of Monday afternoon and most of the evening reading. And, for the first time, she knelt down beside her bed and tried to pray before going to sleep. The missionaries had made it sound so wonderful, so important—and so easy! But she felt strange and ill-at-ease and didn't know what words to use. The only image that came to her mind was that of her father. Yet, strangely, instead of the usual fear and frustration, Janet felt a sense of peace, a relaxed, almost happy feeling.

Tonight, she had decided, she would pray again, and tomorrow—perhaps tomorrow she would speak at last. She was anxious to tell someone! Though exactly what she would say she wasn't sure. Maybe Edwin would have to do; she was still afraid of approaching her mother.

So she knelt by her bedside that night with more of a sense of purpose and peace than she had known since her father's death. But when the morning came, and she arose with a sense of anticipation, a very different set of circumstances were destined to be enacted than what she had planned and hoped for in her mind.

Janet was nearly ready to come down for breakfast when she heard the smashing of glass and the high, almost hysterical shriek which she recognized unmistakably as Helen's. Helen had worked for her mother since before Janet was born; she was solid and sensible and used to Jessie's ways. Janet flew down the long stairs knowing something must be very wrong, trying to fight back the panicky fear that was rising within her.

Janet found them in the library: her mother, Edwin, and Helen, who cowered helplessly in a corner. Her mother had broken things before, but it was one of the precious Chinese vases which lay shattered at her feet. Its mate was precariously careening back and forth on the table; Jessie had lunged for it, but Edwin had caught her arm in time. They were struggling now, Jessie screaming, "I hate him, I hate him, I hate him!" over and over until it sent a chill down Janet's spine. Janet reached the vase and safely straightened it, then replaced it carefully on a high shelf out of the way. Edwin was holding Jessie's wrists now, moving her gently toward a chair, speaking something low and soothing, but Jessie's voice rose above his.

"He's put a spell on Andrew. He's bewitched my boy. Won't he ever leave us alone?"

Edwin had her seated now, and he motioned for Janet and Helen to leave the room.

"What is it?" Janet demanded of Helen once they were outside and the heavy door was pulled closed behind them.

"It's the telegram, miss," she answered, the hysteria still in her voice. "From America. Young Donald brought it out this morning."

"Andrew!" Janet felt herself go sick inside. "Is something the matter with Andrew?"

"Ach, no, the lad's all right, but he sent word saying he was staying on. Can ye imagine? Had something important going, mind you. I canna tell ye how white yer mither went when she read it. She just stood there and tore the paper carefully into little bits. It was awful. Then suddenly, well—then she—"

"Yes, I heard." The poor woman was close to sobbing. Janet led her into the kitchen, sat her down, and offered a cup of tea. She went back into the hall; no sounds came from behind the oaken door. What was going on in there? Oh, Andrew, what could be so important that you can't come home? She stood vigil outside the door a few minutes longer, then walked slowly back up the stairs. The silence was like a weight upon her, and by the time she reached her room she cared no longer about what it was she had been so eager to tell someone—anyone—that very morning.

Once Jessie was forced to sit down and hold still the wild raving stopped. Edwin knew it would. Jessie sat pale and silent, withdrawn now, her eyes almost vacant of expression. He helped her from the chair, and with his arm around her waist guided her up the stairs to her own rooms. The entire way up the stairs he cursed Andrew in his mind as a blithering idiot, and it made him feel a little better. In Jessie's rose and ivory boudoir Edwin settled her into a comfortable divan. Her pride was restoring itself, and what self-loathing she might feel for her behavior while downstairs would be transferred to any likely scapegoat she could find. Edwin knew that. He also knew that he, alone, would escape her wrath, for he was Andrew *in absentia*, the one and only object of her love and adoration.

He went personally downstairs to prepare her a light morning tea. In her present mood it wasn't safe for anyone else to wait on her. He had better keep Janet away for a while. Poor girl. Sad that Jessie's love hadn't been sufficient to really enfold her only daughter, as well as her son. Maybe it was the fact that they were both women, that Janet constituted some kind of a threat. He didn't know.

He brought in the tray and arranged it on the low table at Jessie's elbow. The fire was back in her eyes, and he couldn't help noticing how fine and lovely her features were.

"A woman who's behaved as shamelessly as yourself has no right to look as beautiful as you do right now." He said it as he handed her the cup. She bristled right back at him, but her voice was not as hard as it had been before; some of the pain she struggled so hard to control seeped through.

"You don't know what you're talking about, Edwin. You don't understand. How dare you judge me when you can't begin to understand!" He thought briefly of his own mother, mild and meek and well-mannered, and realized that he felt much more at ease with Jessie.

"Leave me now, Edwin. But stay near in case I want you." It was a tone of absolute command. He gave his usual little bow, almost mocking in manner, and closed the door behind him.

Jessie put down the cup, her hand too unsteady to support it. The silence in the little room was heavy with memories. It was a place of suffering; how many were the times she had faced pain here, alone and comfortless? She had been young when her husband left for America; so lonely, so afraid of being alone at night. How often she had paced between the window and the desk, gazing out at the dark shapes in the moonlight until her eyes blurred, then had sat at the desk, her back stiff and aching, writing page after page to send off to Alexander, wherever he might be. No one dreamed that with him she was a different person altogether. He understood the uncertainty and insecurity behind her domineering ways; he humored her, but with love and respect, his hold upon her tender and personal, and much, much deeper than anyone would ever guess.

But he had not been here when her baby daughter died. Even after all these years she shuddered to think of the anguish of those days, when she had faced the dark abyss of her suffering without his support, not even knowing where he was, needing him so desperately. Now, in death, he had deserted her again. He had known she couldn't survive without him, but he had left her, and this time with no hope—no promised homecoming, no sunrise after the dark. Nothing but Andrew. Without Andrew—she didn't let herself think what she would do without Andrew.

Whatever could have possessed him? Andrew realized—of course he must realize—that the search was only a pretense, a coercion, an insult to be borne. Surely he wasn't becoming involved in the project— surely he wasn't beginning to care? Could the search, itself, induce him to stay away from home? She had known how reluctant he was to leave in the first place. She rose and began pacing the confines of the room. Three months was a long time to wander, a stranger in a strange land. Why wasn't he coming home? Was there something he hadn't told her?

A dozen fancies rose before her eyes as her mind strove to fashion some horrible explanation, some strange reason to account for Andrew's behavior. Unwillingly her thoughts settled on the original Charles. He sailed to America, but he did not return. What had he suffered? What had been his eventual fate? She had lost Alexander. It couldn't be possible that she would be required to bear the unbearable, the loss of her Andrew as well! She paced and paced, torturing herself with her own thoughts.

Edwin found her in such a state nearly two hours later. He entered uninvited, having expected a summons long before. He brought her soup and something to calm her and, at her insistence, moved his brief-case, filled with papers and portfolios, onto her own small desk, promising to work at her side all afternoon, promising not to leave until she awoke. Even then it took her a long time to succumb to sleep. Edwin was up half a dozen times, arranging the pillows beneath her back, giving her a cool drink, drawing the heavy curtains against the light, tucking the silk coverlet around her legs. He didn't mind, though he couldn't say he relished the idea of working at the cramped desk for hours. He felt as though he were in a sickroom; even in Andrew's light, airy study with a frothy ale at his hand it was hard enough to concentrate.

At the end of an hour Edwin was near to distraction. He had moved aside some of Jessie's papers to make room for his own. He was rummaging now for a sheet he had misplaced, angrily attacking the stack as the piece eluded him. His precarious order disintegrated and papers slid to the floor in every direction. Swearing under his breath, Edwin gathered them up again, and it was then that he noticed. The unusual shape and bulk of the folder caught his eye. Here was a piece of luck, a curiosity to while away some time, an excuse to keep him from his tedious work. He had always harbored a lively curiosity concerning the famous will. Jessie must have been going through it for some reason to have it out this way. Well, now he was to see for himself. He removed the starchy sheets eagerly from the folder.

Good heavens, there is a lot of detail! He scanned the pages, a little disappointed as one dry, commonplace paragraph succeeded another. He smiled at some of the stilted, old-fashioned sentences, but even the infamous clause outlining the trust for Charles and his descendants was disappointingly devoid of the romance and color and emotion he had expected there. But there were other papers here as well. Edwin began leafing through them and noticed the date at the top of one of the sheets. 1927. 1927! That was impossible! He smoothed out the pages and read:

Dear Mr. Buchanan:

Pursuant to your request, I have examined the Last Will and Testament of your great-grandfather, Andrew Buchanan. Your great-grandfather left his estate in trust with a provision that 80 percent of the income generated by the trust estate would be paid to his son, Andrew Buchanan, your grandfather. Following your grandfather's death. . . .

A letter from a solicitor, Edwin gathered as he read, outlining the well-known conditions of the original Buchanan will. But why the sudden concern, in 1927? For what purpose? He scanned the paragraphs and came at last to a part which began to interest him:

> Your great-grandfather intended that the required search be carried out generation by generation in perpetuity. It is my considered opinion that this feature of your great-grandfather's testamentary trust violates the rule against perpetuities, a technical legal doctrine which prohibits passing an interest in trust from one generation to the next without end.

Edwin was absorbed, his mind immediately intrigued by the multitude of possibilities this information opened up. He read on:

> Because your great-grandfather's testamentary trust violates the rule against perpetuities, the trust can be declared null and void and the entire trust estate, including the income accumulated for Charles Buchanan or his issue, will vest in you. In other words, you are free to do with the entire estate as you please. . . .

Edwin whistled under his breath. The implications were increasing. *Why doesn't anyone know about this?* This was—let's see—Andrew's grandfather, brother to his own grandmother, Sarah. So the power had been suddenly vested in him! *What did the old lad do with it?* he wondered.

There was a second letter from the solicitor bearing a later date. Edwin picked it up with profound interest and began to read:

Dear Mr. Buchanan:

I understand after talking to you in my office last week that you are intrigued with the idea of finding the issue of your great-grandfather's missing son, Charles Buchanan. I further understand that in spite of the fact that you are under no legal obligation to do so, you intend to continue the search for the missing heirs by keeping the estate in trust as long as you are legally permitted to do so under the rule against perpetuities.

As I indicated to you when we met together in my office, you can set up a will with the same type of limitations as your great-grandfather had in his will and pass the estate subject to the search requirements. You will be limited to passing the estate to your son for his life and then to your grandson. If the missing heirs are not located by the time the estate passes to your grandson, the accumulated income from the 20 percent interest must vest in some person free and clear of trust.

There was something exciting about to happen here; Edwin could feel it. What would this great-uncle do with the accumulated 20 percent, the silently-gathered wealth of generations, which had now come under his power? The letter continued:

Enclosed herewith you will find a will which I have prepared for you containing a trust with provisions similar to those of your great-grandfather's will. The only difference between your new will and your great-grandfather's will is that if your grandson does not locate the missing heirs after he makes his one-year search, the accumulated income from the 20 percent interest will pass to the living issue of your sister, Sarah Buchanan Bain. I have, according to your instructions, added an explanation in the will for your actions in leaving the accumulated income to the issue of Sarah Buchanan Bain. I understand that you have always felt a special tender affection for Sarah Buchanan Bain and you feel that such a gesture is appropriate.

If this will meets with your approval, please feel free to come to my office and execute the same.

The usual formal closings followed, but Edwin's attention was riveted on that one name: his grandmother's, Sarah Buchanan Bain. The issue of Sarah Buchanan Bain. . . . With careful deliberation Edwin reviewed his grandmother's family in his mind. There had been two daughters: Emily, who had died while still in childhood, and Margaret, who had grown into nothing but an old maid and passed quietly out of existence years ago. Then there was Robert, Sarah's only son and Edwin's father. Edwin felt only a vague sense of loathing when he thought of his father. He had died a failure, little more than a derelict. But Robert had never remarried, had never had children other than himself. Edwin was suddenly, overwhelmingly grateful for that one now vital thing which his miserable father had inadvertently managed to do right.

And so the issue of Sarah Buchanan Bain—the only existing issue—sat now with the solicitor's letter clutched tightly in his fingers, struggling to comprehend what this meant to him, consumed with a desire touching on passion, the conviction strengthening within him that fate had tossed his future into his hands—that elusive future which seemed always, tantalizingly, just outside his grasp.

Andrew knew nothing of this will; Edwin was certain of that. No one knew but Jessie, then, and that knowledge must be a sore cross to bear, indeed. Not for a moment did Edwin waver or hesitate. In his mind there were no alternatives, only one clear path which had been handed him in an instant of blinding revelation.

Andrew's grandfather had wrested the power from the cold, hard grasp of the dead man! And he had placed it directly into Edwin's hands. The power was his now, and power was something Edwin was developing a definite taste for. He was prepared for this moment; it had been meant to come! Every man had the right to direct his own future, and Edwin intended on using this new-found power in determining his.

He replaced the papers and returned the folder to its original place on Jessie's desk. He glanced over at his aunt, who was sleeping peacefully and still, and in his mind his own cause seemed just. He believed there were more reasons than one why he had happened to be here, acting Andrew's part, at this very moment when time and circumstance combined to at last open up his way before him.

7

Hurry, Nan, you've got to come and see what came for you this afternoon!'' Hannah smiled at her brother's enthusiasm. Nan decided it must really be something special this time for Jonathan to meet her out here. She closed the car door and tried to conceal her own excitement from Jonathan's eager eyes.

These past weeks had seemed to be right out of a fairy tale. Ever since that miserable phone call the night of the storm, little packages had been arriving from Andrew—clever little gifts that had delighted her heart. The first had been a small box topped with a copper-covered postcard, then filled with half a dozen trinkets made from Utah copper. There had been the rock candy and a small bag of salt from the Great Salt Lake, and an Indian doll with a black-eyed papoose strapped to her back. Nan felt at her neck where the necklace lay safely against her throat—a graceful seagull in flight suspended between delicate links of chain. She hurried her footsteps. What could it possibly be now?

As she opened the screen door Julie's laughter was the first thing to greet her.

"Your Scotsman has really outdone himself this time," she said lightly, with just a hint of mockery in the bright voice. "He's sent you a beautiful bouquet of weeds—as if we don't have enough that flourish here already."

Nan picked up the package carefully, curious now. She had to stifle a grin, for it was true. The strange little flowers looked amazingly like weeds, and without the folder tucked in with Andrew's card she wasn't certain she would have recognized them herself.

"It's Scottish heather," she breathed softly, and held the pale purple blossoms briefly against her cheek.

"Oh." Jonathan was obviously disappointed. "Weird stuff. What did you call it?"

"Heather," Nan replied. "It grows wild in the highlands and along the lonely moors—"

"Spare us," Julie interrupted flippantly. "You can have it as far as I'm concerned. I'd much prefer a dozen red roses myself."

Nan gathered up the flowers without another word and took them to her room, where she carefully read the instructions, excited at the idea that, after keeping them wet for a few days, she could allow them to dry out and preserve them that way indefinitely. She placed them in a vase on her dresser where they were reflected again in the mirror, delicate pale flowers with leaves like miniature pine needles on slender, woody stems. Hannah tore open the small envelope that bore her name and slipped out the card. "To my nut-brown maiden—Andrew," it read. *My* nut-brown maiden. Hannah savored it a moment, then slipped the card inside her copy of Shakespeare; no fear of anyone discovering it there.

She was grateful that something had come from Andrew today. Perhaps it was a good omen. Tonight she had a date with Tom. Though he had hinted at a confrontation on that first night after Andrew left, Tom had since seemed to back off, content to let things ride again. He might have been afraid of scaring her off altogether. She didn't know. All she knew was that the assumptiveness was there again in full force; Tom's physical advances were becoming more and more pressing each time they met. She could no longer avoid the issue. If Tom wouldn't face her, then she would have to take the lead. Much as she dreaded it, there was really little choice left in the matter.

Nan dressed carefully that evening. She had not worn *her* fragrance, lavender, since Andrew left, and now she avoided Tom's old favorite, Tabu, though the bottle he had given her at Christmas, still half-filled, stood on her dressing table with the rest. She chose a safe splash of Roses, Roses and brushed her long hair into loose, natural curls around her shoulders and down her back. Whenever she tried to plan in her mind what to say, everything went empty and blank. She would have to depend on the instinct of the moment and her deep reserves of honest feeling and conviction.

Still, it was difficult when the time actually came. The evening was lovely, the movie a good one, the ice cream sundae fixed exactly how she liked it, and Tom more natural, more fun than he had been for a long time. How was she going to do it? He seemed so unaware, so unsuspecting. He pulled the car off the highway and into the park. Hannah felt her muscles tighten with apprehension.

She watched Tom's profile as he drove. He was good-looking, actually, his light brown hair curling ever so slightly over his forehead and around his ears. His eyes were brown and warm, and he had a wonderful slow smile that seemed to never quite arrive but to be continually happening, giving his face a quizzical look of animation whenever he smiled—which was often, really. He wasn't smiling now; his thoughts were on matters of a different nature. The gravel crunched beneath the warm tires as the car slowed and came to a gentle stop.

As soon as the engine was still the quiet of the park took over. Nan felt engulfed by the dark shadows of the surrounding trees; the incessant high pitch of the crickets began to throb in her head. She was aware of every bird cry, every indistinct rustle in the bushes nearby. It was only a matter of seconds, but before she was able to break the spell and speak, Tom reached for her across the space of darkness separating them. His hands were warm and firm on her arms and he drew her close all too quickly, so that she had to pull herself away from him, his lips brushing her cheek and the curls of brown hair. He gave a little exclamation of surprise, but said nothing as she sat facing him, feeling ridiculously awkward.

"Tom . . . Tom. . . ." He still said nothing; he wasn't going to help her. "It's time, Tom. We can't pretend any longer."

"Pretend!" His voice was rough with emotion. "You know how I feel about you. I've never pretended with you, Nan."

"Oh, yes, you have, Tom. You've pretended you don't see the things that stand between us. You've pretended that I feel the same way you do. And I don't. I never have—and I never will, Tom. You know I never will."

"Please, Nan, don't!" He put his head down against the steering wheel and the anguish in his voice cut Nan with a pain she had not expected. "I know I love you more than you love me, I've always known that. But I'd take good care of you, Nan. You'd be happy with me, I know it!"

It was more a plea than a statement. *What am I doing?* Nan thought to herself. *What am I doing?*

"I do care about you, Tom—but I don't love you. Not in the way you love me. Not in the way that's—well—necessary. I couldn't be happy with you, and you couldn't be happy with me. Not unless we shared that kind of love together."

He raised his head and looked at her. Even in the darkness the intensity of his gaze burned into her. He laughed, a dry, mirthless laugh.

"I could be happy with you, Nan, under just about any circumstances. As long as you were mine."

She felt cold all over and sick inside. "It's impossible, Tom. Please believe me. It could never be."

He didn't answer her. He sat there motionless, stiffened against the blow.

"I'm sorry, Tom. I'm so, so sorry." She touched his arm, ever so gently, but she felt the current of response surge against her fingertips. He cried her name as he drew her roughly into his arms, and there was such a passion, such a pain in his kiss that she could not deny him. Her heart cried out to comfort him, but she knew how cruel any tenderness on her part would be. Gently she pulled away and buried her face against his shoulder.

"I hope that someday you can forgive me, Tom. I never meant to cause you such pain."

He held her to him then with his face against her hair, until at last his arms relaxed and she slipped over to her own side of the car. He started the engine, its throaty, throbbing intrusion pulling them abruptly back into reality. They didn't speak again until he turned into her own driveway and came around to help her out of the car. He paused at the door and she waited, knowing he wanted to speak.

"Nan . . ." he tried to smile, but it was a miserable attempt. Nan could hold the tears no longer. She wiped them angrily away, but he had seen them.

58

"Don't cry for me, Nan, please. I love you. I guess I'll always love you."

It was all he was able to say. He didn't try to kiss her again; he turned and walked away.

Up in her room Nan lay on the bed without turning on the light or getting undressed. She had grown up a lot during the last hour, and she knew it. Love was nothing to tamper with, nor take lightly, nor scorn. The absolute sanctity of human feeling hit her like a jolt. She lay there aching; longing to be able to fulfill Tom's need, hurting for him, knowing that his fulfillment lay outside the scope of her powers. The thin fingers of the heather traced shadows against the mirror, and the thought came unbidden to her mind, the hunger, the fear—the trembling realization that her own happiness, her own fulfillment was beyond her control. Her own dreams could be shattered, just as she had shattered Tom's. For her fate lay within another's grasp; he carried the awesome power to either destroy her or grant her life, according to his own desire and will.

Andrew was discouraged. As disappointment followed disappointment and every promising avenue led only to a dead end, his respect grew for the tedious, time-consuming work of genealogical research. It was eating up every shred of patience he had, and he was becoming restless. He had received only one terse communication from Scotland, a telegram from Edwin in reply to his own: "Things in hand here. Grand move, that! Will wait upon word from you."

The sarcasm in the telegram was evident; Edwin must have been having a deuce of a time. And it was all Andrew's fault, of course. And, in spite of everything, it seemed he might still go home empty-handed after all. But Heber Shumway didn't seem discouraged. This morning he had only shook his head and laughed.

"This is going to be a harder egg to crack than I'd expected, Andrew." He gathered up his papers, his eyes sparkling as if in anticipation. "In fact, I'd say this is one of the biggest challenges I've ever been handed."

They had lunch together at the Lion House Pantry, where they sat beneath a stern oval portrait of Brigham Young. Andrew looked at the strong lines of determination in that face and wondered what a man like

Young would do in his place. Heber Shumway, with his enthusiastic ways, reminded him of what the Mormon prophet might have been like. Despite his impatience, Andrew's own enthusiasm for the project, rather than dwindling in proportion to the defeats they were experiencing, was growing daily. He was beginning to really care, to feel it was important that he, Andrew, uncover the missing link, patch up the gap, restore—restore what?

He left Heber in the plaza outside the Church Office Building, and walked to his hotel. A seagull stretched and strutted, preening itself in the sun. He had come to really enjoy the plucky little creatures. He would give himself until the end of the week, he thought. No longer. He had plans to drive with Alan over the Point of the Mountain south to Provo and to tour Brigham Young University, the L.D.S. university there. *Brigham Young* University. It seemed to Andrew he could feel the influence of the man everywhere he turned. He didn't resent it—he rather liked the intermingled sense of history and destiny that seemed to flavor things here. Tonight he was taking Rebecca Shumway to a play at the Promised Valley Theatre. He couldn't remember what play it was—something Alan had assured him he couldn't miss. He had grown to like Rebecca; she was a lot of fun, and intelligent as well. But every time he was with her he wished it could be Nan, instead.

Inside the hotel he checked his mailbox. There was a letter, a thick letter from Janet! Anxious as he was, he hesitated opening it, fearful of what it might contain, aware that the hopes he was cherishing depended solely on what he read in and between the lines.

Once in his room, he skipped lightly over the mundane news of the weather, the neighbors, what was happening in town—all the light chitchat Janet wrote to entertain him. Finally he found it:

> Mother was a terror the morning your telegram arrived. Edwin was magnificent with her, though since 'the crisis' he's seemed a little tense and on edge. I think living with two daft women must be getting on his nerves.

Andrew smiled at that, remembering all too well his cousin's feelings toward Janet.

> Mother's settled down amazingly well and, though I miss

you awfully, I think you ought to go ahead and do what has to be done. Really, Andrew. As long as you're there, you might as well do it up right. I have faith in you and know—

Andrew didn't complete the sentence, didn't read the sweet, encouraging, sisterly words. As soon as his mind caught the phrase "and do what has to be done," he knew it was the answer he had been seeking. What he wanted to do had to be done. If he could spend long months of his life searching out another man's answers, piecing together happiness for people he didn't even know, then surely his own happiness, his own future was deserving of a little of his time and attention. He picked up the phone, and the desk clerk connected him with an airlines office. Andrew booked a one-way ticket to the Quad Cities—a two-and-a-half-hour drive from Nauvoo.

The entire Shumway family drove him to the airport. It was difficult for Andrew to say goodbye, difficult to express the depth of his appreciation, not only for the things they had done, but for all they had given of themselves. He was weighted with the last-minute gifts of farewell they had pressed into his arms: a copy of Alan's favorite book on fly-fishing, half-a-dozen jars of Lucille's home-preserved jams, a reprint of an old pioneer recipe book tucked into the box with the jam. Rebecca presented him with a pair of exquisitely embroidered pillowcases in the browns and golds and russets Andrew loved. Andrew had never seen the girl flushed and embarrassed before; it became her. He was touched by her thoughtfulness and grateful that he had kept his relationship with her as open and honest as he had. How awful it would have been if he had inadvertently hurt her!

Heber took him aside, giving and receiving last-minute instructions on the work. He handed Andrew a packet of papers and a thick volume carefully gift-wrapped.

"You can open this on the plane, Andrew. You haven't got time here. I'm giving it to you because, well, because—"

It was the first time Andrew had seen the man at a loss for words.

"I'm giving it to you because I know you'll understand the spirit in which it is given. You know how much we all think of you. We'd never want to force our ways upon you. But we love you too much not to at least make certain that the opportunity's there if you want it."

Their eyes met, but Andrew had no opportunity to reply; a dozen hands drew him back into the family circle. There was another series of hugs all around and promises to write and, somehow, he was out the door and halfway up the ramp. He waved unashamedly out his tiny window as long as the plane taxied. Long after he was airborne the warmth of their presence seemed to linger around him.

Finally he opened Heber's package. He drew his breath in amazement. The black leather volume bore a three-lined title—Book of Mormon, Doctrine and Covenants, Pearl of Great Price—and his own name was imprinted in gold in the lower right-hand corner. Andrew knew the volume contained not only the Book of Mormon, but the other Mormon scriptures as well. Inside the flyleaf, in Heber's bold, firm hand, was written the following inscription:

> To Andrew, whom we love as a son, with the hope that you might find within the pages of this volume the peace and joy and truth which we have found.
> With love, your brother and sister. . . .

Both Heber and Lucille had signed their names. Andrew could picture their faces as they lovingly wrapped the book, tucking in their own deep hopes for its success. He knew enough to sense what this meant to them. He held the book for a long time, unopened. He knew he was afraid to turn the leaf, as if, in doing so, he would open up a whole new realm, teeming with knowledge and feeling and responsibility. Was he ready? He didn't know exactly what it was he would face. But he did sense that, once he had faced it—bold, outright—no matter which way he decided, he would never be the same again.

8

Andrew mopped his face with the damp handkerchief for the fourth time. The temperature at the airport had read 102 degrees, humidity 93 percent. But in the little air-cooled car he had comfortably forgotten about conditions outside, eager only to lap away the distance that separated him from his destination. Now, a mere five, ten miles outside Nauvoo, he was stuck with a flat tire. A flat tire in 102-degree weather and no jack! The last customer, so it seemed, had artfully disguised the broken pieces and someone had failed to check thoroughly. Whatever the situation, it resulted in Andrew, stranded on a back-country gravel road, as hot and dusty and frustrated as he could ever remember being, cursing himself a thousand times over for having taken the blasted shortcut, anyway. He sat back in the car with the door open, searching vainly for a way out of his predicament. The only reason he noticed the truck at all was that a thick, choking cloud of dust and exhaust fumes enveloped him when the driver pulled off the road.

"Looks like you need some help." The young man who stepped out of the truck had sandy-colored hair and a face as generously spattered with grease as were the T-shirt and work pants he wore.

"I'd certainly appreciate any help I can get! You wouldn't happen to have a jack I could use, would you?"

It was then that Andrew noticed, as he glanced back at the truck, the faded sign on the door: *Ives' Garage and Towing Service, Nauvoo,*

Illinois. What a stroke of luck! The truck driver already had his equipment out and was bending over the front wheel. Andrew bent down beside him.

"It's a rented car, you see, and the jack is broken—useless."

The driver turned and grinned at him.

"You're just lucky I came by. I was out on a service call—tractor on one of the farms back there. Not many cars travel this road."

"So I've noticed! I was in such a hurry to get to Nauvoo I thought I'd try it."

The driver eyed Andrew with open curiosity. Andrew didn't blame him; a well-dressed stranger with a foreign accent wasn't what you'd expect to find in the area.

"What business you in?"

Andrew chuckled at the thought of trying to explain the unusual business in which he was currently engaged.

"Actually," Andrew replied, his voice more warm than he realized, "actually, it's a personal matter. Here, let me help you."

He took the lug nuts from the driver's grimy hand and rose to get the spare tire from the trunk.

Tom pushed back his hair from his forehead and watched the stranger, and suddenly everything clicked. He should have caught it sooner; the accent, the dark good looks, the expensive clothes and luggage. The man walked around the car, bouncing the tire and grinning. It was hard for Tom to believe that this stranger was at least partly responsible—no, directly responsible—for his own unhappiness.

He felt a ridiculous desire to confront the stranger then and there, longing for the freedom he had known as a boy, when he could have hurled the challenge, "You leave Nan alone, understand? She's my girl!" and then could have backed it with his fists.

It wasn't that simple any more, though. He took the tire and began fitting it into place, trying to ignore the sensations that welled within him when he thought of Nan with this man. The task was over within minutes. He rose and wiped his hands on his pants legs.

"I can't thank you enough, honestly. I don't know what I'd have done if you hadn't come along."

"You'd have been in a pickle, that's for sure."

The stranger had his money out. Tom wouldn't have taken it in the first place; he certainly didn't intend to now.

64

"Please take it," Andrew urged. "It's all I can do to repay you."

The sincerity in his voice was easily discernible. There was something likeable, very open about him.

"It was my pleasure." Tom wouldn't have ordinarily stopped with that: he enjoyed helping people out, and he usually would have added something like, "Stop at the garage if you have any more problems," or "Hope you have a pleasant visit." That was impossible now.

Tom got back into his truck and pulled it onto the road. He could see the little gray car in his rear-view mirror as it followed him toward Nauvoo. He turned the radio on full blast. In fifteen minutes he'd be back in the shop, too busy to think. He stepped on the gas pedal and took the old truck to the top speed it could handle on the pitted gravel road.

Andrew had phoned ahead for reservations. He parked his car outside the Hotel Nauvoo and hurried up to his room, glad for the opportunity of a cool shower before seeing Nan. When he finished dressing, it was close to four o'clock. Should he wait until after the dinner hour? He knew he couldn't bear that. He drove to the florist shop; he felt better armed with the two pink roses and a spray of baby's breath. He had only been to Nan's house briefly before; he had never even met her father. And no one was expecting him now. What if Nan wasn't there?

He parked the car across the street from the tidy brick house. Nan's cat was sleeping on the front porch swing, and a young boy of thirteen, perhaps fourteen, was mowing the large front lawn. The boy turned off the mower as Andrew approached.

"Is Nan at home?"

"Nope," the boy answered. "Nobody but me."

"And that not by choice, I'll warrant."

The boy looked at him blankly before he caught Andrew's meaning. "Oh, yeah," he grinned. "I'd much rather be out swimming on a day like this."

"You must be Nan's little brother. Jonathan, is it?"

"Yeah. And—and you're Andrew!" The boy was getting interested now.

"That's right."

"What're you doing here? I thought you were in Salt Lake City. Nan isn't expecting you, is she?"

"No, no, I thought I'd surprise her."

"You'll do that for sure. I can't wait to see her face. You can stay till she gets home, can't you? She shouldn't be much longer. What time is it?"

Andrew checked his watch. "A little after four."

"Oh, yeah, she'll be here any time now. Come on. Grandma made some lemonade before she left. I could use a cold glass myself."

Jonathan started walking toward the house. Andrew hesitated.

"What about the lawn?"

Jonathan smiled back at Andrew and cocked his head to one side in a manner so strongly resembling Nan that it made Andrew catch his breath.

"I'll finish the lawn after Nan gets home. She'll see to that."

Andrew followed, smiling, and the boy kept up a steady chatter as he walked.

"Nan will have a stroke when she sees you. She sure hasn't been very happy since you left, especially after that business with Tom Briggs and all. You know that necklace you sent her? Heck, she wears it every day. Do you really own a dozen factories and live on a big estate in Scotland?"

Andrew laughed outright. "Not exactly, Jonathan." By the time they were settled at the long kitchen table with their lemonade and a plate of homemade cookies, Jonathan had Andrew telling him all about Paisley and the old cotton mills. The boy had a quick mind, curious and imaginative, and Andrew found himself relating some of the stories of the weavers in Paisley and Kilbarchan, stories he had loved when he was a boy.

They both heard the car pull into the driveway. Jonathan ran to the window.

"It's Nan!"

He turned and saw the excitement leap into Andrew's eyes. They waited, quietly now, for her to reach the door. Andrew couldn't sit still. He rose and paced the kitchen. The front screen opened and swung shut. They heard Nan's voice.

"Jonathan? Are you in here?" Jonathan could see that Andrew was struggling to get himself entirely under control. The boy grinned and remained silent.

"Jonathan, why have you left the lawn half done? Is anything the matter?"

She paused at the entrance to the kitchen with a little gasp. The books she was carrying slipped to the floor, unheeded. She stared at Andrew, unable to speak, for—even in that moment of surprised shock —the realization of what his presence there meant came over her.

Andrew was beside her in moments and took both her hands in his. All the clever things he had planned on saying seemed totally inappropriate now.

"It's all right, Nan. Don't look so stricken."

"That's right. Andrew's just passing through on his way to Scotland."

Jonathan made a comical face and winked at Andrew. Nan laughed then and sank into a chair, aware that Andrew was still holding her hands lightly.

"You didn't tell me. Did something go wrong in Salt Lake?"

"I didn't want to tell you. I was afraid you might protest. I wanted to surprise you. And nothing went wrong in Salt Lake. The work is so blasted slow, I couldn't afford to stay there any longer."

"You ought to be home right now."

"I ought to be right here."

Right here. He really was right here, touching her, talking like this!

"Jonathan, why don't you—"

"I know, go finish mowing the lawn. I'd be glad to." He winked broadly at Andrew as he left the room. Nan raised her eyebrows quizzically. Andrew only smiled and gathered her up into his arms and kissed her, with a tenderness that swept through her entire being.

"You and I have a lot to talk about, Hannah Martin. Is there any place you know of we could slip away to?"

"Well, there's a lovely old willow along the river. Very cool and quiet and secluded."

It was much later when Nan and Andrew emerged from their haven. They had talked of many things, though neither of them dared to broach the subject uppermost in both their minds. Andrew shared with Nan some of his experiences with the Mormons in Salt Lake and some of the impressions they had made on his heart and mind.

"They wouldn't be a bad lot to be mixed up with." He tried to put it lightly.

"You really mean that, Andrew."

"Well, Nan, some of their beliefs are very exciting, very attractive. Like temple marriage, for instance."

He smiled at her teasingly and she felt her cheeks turn rosy beneath his gaze.

"Their ideas about God and progression, and the way they work together—like their welfare system that I just told you about. I'm surprised you don't know more about the Mormons, Nan, living so close to them as you do, and being so interested in their history."

Nan was very thoughtful. "I wonder, too," she replied. "I really wonder why. . . ."

Her voice trailed off. She was thinking of Grant. It struck her, suddenly, that he had never told her anything. Oh, he had talked sometimes about "the Church," safe facts and figures concerning how the congregations were run with a bishop and his counselors, how the meetings were held, what different organizations existed—little items of interest about temples and missions and such. But the actual spiritual doctrine—Nan realized with a shock that Grant had never told her a thing! Why? Surely he cared. She knew he did. Then why had he never even tried to teach her what he believed?

"Nan, I don't know about you, but I am ravenously hungry. Do you think there's any place still open where we can get a bite to eat?"

"Twenty minutes until the drive-ins close. Let's go."

They drove through town with the windows down, and the cool night air teased Nan's hair and ruffled it about her face. Andrew had forgotten how breathtakingly beautiful she really was.

"There it is," he cried, pointing off to the right. "Ives' Garage. That's the place."

Nan felt her pulse begin to race.

"What place? What do you mean?"

They pulled into the drive-in and placed their order. Nan didn't want to appear too curious, but she had to know.

"What were you saying about Ives' Garage, Andrew?"

"Oh, I'd almost forgotten to tell you, Nan. I had a beastly time on the way here today. The car had a flat and I was out in the middle of nowhere. You know how hot it was this afternoon. I had visions of walking ten miles into town when this old battered truck pulled over. It was a lad from that place we passed—Ives' Garage. He changed the wheel in no time. Very gracious, too."

"What did he look like?"

"Oh, yes, I suppose you might know him. He had sandy hair, rather curly, and brown eyes. I don't know what else. A nice smile—so much grease on his face it was difficult to tell much more."

"It was Tom."

"Who, Nan?"

"Tom Briggs."

"And who is Tom Briggs?"

Andrew could see by Nan's face that she was disturbed about something. The name sounded vaguely familiar to him. Had the lad mentioned his name this afternoon? No, he was certain he hadn't.

"Jonathan! Jonathan mentioned that name. That was it!"

"Jonathan! How could he! What did he say?"

"I don't quite recall. Something about you being unhappy and some kind of 'business with Tom Briggs,' that's what he called it."

Nan sighed. She may as well tell him now. But it was going to be a little ticklish. She didn't want Andrew to wonder about her own presumptuousness, to think that it was only because of him she had refused Tom. And yet, without Andrew, what would she have done? Would she have had the courage to say no?

She told him everything and he listened patiently, his eyes dark and concerned. It never occurred to Nan to be anything less than totally honest with Andrew. Something right from the first had created that kind of feeling within her. And so she told him not only what had happened, but how she felt, the understanding that had come to her as she lay in her room, her realization of the sanctity of love.

As she spoke the strength of her spirit lighted her features, and the few trailing wisps of doubt which still clung to Andrew's heart were burned away by the purity and beauty he felt before him. She didn't know what a powerful influence she was having upon him. Finished with her burdensome tale at last, she laid her head lightly against his shoulder, relieved and relaxed.

"I feel very sorry for Tom Briggs," he said softly. "I think I can understand something of his pain." Andrew was shaken by the depth of the compassion he felt for this man who loved Nan. "But I don't think even Tom realizes fully the extent of his loss."

He smoothed her soft hair and held her gently; his feeling of tenderness was too deep for anything more. It seemed at that moment that Nan had always belonged to him, as if something deep within him was struggling into existence, awakened by her presence, stirred by his knowledge of his love for her.

"You'll love him, Andrew, I know you will. I'm so grateful you two have an opportunity to meet each other."

"How do you know where to find him?"

"I pretty well know his daily schedules. It's Wednesday morning —he'll be tending the gardens either at the Brigham Young house or at Brownings. There he is, Andrew—pull over here."

Nan didn't surprise the old man this time. He was leaning on the hoe for a breather and watched the two young people walk across the street together. It was a lovely sight. He looked like just the kind of fellow Grant had always imagined for Hannah. There was only one thing left to make it right for both of them. As soon as they came within earshot he called out, "So this is Andrew. I thought you were in Salt Lake City, young man."

"Oh, Grant! I hoped you'd be working and I could surprise you."

Grant's eyes twinkled and he winked ever so slightly at Andrew. "Why, you know you never surprise me, Nan. Besides, I wouldn't have missed watching the two of you walking together for anything. Prettiest picture I've seen in a long time."

Nan blushed now and stomped her foot at him in her frustration. Andrew liked the old man immediately, and they found it easy to talk together. As Andrew answered Grant's questions about Salt Lake, Nan wandered through the neat rows of tulips and pansies, the tall, old-fashioned hollyhocks in muted shades, and the purple flowering kale. Whenever she looked up at the men talking earnestly together, her heart skipped a little in excitement. Seeing them together like this made her feel warm and happy inside.

As they talked, Andrew could easily see how deeply this gentle man cared for Nan. For his part, Grant was thinking, *He loves her. He's not even trying to hide it. He's admitted to himself now how much he loves her.*

Grant wished he could really talk to the boy, but this was neither the time nor the place. He would have to hope for another opportunity. When they parted Nan hugged him and her eyes were dancing. He squeezed her hand; there wasn't time for much more. He watched them walk off together. He thought of his own youth, aware that his thoughts held no bitter longing or regret.

His years with Ellen had been as sweet and strong and true as a man could ever hope for. But then, they'd started out with a lot of advantages, a lot of help. He wanted the same for Hannah. And that intelligent young man with the warm eyes who loved her—didn't he deserve the opportunity of laying the best life has to offer at her feet? Grant thought so. He just didn't know what he was going to do about it.

When they left Grant, Andrew drove Hannah home to get the Mustang. She had cut down her newspaper work to a minimum, eager to spend every possible moment with Andrew, but this was one assignment she hadn't been able to wheedle out of. She hated to leave him! The day was so fresh and lovely; she felt as though she were throwing it away. They made plans for Andrew to return at six for dinner with the family. The confrontation between Andrew and her father had to come sooner or later, but Nan was so fearful of what would happen that she didn't dare let herself think about it.

Andrew watched her drive away. What to do for all the hours ahead? He was restless. More nervous about this evening than he wanted to admit. Surely their approval couldn't mean so much to him? But he knew how much it meant to Nan, and he didn't want to see her hurt or humiliated in any way.

He drove to the far end of the park. He could always think better when he had someplace to walk. And he needed to think. Here beneath the tall pines and spreading elms it was quiet, and he would be alone. He knew now, beyond doubt, that he loved Nan. But he hadn't told her so. After all, what did he have to offer her? He couldn't ask her to marry him. If he told her the truth, would she understand? He walked with long strides, the pull at his muscles feeling good. He knew he had no choice, but he didn't know if he could bear the silence, as well as the waiting. He couldn't even declare himself to Nan's father! What kind of an impression could he possibly hope to make on the man? And Nan. Nan would have to bear the brunt of the ridicule and misunderstanding that might openly develop after he had gone.

He ran now, kicking at the stones and leaves in his path. If he had his way he would ask Nan to marry him today and take her with him to Scotland. His heart thrilled at the prospect, but his mind knew full well how impossible that would be. His own way . . . he was twenty-four years old, and he had never yet been his own man. Because of an obligation to a dead man his own life, his own desires seemed always pushed around the corner, neglected and unfulfilled.

"Watch out!" The path Andrew was jogging crossed the narrow gravel roadway that wound up through the park, and he shot out into it at top speed. At sound of the sharp warning he veered, barely missing the front fender of the old Chevy. He stopped, catching his breath and trying to take in the scene before him.

The old car was straddling the entire roadway, inching its way, but certainly not forward, for the power that propelled it had little control over direction. One girl pushed from behind, head down, shouting encouragement to her friend who, with a hand on the open door and one on the steering wheel, was trying to move the car and steer it, somehow, at the same time. Andrew stifled his laugh with difficulty.

"Allow me," he said kindly, but firmly, as he reached across the girl, turned the key, and pulled the shift lever into park.

"There. Now let's see what the problem is, ladies."

The girl beside him wrinkled her nose and the little band of freckles that seemed painted there began to dance. Her gray eyes sparkled and there was laughter in her voice when she spoke.

"I'm sorry we nearly ran you down."

"You scared us to death!" The other girl came around the car and leaned against the dusty side in exhaustion.

"I don't think you'd have done much damage at the rate you were going. What seems to be the problem?"

Andrew walked around and opened the hood. It was scorching hot and he winced at the touch of it.

"We can't figure out what's the matter! The ugly old thing is always breaking down—every time we drive it." The girl with the brown pigtails was nearly wailing in frustration.

"Is it your car?" Andrew asked her.

"No." It was the gray-eyed blond with the freckles who replied. "It's her brother's. Personally, I think he must fix it before he gives it to us. He gets such a kick out of seeing us suffer."

"He says it's one way to keep us out of trouble."

Andrew laughed now; he couldn't help it. They were such a pathetic, typical pair of girls. The blonde with the gray eyes wrinkled her nose again and looked at him appraisingly.

"You're Andrew, aren't you?" Her voice was as cool and appraising as her look. It took him by surprise. How the devil did she know who he was? And why this attitude of almost-accusation?

"Yes, I am, lass. You have me at a disadvantage, though. I'm afraid I don't know—"

"I'm Julie. Nan's sister."

"Nan's sister! You're very . . ." He almost said *unlike her*, but thought better of it just in time.

"Very different from Nan. Yes, I know. Everyone says so."

The girl with the pigtails was staring open-mouthed. "I don't understand, Julie. If this is really Andrew, why didn't you recognize him? Haven't you ever met him before?"

"Not really, Cathy. I've only seen him from a distance. Nan was awfully, well, let's just say protective where he was concerned."

It was there still; Andrew sensed the wary sarcasm. Why did the girl resent him? "Nan's told me of you, nevertheless."

"I'm sure she has. 'I've got this frivolous, empty-headed kid sister.' I can just hear her."

Andrew smiled his most charming smile—sincerely, too. The girl was afraid, very uncertain for some reason.

"No," he answered truthfully, "she told me you were pretty and vivacious, with lovely gray eyes, and that you were the best swimmer in four counties."

"That's right! She took first in the freestyle and the medley at state competition last spring."

Julie shot her friend a withering glance, but her gaze returned immediately to Andrew. He looked at her a moment, then said softly,

"Nan's really very proud of you. And she was certainly right about one thing: you have the most beautiful gray eyes I have ever seen."

It was true, but Julie couldn't stand his gaze. She looked away in confusion. Andrew grasped the break in conversation gratefully.

"Let's see if I can be of any help."

He stuck his head under the hood. If it was something basic and easy to spot he'd be all right. If not, he would have to bow out gracefully and find some other way to redeem himself in the eyes of the two girls.

"Come here, Julie. Could you help me a minute, please?"

She came hesitatingly, bending her head close to his. Andrew could sense that the closeness made her uncomfortable.

"Hold right there. That's right. It won't hurt you. Looks like the coil wire has vibrated loose. If I can just slip this wire onto the coil— hold over there. That's it. Great!"

Once together, if nothing else were wrong, he ought to have the old car running again.

"Give her a try, Cathy."

The girl climbed behind the wheel and turned the key. The engine ground sluggishly a moment, then whirred into life. Cathy squealed and clapped her hands. Julie smiled—warmly, he thought.

"You did it. Thanks a lot."

"You're welcome, lass. Listen, I have an idea. Why don't you pull that beast off to the side there, Cathy, and the two of you join me for lunch?"

"Really?" Cathy was delighted.

"I don't know. I don't think we ought to." Julie's coolness was creeping back again.

Andrew decided to play his hand. "Please, Julie. Actually, you'd be doing me a favor. I'm on my own this afternoon; rather at a loose end. And I would honestly love the pleasure of your company."

She studied him a moment before deciding to accept his sincerity. At last she smiled.

"All right. We'd love it, Andrew. Lead the way."

He turned and started back down the path, the two girls following. As he turned he barely caught Cathy's excited whisper.

"Oh, Julie, he's so—"

He didn't need to hear the rest. Julie had been one of the people he was concerned about meeting tonight. It looked as if he could cross that one little worry off his list.

9

If zealous love should go in search of virtue,
Where should he find it purer . . ?

KING JOHN

It was ten minutes to six. Andrew seemed always to be prompt, so he would be here any minute. Nan had hurried home so she could make the apple pie herself. It was one of her specialties. The table was set with the good china and silver, and with linen napkins. A pretty vase filled with violet and yellow pansies and perk, velvety snapdragons rested in the center. Julie had actually offered to arrange the flowers, and now she was asking if she could help. Nan couldn't understand it. She had been so antagonistic before at the idea of having to sit through a dinner with "Nan's stranger." She had called him that constantly, knowing how it upset Nan. What could have caused such a total change?

She handed Julie the tray of tomatoes stuffed with her grandmother's homemade cole slaw. The chicken was baked to perfection, and a pan filled with plump, tender ears of corn boiled and sputtered on the back burner. Nan wasn't worried about the food. But she was worried sick about her father.

After that first caustic remark about the stranger being out for what he could get, he hadn't spoken half a dozen words concerning Andrew. Nan knew he didn't approve, but she had no idea what he felt, or what he would say when he was face to face with Andrew at last. Oh, she had missed Andrew today! If it was this bad after only a few hours, what would it be like when he left again?

76

She was taking the rolls out of the oven and didn't hear the doorbell ring. When she walked into the dining room Andrew was already there. He rose and came over to her.

"I missed you," was all he said. She didn't need any more.

They sat down at the table and her father spoke the grace, as he always did, in that colorless, toneless voice which made praying nothing but a mere formality. As soon as the food was passed and everyone was settled, the questions began.

"You're from Loch Lomond country, Nan tells me. Is that right, Andrew?"

"That's right, sir. My family is in the textile business in Paisley."

"I see. Beautiful country, so I've been told."

"Yes, it is. I think you'd like it. Good farmland, charming old villages, as well as the mountains—and the loch, of course."

"Is that Bobbie Burns country?"

"Not really," Andrew explained. "Burns was born in Ayrshire, further down in Scotland. He died in Dumfries, close on the Solway Firth—a smugglers' paradise in Burns's day."

"I teach a little Burns in my high school literature classes."

Nan was surprised at this revelation on her father's part. Andrew took it up immediately. He was so gracious. He soon had her father talking of favorite poems and ballads and the joys and frustrations of trying to teach such elusive, creative things as thoughts and feelings to a sometimes disinterested class. Nan was hopeful. She had never dreamed her father would talk like this with Andrew.

"Where were you educated, Andrew?"

"Edinburgh." The word was lovely when he said it. "I finished my education there and went right to work with my father. But I didn't have much time. Eight months, actually, before he died."

"Oh, I see."

That was all. Not "That's too bad," or "I'm sorry." Her father bent his head and ate, as though he were through with talking, as in fact he was—for he didn't say another word all evening, except to excuse himself from the table and the room after the dessert had been served. There was an awkward little pause, then Julie spoke—gayly, naturally, as though no strain existed.

"Did you tell Nan about our little adventure today, Andrew?"

Nan caught the note of comradeship in her voice and looked up, incredulous.

"I haven't had an opportunity. Why don't you?"

Amazingly, Julie complied, giving her own clever, colorful account of what had happened in the park. Andrew caught Nan's eye across the table and smiled. So Andrew had charmed Julie, worked through the terrible defenses she had constructed against him. Nan was glad, though she still couldn't believe the transformation he had wrought in her sister. How much more attractive she is, Nan thought, when she is thoughtful and sweet and happy like this.

Andrew said something to Nan's grandmother. Nan didn't catch it, but she could see by the expression on her grandmother's face that it must have pleased her. There was nothing to worry about from that quarter. She was very susceptible to any man with charm, Nan knew. And Jonathan. Andrew had won him over that first day in the kitchen before Nan came home. Nan knew the prejudices her family held were based on ignorance, and she had hoped that just such a thing might happen; they would have the opportunity to meet Andrew and see for themselves what kind of a person he was.

But there was still her father, sitting at the end of the table, totally withdrawn, as if no one else even existed. The light, easy conversation among the rest of them covered up what awkwardness there was. But Nan had to force down her food, and the smile she kept on her face was beginning to hurt. Everyone else seemed to be fine, but she was angry—angry at herself for caring what her father did and thought, angry at her father for spoiling things, for not being everything she wanted him to be, for being so insensitive to Andrew, when it seemed as though there was no need, no provocation at all.

Andrew dried the dishes and teased her grandmother, and looked at Jonathan's airplane collection, which seemed to include a twenty-minute treatise on each individual model. He listened to Julie's favorite song on her new album. It seemed Nan would never get him to herself!

When at last they were alone, Andrew turned to her, his eyes sparkling.

"Thank you, Nan, for tonight. I know how difficult it was for you. But I enjoyed the evening immensely."

She didn't answer, and he cupped her chin in his hand, lifting her eyes to meet his.

"Don't worry about your father, lass. I was more of a success there than you realize."

"What do you mean?"

"I could see it in his eyes. He liked me. And he didn't want to. For some reason of his own he doesn't want to like me at all."

"Why are you so kind to him?"

"I don't know. He's your father, Nan. I can't help feeling kindly toward him."

"You're much too soft-hearted, Andrew."

"You think so? It'll be your own fault, then. I'm too happy, you see, to feel anything but good about everyone."

He took her hand and they walked, the moonlight making a path for them to follow. And Nan's own happiness spilled over and filled up every little crevice of fear and pain, and she wondered if she had ever known what happiness was until this night.

Long after Andrew brought Nan home and she fell asleep, exhausted with the activities and emotions of the long day, her father sat awake in his study at the back of the house. He worked hard at ignoring the thoughts and feelings which brought him pain. But tonight they had assailed his defenses and worked their way inside, and he was forced to face them against his will.

He rose and took a slender volume from one of his shelves. He opened it to the inscription, written in the flourishing feminine hand he had known so well. Even after all these years a picture of his wife came easily to his mind: the delicate, finely molded features of her face, the clear white skin, the brown eyes whose range of expression never ceased to fascinate him. Nan was so very like her. He had watched Nan grow into womanhood, and each year the transformation was more complete, until now she was so much like her mother, in voice and feature and personality, that he could hardly bear it.

Only in his darkest moments did Abraham Martin admit to himself the truth. His love for Elizabeth had bordered on idolatry, and yet that very love had stood between them. He had worked and struggled to educate himself, to rise in the world. But all the things he struggled for came to Elizabeth with ease. *He* was the teacher of English, the one who should be best acquainted with the great writers and the great minds. But Elizabeth could recite poetry to him for hours, and her fine mind grasped many ideas and principles which came to him only with difficulty.

Elizabeth possessed a certain grace and wisdom that astounded him. She was feminine to a fault, sensitive and sweet, yet with a fire to her spirit which made her gentle qualities more endearing still. Abraham had never felt worthy of her; he had known she was fashioned for much better things, much higher ways than he could provide. His resentment of himself grew into a canker that tainted the sweetness of their relationship—the only knowing sorrow he ever caused her. And yet it seemed a poison he was helpless to control. Only when she died and left him did he realize the tragedy of how he had lived—of how he had failed her with his cowardice and weak will.

He shrank away from all relationships now, convinced that his influence would be nothing but a blight upon those he might love. Especially did he turn away from Nan, for as she grew to be more and more like Elizabeth, his pain and self-loathing became a shadow ever moving between them.

The hot room and his own heated thoughts were stifling him. The back door was close; he slipped out into the night, the cool darkness a balm on his mind. He was thoroughly lonely; a man who walked alone by choice. He knew he had woven the strands of his own loneliness by rejecting anyone or anything that might get into his heart. And he knew he had failed. Elizabeth was the light and joy of his being, and Nan was part of Elizabeth, and part of himself, and all his agonized efforts could not destroy the deep love for her which lived within him.

Just like Elizabeth, Nan was too good for him. Tom Briggs wasn't really his choice for her. But in his ineptitude, what better did he have to offer Nan? This Andrew Buchanan was Nan's choice. He was the man of her dreams, drawn to her from the other side of the world. And he loved her. It was easy for Abraham to see how much the man loved her. Elizabeth had never had the man of her dreams. In Abraham's mind Andrew represented his own dream-self, the man he had wanted to be for Elizabeth, and failed.

And Andrew Buchanan would take Nan away. Elizabeth had left him; Nan's presence seemed his only tangible contact with her. What would happen if Nan were to leave him, too? He walked, the grass wet upon his feet and legs, walked tired and comfortless. In the room above him Nan slept peacefully, completely unaware of the love and pain that trembled in her father's heart.

Andrew came for Nan early the next morning. In spite of the heavy August heat, the city was teeming with tourists. And today, this last day, more than ever he needed to be alone with Nan. He told her so, and she fluttered her eyes at him in mock protest. Then she directed him to a place outside of town, a large wooded tract of land where no tourist's foot had ever stepped. They walked until they found a shady spot where Nan could spread a blanket for them to sit. She opened the thermos of cold lemonade she had brought and poured him a cup. He drank deeply, then tried to begin.

"Nan, Nan . . ." he bent closer to her and took her hands. "Nan, I love you. . . ."

This wasn't how it was supposed to be. He should be whispering the words passionately against her hair, with moonlight and music and the scent of flowers in the air. He rose, angry at himself, and frustrated. She rose, too, and came to stand beside him. Her fingertips barely brushed his hand.

"It's all right, Andrew. Go on."

He looked into her clear eyes and the romantic surroundings didn't seem so necessary any more.

"I love you, Nan, and I want to marry you. And I want you to know that I have never spoken those words before, to any other woman."

Her heart was pounding, she felt warm all over, in a tingling sort of way. And yet her mind was calm, and she wondered, *How can it seem so natural to hear Andrew speak these wondrous words to me?* She reached for his hand.

"That's not all, Andrew, is it?"

He hesitated, miserable; wishing that the next part didn't have to come.

"I can sense that you're terribly worried and unhappy about something." She smiled as she said it. "Besides, why else would you say you love me, and then knit your dark brow and glare at me that way?"

He smiled, the adoration he felt for her glowing in his eyes. He led her back to the blanket and sat down.

"My mother," he began, "is an unusual person. No one has really understood her or been able to handle her except my father. She appears to be very overbearing and domineering. But in many ways she's remained a frightened little girl all her life. It's just that people don't see that side of her, or rather, what they see doesn't register as uncertainty or fear."

"It sounds like you understand her pretty well."

"I've tried to. I've watched my father carefully and tried to. Well, Nan, when my grandfather died my parents were both very young. And when it was time for my father to spend his three months in America, in obedience to the requirements of the will, my mother was terrified. She was young and in love, and she tried to be brave, but it nearly broke her heart to let him go. Helen, our old serving woman, was with her then. She says mother hardly slept nights at all. She paced her rooms and wrote long letters to father and wore herself out before she was able to sleep."

"The poor thing." Hannah could picture the frightened, lonely young woman struggling alone in the darkness, unable to control her fears.

"Mother had one small daughter then. Jeannie. She was two and a half, maybe three years old. She had been sick with what seemed to be a cold and an earache. One afternoon she developed a fever. By evening she was burning up. The doctor stayed by her bedside all night. But there was little he could do. It seemed to strike so fast. For two days she hovered between life and death, suffering greatly. In the early hours of morning she died."

"No! Wasn't there something? What about medicines, hospitals?"

"They decided afterward that she must have had some kind of bacterial pneumonia, which developed into meningitis. Only lengthy cultures and tests would have confirmed a diagnosis before her death. You know, even penicillin wasn't widely used back then. It just happened too quickly. Anyway, Mother was frantic. They had sent a telegram to America, to the last address they had for my father, as soon as they realized there was real danger. But the telegram just missed him. It was more than a week before they located him; days later before he was able to make it home.''

"And your mother was all alone. Facing that terrible suffering without him.''

"Yes. The death, itself. The funeral and the burial. Helen says she was totally distraught. Refused to give up the little girl. Apparently it was awful.''

Nan rose, unable to bear the pictures in her own mind. She stood behind Andrew and placed her hands on his shoulders.

"Oh, Andrew, Andrew!''

"After Father returned it was years before she would allow him to be away from her for more than several hours. She accompanied him on all his business trips. She worried if he was ever the least bit late coming home. It was hell for them both. Then I was born. It had been several years since Jeannie's death, and Mother assumed that she would never be able to have more children.''

"So you seemed like a miracle, and all the love and tenderness she had been hoarding was lavished on you.''

"Yes, I imagine that was the way of it. And for the first time she relaxed a little and began to enjoy life again. Then Janet came, too, and you would think she could have forgotten the awful unhappiness of those early years.''

"But she didn't.''

Andrew paused. "No. She harbors an irrational hatred of anything American.''

"How did she ever let you go?'' Nan's voice was barely a whisper.

"I don't know. Father's death nearly destroyed her. My going off to America was little different in her eyes than having me dead, as well. My cousin, Edwin, whom she loves nearly as much as she loves me, is with her now.''

Nan nodded. "That's right. I remember.'' She had never known she would love someone so deeply, and the pain inside was like a raging torrent beating down upon her. "And you're going home tomorrow. And it would hardly do to tell her you've fallen in love with some obscure little American girl. . . .''

"Nan!'' He pulled her roughly down beside him. "You mustn't talk like that! Nan, listen! I'm afraid you're right. I can't possibly tell her that now. I'll go home and somehow get through this whole affair of the will and the trust. Once that strain is out of the way, once she sees I am home safe—well—it's only a matter of months, Nan, until the whole business will be finished with, and then—"

"And then what, Andrew? You'll open up the old wounds and start all over again?"

He took her by the shoulders and held her so tightly that it hurt. But his voice was gentle when he spoke.

"She can only bear so much at a time, Nan. You've no idea how out of touch with reality she can become. It frightens me. I can't tell her now and have you forever connected in her mind with those fears and fantasies that revolve around the old man and his will. There will be ways of introducing you into her life and into her heart. Ways that bear no resemblance to her grotesque, unreasonable images of America."

Nan didn't want to cry. Her throat ached, but she knew she must hold back the tears.

"Scotland is so far away, Andrew. And once you're home—"

"Oh, Nan, do you have so little faith in me and my love for you?"

It was an appeal, a direct challenge from his heart to hers. She looked deep into his eyes.

"Grant has always told me, 'Be patient. Keep your heart in the right place. The Lord will take care of you.' Ever since I was a little girl."

"He told you that?"

"Always."

She pushed back his hair and traced with her finger the line of his forehead, his cheek, his lips, a new and powerful feeling surging through her at the touch of him.

"My heart's in the right place, Andrew. I know it is."

She smiled at him as the first tear rolled down her cheek.

"My heart's in your safekeeping, Andrew. Go home. I'll be ready when you come for me."

He kissed away the little tear. How could he ever tell her of the awesome respect he felt for her? He held her tenderly and wondered, suddenly, if his father had felt something like this when, as a young man, he held Andrew's mother in his arms, knowing he had to leave her, and wondering how he was going to be able to do it.

10

It was so good to be home! Everything had a glow about it. Andrew devoured each familiar, loved scene, realizing how deep his hunger, his homesickness had really been.

There was a great family feast to celebrate his arrival, his mother seeing to it that all his favorite dishes were served: steak and kidney pie with potatoes and cabbage, warm rhubarb tarts for dessert, and the mellow, lingering taste of his favorite port wine. He savored every moment, every taste and sight and smell. Janet was more fresh and lovely than he had remembered her, and he was startled by his mother's proud, regal beauty, enhanced by his presence there.

Edwin might have given Andrew a bad time, but he didn't. "I couldn't have held out much longer," he said laconically, with the sparkle in his eyes, and that was all.

Andrew, sensing his meaning, was therefore not unduly surprised to discover that everything was in order; perfectly organized, recorded, and accounted for. Perhaps Edwin had decided it would be unwise to bite the hand that fed him. Andrew couldn't guess his motives, but he was too pleased with the results to care what had motivated them.

He threw himself back into his work, anxious to be totally engaged, beyond the reach of thought and memory. As he pulled things back together and reviewed them after his absence, he was astounded to discover how wonderfully Edwin had actually managed, and told him so one evening at dinner.

"I hate to admit it, Edwin, but I didn't expect such a spectacular performance as you've given."

"Nothing but the best for you, Andrew." A wry smile played around the corners of his mouth, but Edwin went on eating.

"The best, indeed. If you ever give your best, Edwin, the world will sit up and take notice. You've too much natural ability. You never have to push yourself."

"I had the vague feeling when this conversation began that you were intending to compliment me, Andrew. It's rather turned into a lecture, don't you think?"

"He has you there, Andrew." Janet's eyes were sparkling as she laughed at her brother's discomfort.

"I'm sorry. You're both right. But, confound it, Edwin, you've got a grasp on things it took father six months—sometimes a year—to hammer into me. You're a canny one, Edwin; you've got a head for this kind of business, and you know it."

A slight little bow of the head; a gracious, almost mocking acknowledgment.

"It was gruesome work, that. I don't know how you take it, Andrew."

"I love it. And, in spite of your fantastic coverup, I'd hazard a guess that you enjoyed it much more than you'd ever admit."

Edwin made a face, contrived to express half a dozen things at once, but actually revealing nothing of his real emotions. He turned and spoke to Jessie, skillfully turning the conversation away from himself. Andrew had hit too close to home. Edwin was having difficulties keeping his ambitions and jealousies in check. It would never do for Andrew to suspect the least change, however subtle, the least bitterness. Even too much enthusiasm on Edwin's part would be something to create notice. It was imperative for him to keep the casual, uncaring, charming facade. It was the best protection, as well as the best cover, he could ever wish for.

Edwin cursed inwardly at the cruel twist of events which had placed him at cross purposes with this cousin. Andrew was one of the few men Edwin respected—perhaps the only man he could say that he actually loved. Now their interests stood at odds with one another. Well, he could still achieve his own ends without injuring Andrew in

86

any way. He would bide his time. Too much was at stake to let impatience play him wrong.

Edwin smiled across the table at Janet. She was more beautiful, more vibrant than ever, now that Andrew was home. Twice fate had crossed him: in denying him the name and legacy of Buchanan, then in denying him access to this lovely girl who returned his smile with such innocent affection. This was his last chance: third time's the charm. The game of chance and fortune was something Edwin understood. At last he had a hand to play. And he was prepared to play it to the hilt.

Janet could feel the warmth of peace and happiness spread over the family like an enchantment, a spell. Her mother's eyes danced and gleamed as she had not seen them do since her father's death. Even Edwin seemed more relaxed now that Andrew was here. She had no right to destroy it in any way. Nor did she want to. But every time she met with the missionaries or attended a Mormon religious service she became more and more converted. The more she learned, the deeper her convictions grew.

She watched Andrew now, as he ate his food with such carefree concentration. She had tried to discover his feelings, wildly hopeful that, after his happy stay in Salt Lake, he would be very favorable toward the Latter-day Saints. But she was afraid to ask questions which were too pointed; and she seldom had him alone, anyway, with her mother always hovering near, as if she couldn't bear to let him out of her sight.

Andrew seemed to Janet to be very enthusiastic about the Mormon people, but he never said a word that concerned their doctrine—what he might know of it, or what he might feel about what he knew. And as the days passed, happy, busy, and serene, Janet became convinced that it would be impossible to confide in Andrew. Even if he were sympathetic, even if he wanted to understand, he could never support any action that would upset Jessie, especially now, when things were going so smoothly again.

Andrew's life fell easily back into the old routine. It gave him a sense of security to know what to expect, to realize that every aspect of his life was familiar: something he could anticipate, something he could handle, no matter what problems might arise. After the fog and frustration of his lonely search, it was a joy to work with things he understood and loved. Edwin had agreed to work with Andrew, at least for a week or two. His companionship brought great pleasure to Andrew, having the added advantage of reducing even further those unguarded moments when he was entirely alone.

Sunday, he could see already, would be the most difficult day for him. There was virtually no activity around the place, nothing he could lay his hand to; the lazy hours were like a punishment to him. The first Sunday after his return he had wandered every inch of the place, as if he wouldn't really be home until he had seen it all with his own eyes, felt it and touched it, and reclaimed it as his own.

It had been easy to imagine Nan beside him: standing beneath the ancient rowan tree—Nan had never worn a sprig of rowan berries in her hair—or walking the braes along the placid little burn, thick with moss and bracken, where every breath of air carried the heady fragrance of gorse, mingled with the smells of soil and water and wet leaves from the stream at his feet. He missed her with a sense of incompleteness. And he marveled at the unity of thought and understanding which can exist between a man and woman, inherently, it seemed, with no need for explanation, transcending time and distance, customs and ways, a pure and natural reaction of spirit to spirit, wherein there was no pretense and no guile.

He walked back to the house and his study and wrote to Nan, almost wishing he could remove his own strict injunction. He had asked Nan not to answer his letters, not to write. It would be possible, he guessed, to have her letters sent to one of his business addresses. But he had wanted nothing furtive and secretive. His mother, he knew, would never accept Nan if she felt the girl had been influencing Andrew unfairly behind her back. Everything must be open and honest and considerate to be worthy of Nan. He wanted nothing to jeopardize his mother's appraisal and acceptance when the time came.

He addressed the letter, picturing the slender white hands opening the seal, removing the pages, the brown eyes reading them carefully for what pieces of himself she could discover within. Now that the letter was sealed, he thought suddenly of half a dozen things he might have told her. He almost ripped open the envelope and began again. But it was already the longest letter he had written to anyone in his life. He would let it stand as it was.

He rose, his mind casting about for something to do next. He remembered the bright, busy Sundays in Salt Lake City. Even as a non-Mormon he had had something to do. There had been the Tabernacle Choir broadcast in the morning, and usually a concert or lecture of some kind in the afternoon.

He recalled one Sunday when he had been invited to dinner at the Shumways'. Heber had been detained at some meeting, and they had waited dinner for him; Rebecca had astounded him with a list of the meetings Mormons attend each Sabbath. Priesthood meeting, Sunday School, sacrament meeting, choir practice if one was involved, with a possible youth council meeting or an evening fireside. He remembered feeling strangely alien and left out. There was a way for every Mormon, no matter what he was like, to find his own place, to fit in. Every person seemed needed and appreciated. He had realized then that this was a world all its own and he was only an outsider, looking in.

Janet! Perhaps he could talk her into a game of backgammon. They had done so little together since his return.

He looked for her in her room, but she wasn't there. Coming back down the hall he met Edwin dressed for riding.

"Have you seen Janet about?"

"She went off to Mary's. Probably won't be back till late."

"Mary Cameron? What the devil could she be doing there? Why didn't she tell me she was going?"

"Hey, hey, hold on, man. You're sounding like Jessie herself. The two girls are very thick, you know. Janet spent most of her Sundays there when you were gone."

"She did?" A brief spark of doubt entered Andrew's mind.

"You need'na look so dashed, Andrew. Come riding with us. You probably need the air."

"I've been out walking the grounds from end to end. You're riding with Morag, aren't you?"

"That's right. But we could bear your company this once."

"That's grand of you, Edwin, really. But no thanks. She's a great girl, Morag. You'd do well to keep your eye on her."

"My conclusion exactly." With a flourish he was gone.

Andrew turned back to his own rooms, brooding. He hated to admit it, but there was something amiss between himself and Janet.

The easy camaraderie that had existed between them before was strained now. At first he had taken it to be his own imagination, attributing it to any or a mixture of strains, pressures, and circumstances. But he could ignore it no longer. It seemed as if Janet was purposefully avoiding him.

And then there was that episode two nights ago when he had been in his study until late and had heard footsteps on the stairs. Welcoming the break, he rose to see who it was and only caught sight of Janet as she disappeared into her own room. She was carrying her shoes, sneaking past his door!

Janet had never done any such thing in her life. What could it mean? Try as he might, Andrew could come up with only one solution. She must be seeing some fellow in the village. But why would she be so secretive? Why wouldn't she want him to know? It seemed an unlikely thing for Janet to do, and yet, what other explanation could there possibly be?

Perhaps Edwin, with his casual ways, had kept too loose a rein on her. *But that shouldn't matter*, he argued with himself. He had always felt he could trust his sister implicitly, that her own values and instincts were really the only control she needed. Yet, if he were wrong—or even if he were right—and confronted her, would it only widen the gap already between them?

Was she really safe at Mary's house today, or was some clandestine meeting taking place? Why were human relationships so unstable? His sense of responsibility urged him to act, but his trust of his sister, his tenderness toward her, slowed his hand. *Why must there always be something to agonize about, something to cast a shadow and a fear?* He felt as though his mind was filled with leaping, taunting shadows. He was tired, and he couldn't bear the prospect of being alone. He rose to seek out someone to help him fill the tedious hours yet remaining.

It had been a good day, especially for a Monday, and they had accomplished much. Andrew and Edwin drove home together, the lid down on the sleek silver-blue Healey, the last sun of the August day beating warm on their heads.

Andrew stroked the smooth touch of the wooden steering wheel vibrating against his palms. He loved the feel of his own car beneath him, after the string of nameless, faceless, rented American cars he had endured for months. He shuddered now at the thought and, accelerating slightly, then downshifting, took the steep curve gracefully, the throbbing machine hugging the ground beneath it with ease.

"You're that glad to be home, are you?"

Why was it Edwin could read his thoughts with such annoying accuracy?

"Aye, more than I realized."

"You've spoken little of your experiences in America, Andrew. Was it all that bad? There must have been something good, something worth remembering, surely?"

Andrew smiled, thinking warmly, languidly of the many happy memories he cherished to himself. He glanced at Edwin, wishing he could tell him of Nan, wondering what Edwin's reactions would be. Well, at least he could tell of Salt Lake and Heber Shumway and his experiences there. Those were happy memories, something he could share with Edwin, something pleasurable to recall on this sunny, windswept afternoon.

He began to talk, naturally, confidingly. Edwin listened, expressing approbation, surprise, incredulity—all the proper emotions at the proper times. He wasn't being deceitful, really; it was a charming tale, and Andrew was telling it with sincerity and enthusiasm. Edwin was only being deliberate, marking carefully the names and facts and places which were vital to him. His patience was rewarding him at last. It had taken nearly three weeks, the mellowing influence of family and home, the keen challenge of work to be done, and the exhilaration of a fast car on a perfect, winding road to loosen Andrew's tongue. Such easy, simple facts. But Edwin needed them. Until he had them his hands had been tied. Even as the sports car pulled onto the long gravel drive leading to Bieldmor House, Edwin was formulating the beginnings of a plan in his mind.

The evening was a pleasant one, but Edwin was anxious to be alone, to sort out his eager thoughts away from the scrutiny of friendly eyes. So he retired to his own room earlier than usual.

Andrew did not. He was restless, without knowing why. The hour grew late and the house grew silent, and Janet had not yet come home. With a sense of frustration new to him, Andrew determined to wait up for her return.

The clock in the great hall struck once, deep and reverberating, the small clock on the mantle answering only seconds later. One o'clock. Where was Janet? Andrew strode across the room and drew aside the lace curtains, gazing down at the shadowed drive below. The trees were perfectly still, each leaf and branch imprinted in ink black outline against the moon-brightened sky. He should have confronted her that Sunday, when he first suspected something was wrong. This never would have happened if he'd had the courage to confront her then! His mother and Edwin were long asleep; he alone kept this unaccustomed vigil in the still, dark house.

It had been just after ten when Edwin went to his room, and he had been totally unconcerned.

"She'll be here in good time, Andrew. Didn't she say she would be with Mary tonight?"

Andrew wasn't so certain. There was nothing the two girls could be doing alone this late in the night. Could there have been an accident? No. He wouldn't consider such a possibility.

He glanced at the clock. Seven minutes after the hour. He walked down to the kitchen and built himself a sandwich with thick slices of ham, layered with cheese and pickles and onion greens. But a bite or two was all he could eat.

Twenty-three minutes past the hour. He thought he heard a door click shut. But there was no further sound. He wrapped the sandwich and put it in the refrigerator, and walked out into the hall, his ears straining. Then he heard it. The definite patter of footsteps across the stone flags. Now they sounded hollow against the brick, up the stairs and onto the wide porch. He turned and faced the door just as the handle turned noiselessly and the door pushed inward.

The first thing Janet saw when she looked up was Andrew's face, and her heart sank. *He's worried to distraction,* she thought. *There's nothing for it. He'll have to know the truth, tonight.* With a little prayer and a feeling of almost-relief, she swept over to him and took his hand.

"Oh, Andrew, I'm so sorry. I never dreamed you'd be waiting up. I didn't mean to worry you so."

"What did you mean, then, lass? Just exactly what were your intentions?"

She didn't like the look of hurt and concern in his eyes. Did she also read there mistrust?

92

She tugged gently at his hand, which she still held.

"Come in here, Andrew. We've got to talk."

He followed beside her quietly and flicked on one of the dimmer lamps at a low table, but even then the light seemed blazing and harsh. He sat opposite her, straight-backed and still.

It would be easier if he raved at me and accused me of something, she thought. She sat looking at him, her back so straight that it was starting to hurt, and she didn't know where to begin.

"Well, Janet?" He spoke kindly, and some of the harshness had faded from his eyes.

"Andrew, I was with Mary tonight. We got to talking, you see, and—"

He made a short sound under his breath, and she stopped cold.

"You don't believe me, do you, Andrew?" It was half a statement, half a question.

"Well, Janet, it hardly seems plausible that you two—"

"You've always believed me before. No matter how implausible it seemed. You've always trusted me!"

"Yes, but—" he reeled off a list of things: sudden disappearances, long hours spent away from home, times he had sighted her sneaking quietly into her room. She sat listening, wide-eyed, amazed. He finished with one last accusation which revealed, more than all the others, his feelings of rejection and dismay.

"You've avoided me, Janet, ever since I came home. You can't expect me not to have noticed. Something is missing between us."

She wanted to laugh and cry at the same time. She did neither. She rose and went to him, and knelt beside his chair.

"You're right, Andrew. There is something different between us. And it's my fault."

She saw the worry leap back into his eyes.

"Poor Andrew. I suppose you've been imagining all sorts of dreadful, despicable things, then berating yourself for thinking of them at all." She smiled softly, knowing all too well what misery her brother had been suffering. "Well, the truth will be so much better than anything you expected, that you can't help but be relieved."

She curled up at his feet then, and told him of her activities of the past few months: sessions with the missionaries, meetings at the Mormon chapel, discussions with Mary and her parents, the books and pamphlets and magazines she had read. She even told him of her prayers.

"You remember my dream, Andrew. The one about Father. It came more often when you were gone, and it seemed to grow worse. His eyes were filled with such strange longing. He wandered as though he was searching for something, and sometimes he would call my name. It was awful, Andrew!

"Well, the first time I prayed—you might not understand this— but the first time I prayed I felt that he was near me, and I could picture his face in my mind. But it wasn't miserable, as in the dream. I felt peaceful and happy for the first time since he died."

She paused, swallowing hard, trying to control the emotions which had suddenly overcome her. Andrew sat so still that she wondered, suddenly, if he were really awake and listening to her.

"Andrew?"

"Go on."

"Well, at first when you came home I was eager to talk to you. I thought it a marvelous piece of luck that you had lived those weeks in Salt Lake and liked it so well. But then, as things got settled, and as mother was so obviously happy, I became afraid. It struck me that, even if you wanted to, you would never cross her. You couldn't agree to anything that would upset her again, so soon after you had returned and restored the peace."

"Were you afraid to tell even me? Afraid I might stop things altogether, Janet?"

"I don't know!" She was miserable now—tired, and suddenly unsure of herself. "It's silly, but, you see, Mary and her family are being baptized next week, and I had so hoped—I knew it wasn't really possible, but it would have been so special. . . ."

Her voice trailed off and there was silence between them. Andrew rose.

"Wait here," he said briefly, and was gone.

She could hear his faint footsteps on the stairs. It seemed he would never return. Janet yawned. She was aware again of the dull little ache at the small of her back.

Then he was beside her. He carried a book in his hands. He held it out to her and she took it, the smooth leather feeling cool against her fingers. She held it under the light. The title was easy to read: Book of Mormon, Doctrine and Covenants, Pearl of Great Price. It had Andrew's name printed on it, too. She fingered the raised gold lettering and looked up at him.

"Heber Shumway gave it to me. He's my researcher in Salt Lake."

"Have you read any of it, Andrew?"

"Yes, bits and snatches. It's difficult to leave alone."

She frowned. What was it she detected in his voice? "But you want to leave it alone. You don't really want to read it, Andrew. Why?"

The silence was long. He came close to her and looked down into her eyes.

"I'm afraid to, Janet. I'm afraid I'll believe it."

She nodded slightly.

"I know, oh, I know exactly how you feel."

She thought back to when she had felt the same way, and was shocked to realize that it seemed like a long time ago, that now she had progressed so far that those initial fears and doubts and uncertainties seemed to belong to a dim, unimportant past.

"How much do you actually know about the Mormons, Janet? Do you begin to realize the commitment involved? Mormonism is far more than an ordinary religion, it's—it's—" He was searching for some way to express it.

"It's a way of life," she finished for him. "Yes, I know. I've been warned and reminded of that dozens of times already. How much do you know, Andrew?"

"I don't know. I've been exposed to piles of knowledge and information. But it seems to float around in my head, totally disjointed. I haven't fitted it all together very well."

"I'm nearly through the Book of Mormon," she said softly. "I understand so much more than I did, even a few weeks ago. It's really nothing to be afraid of, Andrew."

She looked at him and realized that her hands were trembling.

"Will you read the books and pamphlets I have? They're very good at explaining, at fitting things together. Will you, Andrew?"

He didn't answer her. What would she do if at last he spoke, and his answer was no?

"Please, Andrew. If you don't, you'll always wonder, for the rest of your life."

Even as he spoke he knew he was embarking on a course from which there was no turning back. Yet he felt compelled, knowing what his answer was going to be, unable to stop himself. "Yes, Janet. You bring them to me, and I'll read them."

He held out a hand to her and raised her to her feet.

"Your hand is shaking," he said.

She put her head against his shoulder and he held her, close and protective, as he had when she was a child. She looked up at him, and there were tears in her eyes.

"I'm happy, Andrew. I don't even know exactly why. But I'm happier than I think I've ever been before."

"I know."

He felt it, too. He didn't know what to call it, but it was an influence very powerful and real. He took Janet's hand and they walked together through the halls and up the long sweeping stairs.

11

All torment, trouble, wonder,
and amazement
Inhabit here. . . .

THE TEMPEST

I haven't seen you all week, Hannah. And don't try to tell me you've been too busy, either. If Andrew was still here I might swallow that line. But you'll have to come up with a better excuse this time."

Grant knew something was bothering the girl. At first he had thought it was just Andrew's leaving, her loneliness, and the frustration caused by the conditions imposed upon her. She had told him much about that last meeting with Andrew; what had passed between them, what her feelings were now. She had seemed very strong and sure and happy. Grant felt certain that her problems had nothing to do with Andrew and their relationship. What could it be, then, that was bothering her so?

"Grant, I need to talk to you."

He looked down into her serious brown eyes. *I suppose that's why she waited to find me at home,* he thought.

"All right, Nan, come inside."

The living room was darkened and cool, the hum from the window air conditioner seeming loud in the stillness. She faced him across the room and smiled slightly, wondering how to begin. She had never been uncertain with Grant before.

"Grant, why haven't you ever told me anything about the Mormon Church?"

The question hit him like a mighty weight hurled right at his heart. He was grateful that she gave him no time to reply. She went on to tell him of her conversation with Andrew down by the river, of her sudden realization that she knew nothing about Mormon doctrine, that he, Grant, had never shared that knowledge with her.

"I began thinking back over my childhood," Nan continued, her voice warm and intense, "and I remembered a time or two when I had picked up pamphlets and booklets from the various buildings and brought them home to read. My father took them from my hands, tore them in halves once, and said quietly, 'Such materials are not allowed in this house, Hannah. If you wish to maintain the privilege of roaming free around the old city, you must refrain from taking or even looking at these things. Do you understand?' He flourished the papers above my head, and I nodded in agreement. Then he walked off to dispose of the hateful things, and we never mentioned it further. I don't remember, but I guess I finally stopped bringing them home altogether."

She paused, and Grant realized that his heart was pounding and his hands were clenched. He wasn't prepared for this encounter. Not yet. What had brought it on?

"Last week," Nan continued, "I went to the visitors' center and picked up a copy of every pamphlet I could find. I bought a copy of *A Marvelous Work and a Wonder* and a paperback copy of the Book of Mormon. I drove down to the Seventies Hall and sat on one of the benches and read for hours. I've been reading ever since, Grant, whenever I can get away. I've got a lot of questions, and I want you to answer them. And the first question is—"

She hesitated, not wanting to sound disrespectful or demanding, he knew.

"The first question is, why haven't you told me anything before?"

He didn't look at her; the tears were gathering in his eyes, and he didn't want her to see them. For perhaps the first time he felt like a weak, ineffectual old man. How was he going to work this? What was he going to say?

"Nan, have you always trusted me?"

She made a little motion of assent.

"No, answer me, please. It's important."

"Yes, for as long as I can remember I have trusted you perfectly."

"Have I ever failed that trust, in any way that you can remember?"

98

"No."

"Then all I can tell you now, Nan, is to continue trusting me. Do you believe that I believe Mormonism to be true? That I have a testimony of it? That I believe it to be something wonderful and good?"

"Yes, yes, I believe that, although you've never actually said so to me before."

"Do you believe that I would give you, would share with you anything good, anything worthwhile that I could?"

"Yes!"

"Then trust me, Nan. For a little while longer trust me, my dear."

"All right, Grant. Surely I can give that much to you, you who have given so much to me."

She rose and crossed the room to kiss him, and it was then that she saw the tears in his eyes. Her mind was racing—imagining, searching, wondering vainly what great mystery stood between them that she had been totally unaware of before. She bent and kissed him on the cheek and hugged him a moment, disturbed by how frail his shoulders felt.

She drove straight home, her mind muddled and unhappy. She had never felt such a great sense of unrest before. There was a letter from Andrew, but she didn't want to read it in this kind of mood, so she stuck it in her purse to save for later. She swept the sidewalks and the patio in back, cleaned the bathrooms and washed her hair. Her mind was so clouded that she couldn't think, so she worked as hard as she could, then bathed and dressed for her appointment in the late afternoon.

"I won't be back for supper, Grandma. Don't expect me until dark."

"I never expect you, Hannah," the older woman replied, her voice warm with affection, "until I see you walk in the door. I've known better than that for a long time now."

Her interview was fascinating. An older couple on the outskirts of Warsaw had three giant wolfhounds, and she stayed nearly two hours romping with the great dogs, taking pictures, recording facts. She hadn't realized that the wolfhound could trace his origins back to the Sack of Delphi in the year 273 B.C., and that he was known to have accompanied Christopher Columbus on his voyage of discovery to the New World. The gray-brindled dogs who nuzzled her and licked her hand weighed nearly two hundred pounds and stood on all fours higher than her waist. Nan was awed by the tales of what grim, fierce hunters these dogs could be, and she was at the same time touched by their gentle, loving, frolicking ways.

How she wished she were seeing Andrew tonight, and could tell him all about what she had seen and learned! He would be fascinated, concentrating on every word, knitting his brow as he listened, his blue eyes sparkling beneath the black eyebrows. Perhaps he would even know some stories about wolfhounds himself. Did they have Irish wolfhounds in Scotland? Oh, how hard it was, not to be able to communicate with him at all!

She remembered his letter then, tucked safely in her purse. It was the second letter; he had written one each week since his return to Scotland. She hadn't anticipated as much, believing the old myth that all men are miserable letter writers. She smiled to herself as she drove back to Nauvoo, remembering the fat envelope bearing two foreign stamps and addressed to her.

Julie had made a fuss and Jonathan had teased her when she opened the first letter. It was the longest letter she had ever received. And when she read it, it was just as though Andrew was right there beside her, talking to her. She could see his eyes and hear his voice, and it was both wonderful and painful at once.

She turned now onto Young Street, then right down Partridge and pulled into the parking lot of the visitors' center. She walked the red brick path around the building to the south side, where a park-like area enclosed the grouped statues the Mormons had placed there in tribute to women. There were only a few people sitting or walking among the figures and the gardens, and the air was peaceful, heavy with the fragrance of the flowers and of grass.

Nan sat on one of the benches and opened Andrew's letter. For long minutes she was lost in the world it created for her. He wrote almost as charmingly as he spoke. Bieldmor House, the rowan tree, his Paisley office, the funny little lawyer with the wart on the end of his nose (or solicitor, as Andrew called him)—they all came alive under Andrew's pen.

At last Nan carefully refolded the pages and slipped them back into the envelope. A wave of loneliness swept over her. She missed him so much. She glanced up at the large bronze figure of the woman before her. The figure looked confident, her features sensitive, yet strong. Her long hair and the folds of her dress seemed to sweep behind her; the eagerness on her features and in her eyes was so lifelike that it was entrancing.

All about Nan, in startling array, stood Woman, in the many dimensions of her life: the young girl and boy courting, the woman with her infant, youthful parents reaching out eager arms to an uncertain, toddling child. Each statue had a spirit Nan could feel. She walked over and stood before the statue of the woman with a baby on her shoulder, and she thought of Jessie Buchanan. How much Nan had in common with this woman who didn't even know of her existence, much less of her love for Andrew, of her patient and painful waiting for the return of the man she loved! Would Jessie Buchanan ever know? and, knowing, would she understand?

Nan walked the circular flow of paths around the statues, deep in thought. She paused by the figure of a woman reading, an open book on her lap, her eyes gazing off, intelligent and deep. It was one of Nan's favorites. Close by was the figure of a woman kneeling in prayer. The lines were graceful and dignified. Nan stood beside the figure for a long time and knew it represented, perhaps more than all the others, the Mormon woman, who knew how to talk to her God, who knew what to say and how to say it, and who believed that her voice would be heard. An aching kind of self-pity rose in her throat, and she wished fervently that she was one of those fortunate women who knew and understood, who had someone higher she could turn to. She stood staring at the statue, wishing she, too, knew how to get down on her knees and pray.

It was ridiculous. He shouldn't be going at all. But what the old man said had startled him. He pulled up in front of the tidy little house, walked up the path, and rang the bell. He felt angry and foolish and somewhere, deep inside, afraid.

Once inside the man's house, encountering him face to face, Abraham Martin was surprised at how much the older man had aged.

"It's been years since—" Abraham hesitated, realizing too late that any way he finished the sentence would be awkward.

"Yes, it's been years since we talked together, that first and last time, and I suppose you remember it as well as I do." Grant Morgan smiled as he said the words, but his voice was serious.

Abraham remembered well. When he had first figured out that Nan was enchanted with the older couple, that they loved and spoiled her, he had been jealous, very jealous. He had watched her and questioned her, trying to find some half-way legitimate reason to forbid the relationship. But everything he had learned about it was so positive in nature that he could find no excuse for forbidding it.

Then one day Nan came home talking a bunch of nonsense about God and spirits and angels not having wings. He couldn't remember it all now, but it hadn't mattered. It was all the excuse he needed. He had gone straight to the old man and forbidden him to associate with his daughter. He squirmed a little, even now, remembering what took place.

With gentle firmness Grant had reminded him of the girl's needs and asked him outright what it was he objected to. He had sputtered and spurted until Grant said it for him: religion. Yes, it was that infernal Mormonism he objected to, all right. He wasn't going to have anybody infesting his daughter with that. Then Mr. Morgan had given him his solemn oath that he would never speak a word of religion to Nan, if Abraham would only allow the relationship to continue, allow him and his wife to love and mother the little girl. Even the wife had come into the room and given her promise as well.

What could Abraham do? His own guilt at rejecting and slighting his daughter was too strong for him to deny them their determined request. He had questioned Nan occasionally through the years, but he had trusted Grant Morgan, knowing he would keep his word no matter how difficult it might be.

What was the old man saying now? Abraham forced his thoughts aside and listened.

"So it's like I told you over the phone. I have kept my promise all these years. Though I could see many times where my knowledge could have aided Nan over some difficult time, eased some pain, helped offer some strength, I have never done or said a thing that had the direct mark of Mormon doctrine upon it. Except sofar as my mind and personality have been influenced by the doctrines I believe in, I have never given Nan one particle of the great store I have had available to give."

102

"What are you trying to say?" Abraham felt the implied criticism, the accusation behind the man's words. And he knew in his heart it was justified.

"I suppose I'm trying to tell you that I've wanted to teach the principles of my religion to Nan, and it's been the most painful burden of my life to deny both Nan and myself that privilege.

"But now, Mr. Martin—now Nan has come to me. She has come to me entirely of her own free will. And I feel the time has come."

Abraham looked at the man. There was no antagonism in Grant's eyes, only kindness and a deep sorrow.

"I'm sorry. I could never approve such a—"

"Yes, you could! Nan wants to know! Do you suppose I am the only source she can turn to?"

He paused a moment, then looked straight into Abraham's eyes. "In a few weeks Nan will turn twenty-one. I am free then. You may not remember, Mr. Martin, but the promise was to hold true only until Nan turned twenty-one. You set the date yourself. You felt eighteen— even nineteen—was still too young. *You* set the date and agreed to the terms. In a few weeks I will be free to speak."

"Then why did you even call me here at all?" There was anger in Abraham's voice and, behind the anger, pain. Grant's voice was soft and warm when he replied.

"Because you have the right to know. You're her father, you have the right—"

"What difference does it make? If she's twenty-one in a few weeks and can choose for herself, then what does it matter?"

"She's your daughter, and you love her. I'd rather teach her knowing that I have your agreement. Not your blessing—not your actual approval. I know I can't have that. But I want you to know and, I hope, to understand. I'd rather not do this thing against the barriers of your bitterness and pride."

"You speak plainly, Mr. Morgan. And you ask much."

"Well, old men have the advantage of knowing that pride is the enemy of happiness and, often, so is time. And, in case you haven't realized it, Mr. Martin, I love Nan, too."

So it was here. When Abraham made that agreement years ago, twenty-one was so far in the future, so unreal. Now, suddenly, Nan was there. She was growing away from him in every way, it seemed. He should have expected this.

He looked into the old man's eyes and read concern there and felt, uncomfortably, that some of it was for himself. He knew Grant Morgan was showing him more respect than he probably deserved. He knew he had lost. Could he give up gracefully?

He rose, walked over to the other man, and extended his hand.

"I appreciate your honesty. You have my—what did you call it?—acceptance. Yes, I accept the situation. I accept the fact that, after all these years, you have won at last."

Grant laid his hand on Abraham's shoulder.

"You feel you are losing Nan, I know. You feel this will alienate her from you. I know how deeply you love her, Mr. Martin. You might be able to hide it most of the time. But I can read it in your eyes. This won't take Nan from you. Wait and see. More than ever before she will love you and belong to you—and understand."

The old man's words, the feeling in his voice, brought tears to Abraham's eyes. He was terrified at the prospect of losing control, of revealing so much of himself to this powerful old man. He reached the door with difficulty. Grant managed to squeeze his arm and thank him before he left. Abraham hadn't felt so much kindness and warmth from another human being in a long time. It was like a salve to his troubled spirit, and he savored the feeling as long as he could before it diminished and at length faded away.

The next day was a busy one for Nan. She had purposefully taken on as much work as she could handle, trying to lose herself in what she was doing, giving herself as little time as possible to think or dream or feel sorry for herself.

It had been a long day, but she had accomplished much. She arrived home hot and tired, but with a satisfied feeling inside. Gratefully she sunk into the porch swing, which was shaded now in the late afternoon, and rocked with the cat in her lap, watching a droning bee in the tall hollyhocks at the edge of the porch. The lazy tranquility was a delight. She closed her eyes and drank in the cool feel of the air on her arms and the marvelous smells that mingled, defying identity: the cat's warm fur, the hollyhocks, the roses on the trellis nearby, wet grass and water where the outdoor faucet dripped. She loved trying to pick them all out.

Then she heard it. At first she couldn't identify the sound. A low, toneless drone. But where was it coming from? She listened more closely and heard the tap, tap, tap of a drum growing louder. Then suddenly a burst of music that made her feet want to beat. Her bagpipe record! She nearly laughed out loud.

It was the album Andrew had sent her only a few days ago. The Royal Scots Guards, or something. She loved the haunting melodies they played, and the brave, surging battle songs. Andrew had written that one either loved the skirl of the bagpipes, or one definitely did not! Hannah loved it. She listened long hours in her room alone to the sweep and sob and cry of the pipes, and the longer she listened, the more her heart would leap and her skin would tingle to the weird, entrancing sounds the bagpipes made. But who could be listening now?

She rose quietly and pressed her face against the screen, trying to see inside. At first, after the brighter light outdoors, everything was dark and indistinct. Then she picked out a form lying full length on the living room couch.

Slowly she pulled open the door. It squeaked once, but the form didn't move. The bright, marching music drowned out all other sounds. She tiptoed quietly until she was standing right at his head. Jonathan had his eyes shut, totally engrossed in the music which surrounded him. Hannah dropped noiselessly to her knees, put her face close to his, and whispered in his ear, "Why, laddie, if I'd only known. . . ."

Jonathan jumped. His eyes shot open and he sat straight up, blinking and grinning foolishly. Nan laughed.

"If I'd known you liked the bagpipes so much I'd have asked Andrew to send you a record of your own."

Jonathan scowled and threw a pillow at her. Nan ducked, laughing again, and sat down beside him.

"I'm sorry, Jonathan. I couldn't resist it. After all, you were merciless, you know, making such fun of the pipes when I played the record that first time."

"I know. I thought they were the most awful thing I'd ever heard. Sounded like a bunch of untuned violins, and it hurt my ears."

"Well, what happened?"

"I don't know. I'd listen from a distance when you played the record in your room at night. Sounded muffled and eerie and neat that way. So I decided yesterday to try it again. I sat through the whole record, both sides. By that time I was hooked.''

Nan's eyes were dancing. ''I'm glad, Jonathan. You may listen to the record any time you like.''

It was one little thing of Andrew's, at least, that she could share with someone else. She rose to go to her room.

''Oh, Nan. There was a telephone call for you. Just a little while ago. He said it was important and for you to please call back.''

''Who was it? Do you know?''

''He didn't say. But he sounded too old to be a boyfriend, that's for sure.''

Nan picked up the paper and looked with curiosity at the number Jonathan had written. Her heart jumped. This was Grant's number! She had recognized it in an instant. Something must be wrong! He had never, in all the years she had known him, tried to contact her at her home.

Quickly she dialed the numbers, listening impatiently to the long, droning rings. At last she heard the click of someone picking up the receiver, and his voice penetrated the vacuum between them.

''Grant? I'm so sorry I wasn't here when you called. Is anything wrong?''

''No, Nan. No, I wouldn't say that at all. What are your plans for the evening, young lady?''

His voice sounded strong and merry, almost as though he were about ready to laugh at some private joke.

''Plans for this evening? Well, I don't have any, actually. I just got home a few minutes ago.''

''How long before you can be ready to come over here?''

''Come over there? Well, I don't know. Dinner's almost ready. I'll have to help with the dishes, but I guess that's all. Is anything the matter, Grant?''

He did laugh now, and the sound warmed Nan's heart. ''No, Nan, heavens, no. How long then until you'll be here?''

''Oh, say an hour, an hour and a half at the most.''

''Well, hurry, Nan. I don't know if I can wait that long. I've been waiting a mighty long time as it is. When you come, Nan, I'd appreciate it if you'd bring along all those pamphlets you've been reading,

106

and it might be a good idea to bring your copy of the Book of Mormon, too. And plan on staying for a while, Nan, can you do that?''

"Yes, Grant, but—''

"No buts, Nan. Just do as you're told. Oh—and one more thing. Bring along your questions. They're going to get answered this time!''

Nan hardly heard him say goodbye. Her heart was racing. What miracle was this? She ran upstairs to gather her materials, and to write down some of her most important questions in case, in her excitement, she forgot them.

12

August was quickly blowing itself
away, not warm and calm as one might hope, but breezy and cool, with
soggy rains and leaden skies.

Edwin's plans were complete, and he was anxious to begin. He
was impulsive by nature, so he approached Andrew as Andrew would
expect him to do, and it came off beautifully.

"You've got the bull by the horns, Andrew. I'm only trailing
behind. Aye, and it's far too long I've spent in one place as it is."

"You've set a new record for yourself, I'd dare say. How long has
it been?"

"Three months and twenty-four days to be exact, and that in another man's shoes, trying to keep two women happy at once, and
working like some sort of a fool."

Andrew threw back his head and laughed.

"All right, all right, Edwin, you've convinced me. Will you be
going home for a spell?"

"I'm nothing but a nuisance there, and well you know it. I'm
bound for the North instead, fishing off the isles and evenings in
Portree."

"I know, I know, surrounded by the beautiful highland lasses they
raise up there."

"Jamie MacDonald will take good care of me, aye."

"And you'll find more mischief together than I like to think of."

108

And so they bantered back and forth, Edwin as casual and clever as always, but at greater effort than Andrew would guess.

It was difficult for them all to let him go. Jessie thanked him warmly, more humbly and sincerely than was her wont. A certain understanding existed between them; it always had. But after what they had shared together, endured together these past months, it was deeper, more personal than before—more than either had ever anticipated it would become. Janet was tender, as sweet as she had ever been, assuring Edwin he had earned a good rest, sending him off with all manner of motherly admonitions and kind advice.

"Don't stay out of touch too long," Andrew told him, and their eyes held briefly.

Edwin decided to drive the old black Magnetta into Glasgow; he would leave it at the Queen Street Station, where Andrew could send someone after it. Andrew stood in the drive watching him go, and after the crunch of the wheels on the gravel had stilled, the hot day seemed to close in, and there was a lonely kind of quiet about the place.

Andrew spent the evening with Janet and his mother and, in spite of their efforts to be pleasant and lively, he felt as though an added responsibility had been passed over to him. Andrew might have the know-how, the precision, and the maturity to be responsible for keeping things going smoothly, running well. But it seemed to him that Edwin carried the spirit, the humor, the cleverness and grace. Andrew had always been more serious; too serious, perhaps. How was he going to replace the lightness that Edwin's departure had seemed to remove?

Jessie retired early to bed. Andrew followed soon after, and lay in his tall, four-poster bed and read again the Joseph Smith pamphlet, then picked up the one called "Which Church Is Right?" He had read perhaps half a dozen in the three days and nights since he and Janet had talked.

He had covered not more than a page or two when Janet knocked and came in with two cold drinks and a book called *A Marvelous Work and a Wonder*. They began to talk. Janet knew more than Andrew had realized. She could even answer many of the questions which were forming in his own mind. They shared their feelings and reactions to the things they were learning.

The hours slipped away as the brother and sister quietly talked.

Andrew was stunned to hear the mantle clock strike an insistent twelve. He sent Janet off to her room to sleep, no longer wondering how it was that she and Mary Cameron had been able to talk, on and on, into the small hours of the night, about these new and fascinating doctrines which were now unfolding before him.

Edwin drove into the railroad station, parked the Magnetta, and locked it. He walked toward the big double doors with a heady feeling both of freedom and power. His contest with Fate had begun, and the exhilaration he felt was difficult to control.

He held the door open for a pretty girl, but the smile he gave her was less charming than usual, for his thoughts and energies were totally absorbed in the challenge which had been placed into his hands. At the ticket office he checked the schedules and times carefully. He took a place in one of the lines, chafing for his turn to come. When he was at last before the desk, he leaned his elbows on the marble ledge and smiled at the girl.

Yes, he wanted a ticket north. Well, he was actually heading for the farthest reach of the isles. Had she ever been fishing off Skye? Ach, that was a shame. The spray blew against the great black cliffs, the sun was warm, and the clean air carried the smell of the heather down from the hills.

He painted a pretty picture for her, and she smiled. He asked every question he could think of, with a sincerity and enthusiasm difficult to resist. At last he took his ticket, making sure his fingers touched hers briefly in the exchange.

"I'll post you a card from Skye," he told her, holding her eyes with his own jaunty gaze. She laughed a little and blushed. Edwin walked off, the next person in line moving into place. He was well satisfied with his performance and with the girl's response. She would not soon forget that she had sold him a ticket to Portree.

He waited a few minutes in the lobby, bought a drink, scanned a newspaper casually. Then he chose a line as far from the first as possible. As he waited his turn there was hardly a trace of his lively, whimsical manner. His eyes were dull and his face was down.

He asked for a one-way ticket east to Edinburgh, paid for it, and took it without a word. The next person pressed forward, the line shifted and moved. Edwin tucked both tickets inside his pocket and followed the porter toward the train.

As soon as the train ground and shuddered to a stop in Edinburgh, Edwin was on his feet. He took a taxi to the Prestwick Airport and bought a ticket on a nonstop flight to New York City.

He had previously arranged for a passport and visa in Glasgow. Everything was in order and it looked promising that, within an hour or two, he would be on his way.

He took a seat and opened his briefcase on his lap. He pulled out his list and thumbed through it until he came to the name he was seeking: Heber Shumway, Salt Lake City, Utah. None of the other names and materials he had gathered seemed important beside this one name. This was the only researcher still on the case. This man was Andrew's trusted friend. He would be working diligently and well. And so the sooner he was stopped, the better.

When at last Edwin boarded the plane he was tired and hungry. He accepted the meal from the stewardess gratefully, with only the briefest of smiles. After eating he settled back into the seat. It was wonderful to close his eyes and relax, knowing that the great winged creature he rode was soaring above the clouds, across land and ocean, swallowing hundreds of miles each hour as it went. Soon enough he would be where he wanted to be and it would be time to move. Now he was sitting it out in the wings, letting the big plane do its part. *When the time comes for the next scene to begin*, he thought to himself, *I'll be ready.* The plane slipped into a bank of clouds and everything was hazy and gray. In the darkened quiet around him Edwin slept.

The room at the hotel was not to Edwin's taste, but it was new and clean and airy, and would suit his purposes well enough. He had chosen a hotel a few blocks away from Salt Lake City's downtown area, avoiding the Hotel Utah or any other place too close to where his cousin had stayed.

He smiled to himself when he recalled how easy it had been to spot the places Andrew had told him about: the grounds of the Hotel Utah blended right into the grounds of the Church Office Building, as did those of Brigham Young's Lion House that Andrew had spoken of so often, and it would have been impossible to miss Temple Square. He even asked directions to the Shakespeare Dinner House where Andrew had eaten. He couldn't help feeling a little smug as he sat there, enjoying his meal. Whatever would Andrew do if he could see him now? Edwin felt strangely *like* Andrew, just as he had felt during those weeks at Bieldmor House when Andrew was away.

He pictured Andrew—serious, conscientious Andrew, wandering the city, doing his job with such sober thoroughness. Even if Edwin had known what he now knew *before* Andrew left on the search, he could have saved him nothing. No, Andrew was too replete with integrity for that. Too bad!

Edwin contented himself with imagining Andrew's surprise when he *did* learn of the new will and the terms it involved. He'd be overjoyed to see Edwin come into his own and disgusted, perhaps, at the waste of his own time and efforts. That is, if that confounded researcher didn't mess things up! Edwin was too much of a realist not to face the possibility of someone turning up some flesh and blood Buchanan, lost these countless years; some dense American who would blink his eyes at the luck which had dropped a fortune into his lap, never knowing that he was cheating Edwin of what was rightfully his.

That's why he was here. That's why, first thing in the morning, he would drive to the address he had copied from the Salt Lake telephone directory. That was the prime item on the agenda: to locate Heber Shumway and identify him, and to discover his schedule and where and when he worked on the Charles Buchanan files.

It took Edwin three days to establish the pattern of Heber Shumway's activities. It was a tedious, boring business, fraught with inactivity. But by the fourth day Edwin felt confident enough to make his move.

He had also studied the pattern of things at the genealogical library and the building which housed it, and he chose a propitious time just before noon when there was a great milling and thronging of people. In the library itself people were rising from their working areas, leaving their papers, folders, and microfilm boxes either strewn on the desks or placed in careful order, awaiting their return. Heber Shumway, Edwin had discovered, was not so careless. He never left his materials untended—*except* for the brief periods of time required to return rolls of microfilm and select new ones. Three minutes—six minutes at the most.

Edwin situated himself at one of the little tables and spread an impressive-looking array of papers around him, selecting a roll of microfilm completely at random to feed into the machine and occasionally turn, with apparent great interest.

From where he sat he could see Heber Shumway from the corner of his eye; but he was back and to the right of the man and was entirely outside Heber's range of vision. Earlier, during one of Heber's brief absences, Edwin had carefully, quickly walked behind the row of desks where Heber worked, making certain that the file on which Heber was working bore the Buchanan name. But so much still depended on chance! The chance—the risk was like a tonic to Edwin's blood; it was the waiting that played havoc with his nerves.

Any time within the framework of an hour would do. If Heber Shumway rose and left at any point during that time, then Edwin could make his move. But the minutes ticked by, people came and went, exchanging greetings or quiet conversations along the narrow aisles. Heber Shumway never lifted his head.

At last the clock spelled Edwin's defeat. He rose as slowly and nonchalantly as he could, gathered his papers together, and left the building. There was one more possibility that day—between four and four-thirty. One of the busiest times at the library was the period from roughly two to four o'clock in the afternoon. Then there would be another great emptying of people, and enough activity and congestion that he could probably carry out his plan.

But when he returned to the library, Heber was not in the same place he had occupied that morning. It didn't seem that Heber had returned to the library yet at all. It was long after five when Edwin finally located him, and nearly seven before the man rose and stretched and went off in search of new materials.

Edwin felt himself growing angry, and he knew he could not risk that kind of self-indulgence. He left the area and weighed the various possibilities in his mind. It was dangerous, he felt, to trail the man too long. The possibility of Heber Shumway spotting him and recognizing his resemblance to Andrew grew stronger every day.

Tomorrow was Friday and then Edwin would face a long, wasted weekend, and who was to say that the man would pick up the same schedule at the beginning of the new week? What if he worked on someone else's case on Monday?

The library closed at ten, Edwin knew. There would be the rush and confusion then of everyone leaving, but he would be without the additional confusion of workers from the Church Office Building and crowds walking the downtown streets. However, he would have the advantage of the darkness into which he could disappear.

Ten o'clock. In the three days Edwin had watched him, Heber Shumway had never stayed at the library that late. What kind of chance was there, he wondered, what kind of a chance that Heber Shumway would decide to stay until closing time tonight? Whatever the chance, Edwin decided to take it.

He took a drink from one of the fountains and walked the long stretch of the lobby, pausing briefly beside the large, colorful mural, then lingering to study the lovely, oversized painting at the far end depicting in delicate strength the waters and islands of the Great Salt Lake. He read all the detail on the small-print plaque, but none of it registered. He realized that his hands were moist and his muscles tense. He walked out into the open air, pacing back and forth along the broad fountain in the plaza.

At 8:30 he returned to his vantage point and began watching Heber Shumway. At 9:15 Heber rose and left; he was gone four minutes and twenty seconds. At 9:35 he leaned back in his chair, ran his fingers through his hair, and looked up at the big black clock on the wall.

From where he sat Edwin could hear Heber sigh. The man was tired. He had had enough. His back probably hurt and he was probably missing his favorite television program. Or perhaps his wife had a hearty snack waiting for him at home. Would he decide to call it quits, or would he hang in there for another twenty-five minutes?

Edwin held his breath. The chair legs fell back against the floor and scraped into place. Heber hunched over the machine in front of him and began to turn the knob, feeding the microfilm through. Edwin let out his breath and began to plan every minute aspect of the move he was about to make.

Nine-fifty. The pleasant ladies glided between the tables, announcing closing time. Would the patrons please begin returning their materials to their proper places? Heber Shumway pushed back his chair. He had five boxes of microfilm stacked in his arms. His papers were still strewn across the desk.

As he rose, Edwin rose, and by the time Heber had disappeared around the corner, Edwin was beside the desk. Four seconds. He had to gather the materials neatly. He couldn't afford to occasion any suspicion, or even particular notice of any kind. Seven seconds. The folder was in his hands. He noted with satisfaction how fat it was. He slipped it inside his briefcase and clicked down the lid. It seemed the loveliest sound he had ever heard.

He turned and walked quickly, in a direction away from where Heber Shumway had headed, away from the rows of neatly filed microfilm, toward the swinging door, past the check-out girl. Edwin hesitated and gave her a brief, bright smile. Now that he was in the midst of action he felt confident and bold.

He was outside the large exit door and in the lobby now. He walked with a briskness, but he did not hurry. He smiled at people in passing, but he never paused to look behind. He was outside the building now, and the cool night air held the headiness of wine.

Not until he was inside his car did Edwin allow himself a moment of satisfaction. He had carried it off to perfection! But he was smart enough to know that, after such a winning performance, a smooth exit was the next point to be navigated. He drove the city streets, triumph glowing inside him, but his hands were cool and his head was clear. He drove south, away from the city, away from the direction of Heber Shumway's house. He noticed the neon lights of a large discount store and headed in that direction. The store was closed, the mammoth, litter-strewn parking lot vacant except for a scattered car or two. He pulled around to the back and stopped the car.

Edwin opened his briefcase and removed the file. It felt solid and heavy in his hands. He slid out the papers and checked several, just to make certain that the research involved was really that of Charles Buchanan. He didn't want to trust himself any further than this; he wanted no incriminating evidence floating around in his brain, something that might surface unexpectedly and betray him. By twos and threes he gathered the papers and tore them in halves, then in halves again. In the indistinct light from the parking lot floodlamps Edwin couldn't really distinguish the words on the pages, and he wasn't trying. The final papers torn, he pulled the car close to one of the tall green garbage bins and pitched all the papers carefully over the edge. One more step was completed. The next thing was to get out of this place.

Edwin returned to his hotel and quickly gathered his belongings, which were already arranged for quick departure. In a short time he was checked out of the hotel; or rather, John MacKenzie was checked out. Edwin's passport was, of necessity, in his own name. But John MacKenzie, who had played alibi for him in other, less hazardous adventures than this, had booked the hotel room and rented the car; he took a precaution in every available way.

He would have to take his chances on an unbooked flight to New York. But the airport was such an anonymous place, and he shouldn't have long to wait at this time of the evening. He pulled onto the freeway heading north, turned on the radio, and settled back, relaxed. He followed the signs for the airport, veering to the left and heading west, away from the city.

The lights fell away behind him, but he didn't look back, and he spared no thought of farewell for the city he was about to leave. He had done his work and done it well, leaving as few traces of himself as possible, taking away with him no more care, remembrance, or impression than was necessary.

13

I sometimes do believe,
and sometimes do not;
As those that fear, —they hope,
and know they fear. . . .

AS YOU LIKE IT

I want to be baptized, Andrew.''

The air was warm and the day was still. The pond at their feet lapped lazily against its grassy banks. Janet's voice sounded small, like an unwanted intrusion, quickly swallowed by the lulling quiet into which it fell. Somewhere a skylark called, sharply reminding Andrew of the piercing cry of the seagulls swooping low over the streets of Salt Lake City.

"We've discussed this already, Janet. You know how impossible it is.'' His voice was gentle and low. She could barely hear his words, but his answer was clear enough.

"But it's different now. It's more important than it was before.''

"What do you mean, Janet?''

The skylark flew, trailing its bright, piercing cry until it hung, a vague echo against the immensity of blue which had swallowed the graceful form. Andrew wished he didn't have to hear what Janet had to say. He forced himself to sit still and listen.

Three nights after Edwin had left, Janet finished reading the Book of Mormon. She read carefully the final words in Moroni and accepted his powerful challenge to ask concerning the truthfulness of the book and the principles it contained. On her knees she prayed, longer and more sincerely than she ever had before, and when she arose the testimony which had trembled within her, hesitating and weak, had become a burning, certain reality.

117

At first she had known nothing but a sense of strength and gratitude and joy. But now as she tried to explain her experience to Andrew, she realized with painful clarity that she stood alone. It was impossible for him to understand what she felt in her heart and knew in her mind. It was impossible for him to understand how it had happened, or how valid and real the experience had been. So she hesitated a little now, praying that Andrew would feel what she felt, and at least begin to understand.

"Last night I was reading about temple work and baptism for the dead," she began. "Members of the Church can be baptized in the temples for their loved ones who have died, who haven't had the opportunity to hear the gospel and be baptized for themselves. It seemed like such a beautiful principle. I fell to sleep thinking about it. And while I was sleeping I dreamed about Father."

"The same dream as before?"

"No, Andrew, no! That's what I have to tell you! He was standing outside a building, a beautiful white building which seemed to glow and shine. Father wasn't alone; he was talking with a little group of people, and they were all dressed in white.

"After a moment or two he turned and seemed to look at me. I realized then that he had an open book in his hands, but I couldn't see what the book was. He smiled at me, Andrew, and it was the most magnificent smile I've ever seen—so full of happiness and life. I started to speak to him, to ask him what he was doing and where he was. I felt excited, because I knew, if I just could ask him, he would answer me!

"But I woke up then. I knew instantly that I was awake, and it occurred to me that this was the answer to those terrible dreams which had come before. This was what Father had been searching for, Andrew—the gospel, the truth! Maybe because of him I was able to find it, too. I don't know. But I know, Andrew, that he's accepted the gospel, and he wants us to do his temple work for him."

"Us?" Andrew's voice was sharp and his eyes, which held hers, were hard and bright.

"Yes, Andrew, us. In the temples women do the work for women and men do the work for men. It's you who would be baptized for Father when the time came."

"Aren't you rushing things just a little?"

118

Why was he feeling angry, as though someone was trying to corner him? He rose and began pacing, his hands thrust into his pockets. He couldn't understand what was making him so unhappy, and when he saw Janet's face he felt immediately guilty and ashamed.

"Yes, Andrew, I am rushing things. I know I am. But it's so hard to be patient—" Her voice began to tremble, and she stopped speaking. She wasn't going to cry, not now. She rose and walked over to Andrew and took his hands.

"I'm sorry, Andrew. You've tried so hard. And you've been progressing so quickly, in spite of all the other things you have to think about and do. I shouldn't push you, I don't mean to push you—"

She hesitated, but he didn't speak. *What's the matter with me?* he thought angrily. *Why am I being so selfish, so unkind?*

This isn't like Andrew, she thought. *What did I say to drive him away from me like this?*

She pressed his hands once, then turned to go. After a step or two she turned back.

"Andrew," she said, and something about her voice made him look up. "In January, Andrew, I'll turn eighteen. I'll be of age. If nothing happens before then, I'm going to approach Mother myself. I'll wait that long. But I won't wait any longer."

She turned and left him, walking silently across the thick grass. He had never seen her look like that or talk like that before. What was Mormonism doing to her? Andrew knew, instinctively, that he was still afraid; afraid of what Mormonism would do to him. Afraid of the knowledge and the responsibility which went with it. Afraid of the discipline, afraid of the change. If Janet's dream was indeed true, it disturbed him to think of his father, somehow, as well as of Janet, waiting and watching, *expecting* him to accept Mormonism as being true.

Three fat flies rose arguing in short, angry drones in the grasses at his feet. He gazed at them unseeingly, his annoyance growing. He wondered if his mother would grant her permission for Janet to be baptized. Would she, if he approached her in the right way, with kindness and enthusiasm?

Andrew didn't want to approach his mother, and he knew why. He didn't want to do anything to jeopardize his and Nan's situation. It was difficult for him to admit that it didn't really matter how much

Janet wanted to join the Church. All he really cared about were his own desires, his own driving needs! Get over this matter of the will, and then Nan. Nan! She was so much more important than anything and everything else!

Andrew felt little and petty and disgusted with himself. He turned to walk back to the house, his feet feeling heavier with every step. Halfway there Janet met him, breathlessly informing him that he had a long-distance call, person-to-person, from Salt Lake. Even before he took the phone and heard the familiar voice on the other end, Andrew knew it was going to be bad news.

When Heber Shumway left his desk in the genealogical library that Thursday evening, he had intended on replacing as quickly as possible the microfilms he had been using, then returning to gather his materials and head for home. It had been a long day and he was tired, and it seemed he and Lucille hadn't spent ten minutes alone together all week.

But he had unexpectedly met an old school friend from college days. It had been years since they'd seen each other, so they stood a few minutes in the aisle and talked until one of the girls interrupted, kindly reminding them that it was after ten o'clock and the library was due to close.

Heber hurried back to clear his desk. Surely this had been his place? Of course! But all the desks in front of him were empty, clear. He discovered his briefcase slid under the table, but the folder and papers he had been working on, which he had left for such a brief time, were gone. It was incredible! He decided it must have been some kind of a mistake.

Heber immediately reported the matter to the front desk. Most of the patrons were already gone, but an announcement was made, none-theless. There were questions and searches, and questions again. Surely someone had taken the materials by mistake. Were his name and address on any of the papers? Well, then, someone would prob-ably call him and report the error. Yes, the library would inform him if anyone called there concerning the matter.

It was late when Heber finally arrived home, with no appetite for the steaks Lucille had ready to broil. He waited, with a sick feeling in his stomach, for the phone to ring. He prayed, trying to submerge his own feelings of guilt. If only he hadn't stayed to talk with Bob Harrison! Heber prided himself on how meticulous he was; he had never left his papers untended for more than a minute or two. And this time, this one time. . . .

He awoke early the next morning and prayed again, then drove downtown and checked in the library, searching once more the desks and shelves and aisles near the area where he had worked. The ladies at the library promised to call just as soon as they heard anything. Heber checked with the library personnel again on Saturday and cancelled his plans to take Lucille to a movie that evening, so that he could be home in case someone called.

No one called. Not Saturday night, nor all day Sunday, nor late Sunday night. Monday morning Heber woke up knowing he could delay no longer. He checked with the library one last time. He knew he would have to call Andrew.

Andrew replaced the phone thoughtfully. What a strange, strange thing to have happened! Poor Heber. Andrew had assured him that he held him entirely blameless in the matter. But why did he feel so disappointed, as though something he really cared about had been lost? It was a ridiculous, illogical way for him to feel. And it was hopeless now, Andrew knew. The time it would take to recopy, research, and validate lost information—well, it was entirely prohibitive: there was just not enough time left before the end of November, when the search would be legally ended and out of Andrew's hands. Time had the upper hand now and, with the steady ticking of each second, each minute, time was winning the game.

And yet Andrew had told Heber Shumway to continue, to make what efforts he could right up until the deadline arrived. He knew it was fruitless, senseless, but he couldn't force himself to admit defeat, to call things off, to succumb. Andrew realized he had been harboring a secret hope that he would be the one, somehow, to unearth the old mystery, to bring to light people who were a link to him and his.

Janet was anxious to know what had happened, and Jessie had joined her. Andrew walked into the next room and told them, as briefly and unemotionally as he could.

Janet was shocked—very concerned and sympathetic, even though he had behaved so insensitively toward her only a few minutes earlier. His mother didn't say a word. He turned to her and saw that her eyes were dancing and that a little smile played around the corners of her mouth. *She's happy,* he thought suddenly! *The news pleases her!* She walked toward him now and placed her hand on his shoulder.

"It's a good omen, Andrew. Don't be concerned. You did all that could possibly be required of you. It's a good omen for us, at last."

With that Jessie seemed ready to dismiss the matter. She turned and asked Janet to accompany her to help prepare the dessert list for the cook. As she followed, Janet gave Andrew one last kind look. Then he was alone.

Andrew realized that neither his mother nor Janet was probably aware of the intense personal interest he had developed, the desire— illogical though it might be—for discovery and success in his search. He realized that he was, in a very real sense, alone.

He walked out to where the shiny Healey was parked and climbed inside. The leather seat seemed to fit his body perfectly; it was comfortable, snug, and secure. He drove the lonely stretches that he knew so well, not hearing the birds or seeing the trees, not noticing Ben Lomond rising ragged above the darkening loch. He flung back his head and let the wind tear at his hair and whip tears into his eyes. He drove fast, without thinking, only smelling the fragrance of the clean, cool wind, only feeling its rough fingers pass over and around him.

When at last he came home his mind was again at peace. He went straight to his study and started a letter to Nan. Into it he wrote all the agonies and struggles of his heart, all the disappointed desires, the frustrated plans, all the feelings of defeat and inadequacy. While he wrote he could feel her beside him, and her comfort there.

When the letter was sealed, he still didn't feel like sleep. He polished his brown Oxfords and his Wellingtons. He fiddled with the catch on the thistle badge which held his plaid in place. It was sprung and bent. He would have to remember to take it to his jeweler before the Highland Games next month.

He was restless still, but there was nothing else he could find to do. He straightened his desk a little, but that was too much like work. Then he spied the leather-bound scriptures Heber Shumway had given him. Gingerly he picked up the book, sat down, and began thumbing through the pages.

He was near the end of the volume when a phrase caught his eye: "The ends of the earth shall inquire after thy name. . . ." The page was headed Section 122: "The word of the Lord to Joseph Smith, the Prophet," he read, "while a prisoner in the jail at Liberty, Missouri, March, 1839." The section was short, only one page in length. Andrew decided to read it through.

When he had finished, he sat silent, overcome by the myriad emotions flooding through his being. Never had he read anything so exquisite before. So powerful, so compassionate, so full of love. He felt ashamed, thoroughly humbled, yet strangely comforted by that phrase which was to remain forever vivid in his mind:

> . . . and above all, if the very jaws of hell shall gape open the mouth wide after thee, know thou, my son, that all these things shall give thee experience, and shall be for thy good. The Son of Man hath descended below them all. Art thou greater than he?

A picture of the Carthage Jail came to Andrew, and the spirit of the man who died there seemed to rise from the pages of the book, so that he became very human and real and powerful in Andrew's mind. This Joseph, Andrew knew, was no ordinary man. He had sensed that from the beginning, walking the places Smith had walked, seeing the things he had built, reading the words he had spoken, realizing that thousands of people lived their lives and prospered according to the principles this man had taught.

Andrew believed in heroes. He had been brought up on the noble deeds of William Wallace, Robert the Bruce, and others, and had developed an early respect for greatness and sensitivity and excellence, wherever it may be found. He believed some magnificent personalities were sent to earth with a special mission to perform, endowed with capabilities to see things and understand things not understood by common man, endowed with the capacity to perceive and suffer and sacrifice beyond the ability of others, and blessed with the greatness of heart to do so.

Some of the things Andrew had read and liked, read and believed in, came now to his mind: marriage in the temple which would last for this life and the next; life before this one and the kingdoms after death, divided so logically according to the works and levels of achievement a person attained here; the Mormon concept of God as a loving Heavenly Father, an exalted man, somehow, with a body which had been refined and glorified.

The beauty of these principles seemed to enfold Andrew, and because he had a feeling he could trust the man who had revealed them, Andrew opened his heart and let their influence settle upon his soul.

Long he sat there thinking, and then he began to read. Not the Book of Mormon, but the Doctrine and Covenants, the words of the Lord to his prophet, Joseph Smith, and to the early Saints. Andrew didn't feel particularly comfortable with the Nephites, but he did with the early Mormons. He felt as though he knew them, could understand some of their hardships and picture their triumphs and joys. Their lot had been similar to that of his own people so many times in Scotland's past. Page after page he read, into the quiet hours of the night, unmindful of time, unmindful of fatigue, totally engrossed with the beauties and truths unfolding before him.

When at length he set aside the book and stretched out on his bed, it was only to think over the things he had read, the thoughts and impressions which had come to his heart. Andrew knew now, and admitted it to himself at last, that he was becoming converted to Mormonism, and the realization brought no fear. For the first time there was no struggle, no bitterness, no fear. With a deep sense of peace, Andrew slept.

During the next few days Jessie seemed to bloom. Andrew noticed the change and marveled at how his news had appeared to dissolve all the tense, bitter waiting; his mother was relaxed and warm, more her old self than Andrew had seen her since his father's death. It was September now, less than three months until the dreadful year would be ended, and he knew how anxious his mother was to put it behind her as a thing of the past.

Three more months and it would be a year since his father died. Andrew was aware of how much he had learned and matured during that time, and it gave him a deep sense of strength and satisfaction. He marveled at the way of things, knowing in his heart that he could never consider that his search had failed. It had already brought him two precious things: Mormonism, with the principles it embodied, and Nan.

The phone rang, interrupting his thoughts. His spirits lifted as he recognized the voice on the other end.

"I'm at the station in town. Will you send someone to collect me, or shall I keep on going? If you don't think you're ready to put up with me again as yet, there's always Aunt Alice in Edinburgh or Gavin MacGregor over Lanark way."

"Edwin, you scoundrel! Tired of fishing already, are you?"

"It's yourself to blame, Andrew. You got me so used to working that I'll never be able to enjoy sheer leisure again. Ach, and none of the lassies are as bonnie as Janet, I'm afraid, nor as intriguing as Aunt Jessie can be."

"We'll be there in half an hour. It'll be grand to have you home again!"

Edwin put back the receiver and sighed in sheer relief. Things were all right. Andrew must know of his loss by now, but he must be totally unsuspecting to offer Edwin as warm a reception as he had. Yes, everything would be all right. He walked toward the station doors, more anxious than he wanted to admit, and stood where he could sight the black Magnetta as soon as it drove into the station.

"Brad, let me see that ring. For heaven's sake, where did you get it?"

Brad smiled to himself. It was always the same. The first thing, and usually the only thing, people noticed about him was this large, impressive, unusual ring. He wanted to answer, *It's a long story. Actually, I don't know where the ring came from.* Instead he only said, "It's been in the family for years, handed down from my great-grandfather, who crossed the plains."

"Where would a Mormon pioneer get a stone like that?"

It *was* an unusually large diamond, set in what looked like cupped petals of a flower, unfolding just enough to reveal the exquisite jewel inside. On either side a gold tendril wound its way outside and around the carved blossom, and in each tendril a blood-red ruby winked and glowed. It was by far Brad's most valued earthly possession. He had taken the ring to a jeweler last year and been shocked when the man appraised it at nearly the price of Brad's home.

But it was not for a monetary reason Brad prized the ring. He had loved it since he was a little boy, and when he had first learned that one day the ring would be his, he had slipped upstairs to his parents' room and carefully lifted it out of the case where his father kept it. He remembered still how heavy and solid the ring had felt sitting in his hand. That was long before he knew the story of the ring and the lost ancestor to whom it seemed the only existing link.

Brad now kept the ring in a safety-deposit box at the bank, loathe to risk losing something of that much real and aesthetic value. But he hated to keep it there, where he couldn't see it always. And on every conceivable occasion—for anything that could be construed special—he would remove the ring from its darkened place. Beauty, Brad believed, was meant to be seen and enjoyed.

It was light that lifted the jewels out of themselves, that made their beauty come to life! He never tired of watching the play of light in the crimson rubies and the depths and caverns and crevices of the exquisite diamond they flanked. Brad felt different, somehow; more whole, more alive himself, when the ring was on his finger.

He looked at it now with a kind of resignation. It was over two months since he had made his private resolution. Two months and nothing had happened. Well, that wasn't entirely true. A lot had happened inside him. He had learned what discipline really meant, and patience. Even Jenny and the children noticed how much more patient and sensitive he had become.

It was almost as if, in searching for some lost and unknown ancestor, he was beginning to really find himself and know himself for the first time in his life. Actually, he had never been quite so happy and self-assured. Perhaps that was the purpose of his crazy search, after all. Maybe it wasn't important for him to find his answer here and now. But it was important, he knew, to find himself and to fulfill his eternal potential as he discovered it.

But he had lived with this thing on his mind every day for weeks now, and he was loathe to entirely desert the idea, to give it up. It certainly wouldn't hurt to continue praying and working; he was even a little concerned for fear his grasp on things might slip, otherwise. He didn't want to lose this new strength which had come into his life.

The clangorous voice of the school bell interrupted his thoughts. Three o'clock already. He watched the kids pour out of the narrow doorway, jostling and shoving and merging together—yet each of them, he knew, was so entirely different and distinct. He wondered how many of them knew who they were, or how many even cared, for that matter. They disappeared through the open door at last, but their voices reverberated through the halls, bouncing against the walls in a harsh and hollow chaos that pounded in his ears.

How many of those kids out there will live and die and never really discover themselves, as I'm beginning to discover myself right now? The thought disturbed him. He glanced back at the clock on the wall behind his desk. Another hour and he would be heading home along the freeway. It was Jared's birthday tomorrow. Brad had the new glove and softball for the boy hidden safely in his trunk. He'd probably take the whole family to Lagoon to celebrate, or maybe to Liberty Park. It would be less crowded at the park, and Jenny loved to wander through the aviary. He'd let Jared make the decision.

Brad found himself getting excited as he thought about his family, and it struck him how lucky he was. He'd been around enough to know how many unhappy marriages there were in the world, and even within the Church itself. Funny. He'd thought this same thing half a dozen times over the past couple of months: maybe he couldn't tell his children exactly where they came from, but he could help them to discover themselves, find out who they were inside. Not every man could offer that service to his family; surely, that kind of a heritage was worth more than a bona fide pedigree. Brad hoped so, because it was all he could give them right now. Anything beyond that lay in the hands of the Lord.

14

She had never missed Andrew more. It was the twenty-third of September and she was twenty-one years old today. Nan believed in "special days," and she daydreamed of the ways she would make birthdays and holidays special for her own children when they came. The first snowfall in winter, the first lilacs in the spring—so many things could be special if you only looked at them that way. And few days ought to be as special as the day a girl turns twenty-one.

Her grandma was baking a cake, she knew, and there would be presents at her place at dinner, but that would be all. Her father was acting strange and withdrawn, as though the idea of her having a birthday upset him, somehow. Julie was working at the local Dairy Creme until four, and Jonathan had gone off swimming with his friends. There was no one to talk to and nothing to do.

Nan walked down Parley toward the river. "Teardrop Lane" this road was called when thousands of Mormons walked its length for the last time, pausing from time to time to look back at their tall brick homes, their yards and barns, their schools and businesses—all the beauty and prosperity they had built with such excruciating labor where only a disease-infested swampland had stood. No one could have told their thoughts as they gazed back for the last time, then turned to face the expanse of frozen river which marked the beginning of an entirely new and different way of life, more difficult than anything they had yet encountered and overcome. Nan walked in the heavy stillness, wondering how many tears had been shed by the men and women and children who had walked this lovely path.

She turned and walked alone beside the river and felt sorry for herself. It was still muggy and warm, and the long summer had dried the edges of the river, shrinking the line of water and leaving long stretches of dank mud and grasses, strewn with rocks and bark and broken glass and, occasionally, a dead fish or two. Nan stopped by the willow and tried to remember what it was like the first time Andrew had kissed her beneath this tree. She closed her eyes, but it was difficult to picture his face.

What was he doing today? Working at his offices until late? Or perhaps it was lovely weather and the family was taking a picnic lunch to the lake, then climbing the nearby hills, or fishing from a boat. Andrew would laugh and tease and love every minute of it, never knowing that she was walking, quiet and alone, beside the dirty summer river, while the endless minutes ticked away, and she turned twenty-one with no one to even notice, and no one to care. She luxuriated in her own melancholy, as the only companion or comfort she had.

Finally she went home, showered, washed her long hair, and dressed in a pale summer dress for dinner, determined that no one should guess her feelings and know the loneliness of her heart. She stopped to look at herself in the mirror before going downstairs and was startled by how pretty she looked. Her eyes were deep and warm, the line of her nose thin and fine. None of her inner sadness seemed reflected in her features. Her dark hair shone and her skin was delicate and clear.

"I don't look twenty-one years old," she said out loud.

She turned from the mirror, then caught her breath, for the little oval portrait of her mother had attracted her glance. She went to the dresser and picked it up. The mouth was much like her own, and the nose, though the eyes—she hesitated, then walked with the picture back to the mirror and looked closely at herself again.

Why, her eyes were exactly like her mother's eyes! She had never seen that before. In fact, she looked amazingly like her mother had looked. That picture had stood on her dresser since she was a child. She had always thought her mother was the most beautiful woman she had ever seen; why hadn't she ever realized that she looked like her mother? She held the picture tenderly a moment longer, then gently put it back in place.

Mother, she said to herself, *I'm twenty-one years old today. I'm a woman now, like you. I think I'll pretend that you can see me, and I'll be sweet and gracious and beautiful as you would have been.*

She walked down the stairs with her head poised; it was crazy, but she felt suddenly older and graceful and beautiful, as she had never felt before. *I feel like my mother*, she said to herself and knew, somehow, that it was true.

When she walked into the dining room everyone else was waiting. She thought she heard Julie catch her breath, and she did hear Jonathan give a low whistle. Her father stared at her, not taking his eyes away, until she began to feel uncomfortable and awkward again. Nan took her seat and her grandma mumbled, ''You don't have to go looking like a woman overnight like that, Nan, just because you've turned twenty-one.''

Nan smiled at her and the old woman stammered and dropped her eyes. *They're all uncomfortable around me*, she thought. *Have I really changed, then? Can I be so different so suddenly?*

She didn't realize that the change had been gradual, much like the unfolding of a perfect bud when, with one warm night, the petals suddenly stretch into full bloom, and the rose is a bud no longer; the beauty, the transformation, is there for everyone to see.

She opened her gifts with honest delight: a purse from her grandma, stationery from Jonathan, a new set of earrings from Julie. Everything pleased her; the slippers her grandma had knitted, the Mary Stewart novel Julie had gone clear to Warsaw to find. There was even a gift from Tom. Tabu perfume and a box of her favorite chocolates. Tom, left out and forgotten, but giving to her still. They were all giving to her, loving her, and she felt so ashamed.

There was one last gift, and she knew it must be from her father. She opened it with trembling fingers, and found inside a delicate pen and pencil set and a leather-bound journal with her name engraved on the cover. She tried to thank him, but it was difficult to speak. Impulsively she rose and went to him and threw her arms around his neck, hiding her head against his shoulder, embarrassed by her own emotions. She couldn't remember when she had last hugged her father, but she realized he was holding her so tightly that it hurt, and she could feel the great effort he was making to control himself.

She kissed his cheek lightly without looking at him, then hurried back to her chair. Jonathan said something, clever and normal—she had never been so grateful for his awful humor before! Her grandma began bringing out the food, and the crisis was past. But Nan was afraid to meet her father's eyes again, and whenever she hazarded a look in his direction, she realized that he was avoiding looking at her directly, too.

The meal went beautifully; every dish was one of Nan's favorites, cooked only as her grandma could cook. As they cleared the dishes for dessert, Nan noticed a slender envelope under her plate. She opened it and slid out the paper. Written in a shaky, scrawling hand was the special invitation to "ice cream, cake, and company" at eight this evening, signed by Grant Morgan, dated Saturday, September 23, 3:00 P.M. She looked up questioningly, the paper in her hand.

"He brought it by this afternoon. Asked me to give it to you," her grandma said.

"Did you know about this, Father?" she asked.

"Yes, yes," he answered, still not looking at her. "I think it would be fine if you run over there for a while this evening. The old man probably needs a little company."

Incredible! How could her father possibly be sitting here calmly approving her spending the evening with Grant? She had suspected since Grant's phone call that her father knew of her meetings with the old Mormon; knew, too, that he was talking to her about religion, about all the forbidden things her father had been so adamant about for so long. Nan felt as though she didn't understand anything any more, but right now it didn't matter, for there was a strange, happy glow about her and she didn't want to do anything to make it go away.

"Good grief, I forgot it! I hid it upstairs in my closet, and I completely forgot it! Stay here!" Jonathan dropped his fork and disappeared.

"The dummy," Julie muttered under her breath.

When he returned, Jonathan was carrying a package, wrapped in brown paper, tied with a string, pasted with half a dozen foreign-looking stamps. Nan's heart gave a little flutter, then seemed to stand still.

"What is it?" she said, and her voice sounded small.

"Give it to her, you idiot. This is no time for horsing around."

Jonathan gave Julie an unkind look, but he handed the package to Hannah. It was addressed to her, and the name in the left-hand corner was Andrew's, of course. She just sat there, holding it, while her heart started beating again.

"It's a birthday present. Why don't you open it?" Jonathan sounded eager.

Hannah looked up at her brother, incredulous. "How can it be a birthday present? Andrew doesn't know when my birthday is."

"Oh, yes, he does. He's no fool! He doesn't let the grass grow under his feet, like Grandma always says."

"What Jonathan is trying to tell you, Nan, is that Andrew asked *him* when your birthday was before he left." Julie lifted her eyebrows and glared at Jonathan.

"That's not all he asked me, either. He asked a lot of other questions—strictly man to man."

Jonathan wanted to be able to blurt right out that Andrew had asked him to take special care of Nan, watch out for her while Andrew was gone. Then they'd know how much Andrew respected him and appreciated what he was. But he had given Andrew his word, and he sensed, besides, that a statement like that at a time like this wouldn't really do much toward the furthering of his own already precarious position with his sisters.

Nan excused herself quietly and slipped away to her room to open the little gift. Inside the layers of thin tissue paper was a fine glass bottle of heather-scented perfume, with a red plaid label. The little black case beside it held a delicate silver pin, finely formed into the shape of a thistle, with exquisite detail. She held it in her hands, then opened Andrew's note and read it through and knew again, as surely as she had known it that morning in the woods, that Andrew loved her, that his love was real and deep, warm and secure.

She read the note once more, then she got out some of Andrew's old letters and read them through again, and she took out her favorite notebook and the new pen her father had given her and wrote to

Andrew, penning all the thoughts and hopes and feelings she had wanted to tell him since he left.

She was amazed when Julie knocked on her door and reminded her that it was nearly eight o'clock. She sealed the pages in an envelope and wrote Andrew's name on the outside, then hid it carefully on the shelf behind her books. Someday she would give it to him, perhaps. It was enough for now that she had written it, that she knew it was there. She rose from the desk to get ready to keep her appointment with Grant.

It was fun being with Grant. They didn't talk about religion as much as they usually did lately. They got rather carried away reminiscing, and the years seemed to crumble aside as they relived the experiences they had shared together. Hannah felt like a little girl, young and lighthearted and carefree again.

Then suddenly Grant rose, with a twinkle in his eye, and told her he'd be right back. In a minute he reappeared with a package in his hand. But he didn't give it to Nan right away. He sat down and cradled the gift in his big hands as he spoke.

"I've waited a long time to give this to you, Nan. It's from both me and Ellen." His eyes glistened and the smile began to tremble ever so slightly. "I remember very well the morning she picked it out. We were in Salt Lake visiting Matthew and his new bride. We'd stopped at a bookstore, and Ellen picked up this very book and asked me if I liked it. 'I think Nan ought to have one of her own, Grant, don't you?'

" 'Now, Ellen,' I told her, 'you know we can't give anything like that to Nan.'

" 'Maybe not now,' she said, 'but we'll buy it anyway and tuck it away, and if we have to wait until she's twenty-one, we'll wait, and give it to her then.' "

He handed it to Nan and she took it wonderingly, her own eyes filling with tears.

"I guess she didn't quite make the wait, Nan. But she'd want me to give it to you today."

"It doesn't matter, Grant. You know she's here as much as if she were alive, and sitting there in her chair knitting."

A tear escaped down his cheek, tracing a crooked course among the wrinkles and folds of skin.

"I'm glad you can feel it, too, Nan," he said softly. "I thought perhaps you might."

She tore the paper and folded it gently back to reveal a blue volume, hardbound, with the title *Book of Mormon*; her own name embossed in delicate gold letters at the bottom of the cover. She touched it gently, reverently.

"How old was I then, Grant?" she asked. "When Ellen bought the book, how old was I?"

He thought for a moment. "Twelve. It was the autumn right after you turned twelve years old."

She picked up the book. Nine years, she thought. Nine years this book has laid in waiting for me, storing up all the love and faith of a woman who loved me and wanted to give to me, and who would not be denied. She looked into Grant's eyes, and everything that couldn't be said in words passed between them. Nan marveled at the beauty this special day had brought, wondering at all the choice things which had come to her because the times and seasons had rolled their course to this hour, and she had become twenty-one.

It was late when Nan was finally ready for bed. She had recorded a long entry in the first pages of her journal and said her prayers and read two chapters in the new Book of Mormon with Grant's and Ellen's names in the front.

There was a soft knock on her door. She knew it was neither Julie nor her grandma, and it certainly wasn't Jonathan. She pulled on her robe and opened the door. Her father stood there. He looked suddenly tall to her and big, framed in the doorway like that.

"May I come in?" She nodded and stood back to let him pass. He pulled out the chair from her desk and sat down awkwardly. Nan perched on the edge of the bed, not knowing what to say. He looked around with interest, noticing the shelves of books, the little oval of her mother she had studied with such careful interest only hours earlier.

"It's a long time since I've been in this room," he said thoughtfully. He walked over and picked up the little photograph.

"I'd forgotten you had this," he said. He studied it a moment, then looked up at her. "Are you aware of the likeness? You're so much like your mother, Nan. Not only in physical appearance, but in almost every way."

"Am I? Am I really, Father? Tell me about her. Something—anything. Please."

He hesitated and she held her breath.

"I've never really talked about your mother before. I don't know if I can."

She was silent, praying inwardly. Finally the words began to come. Slowly at first, and awkwardly. Then he seemed to forget himself, and Nan as well, and she could see that as he talked her mother came alive for him again and was the only person he was aware of. Her mother began to come to life for Nan, too. Through her father's words her mother took on form and feature, personality and mannerisms, and Nan felt as though she were getting to know her mother for the very first time. At last the words ran out and her father stopped talking, exhausted, the photograph still in his hands.

"Thank you," Nan said softly. "I know that was hard for you, Father. Thank you so much."

He looked at her, as though seeing her for the first time. He rose and replaced the picture and she saw that he had something else in his hands. It was a thin brown book, old and worn. He placed it in her lap.

"Emily Dickinson's poems. Your mother's copy. I think she would want you to have it, Nan." She couldn't speak. *And I thought this day was complete and perfect before!* she thought.

"Thank you, Father," she managed at last. "I'll treasure it for the rest of my life."

He was at the door. He was leaving! She jumped to her feet and placed her hand uncertainly on his arm.

"Father, will you come again and talk to me about Mother? Please?"

The struggle on his face was visible and told her much that he could never have spoken to her, time without end. At last he nodded.

"Yes, Nan. I think I'd like that very much."

He closed the door gently and she was alone. She stood against the door trembling, clutching the precious volume to her, her mind too full of wonder for thought.

At last she curled up on her bed and opened the book and found the date and her mother's signature in that beautiful, flowing hand. She scanned the pages, reading a poem here and there, wondering which were her mother's favorites and why, and what they had made her think and feel. Her mind and heart and spirit were exhausted, overcome with the intense experiences of the day. At last she slept, the book open beside her to the little verse she had last read before closing her eyes:

> That such have died enables us
>   The tranquiller to die;
> That such have lived, certificate
>   For immortality.

Her last thought was of the two noble women who had died, and yet lived on somehow, who loved her and watched over her. And because she knew how truly they were there, she would never be entirely afraid or entirely lonely again.

15

Nan had only been dressed a few minutes and was starting down the stairs to eat breakfast when the phone began to ring. Her grandmother came to the bottom of the stairs and called up to her, "You'd better go back and answer that, Nan."

Jonathan was in the hall and closer to the upstairs phone than Nan was.

"I'll get it," he offered.

"No," her grandma retorted sharply. "It's not for you. Get it, Nan, hurry."

Puzzled, Nan fled back and reached for the receiver. "Hello," she said, breathlessly.

"Hello. You don't sound any different, even though you are twenty-one now. But your grandmother said last evening that you look like a woman suddenly, and that you're lovelier than ever before."

"My grandmother said that? Oh, Andrew, did you call while I was gone? Did I miss you?"

"I'm afraid so, lass. It was my own fault, that. I should have made more careful arrangements."

"But Grandma didn't tell me! Of course, she was asleep when I came in."

"I think she wanted to surprise you. So you couldn't keep from celebrating your twenty-first birthday even though I wasn't there to help you! Who was the lucky man?"

Nan loved the lilt to Andrew's voice when he was teasing her.

"It was only Grant, and you know it. Grandma told you, didn't she? But I had a lovely time. Oh, Andrew, I can't believe you've really called me, all the way from Scotland. You sound so wonderful and real! It's hard to believe you're so far away."

"Well, for a few minutes at least, pretend that I'm not. Relax and tell me about your birthday. I'm anxious to hear."

Nan tried to, though it seemed incomprehensible to her that people could talk casually and at such length when every minute must be costing an awesome sum. It had been easy last night after supper to write down her thoughts and feelings for Andrew's eyes to read, but it was much more difficult now to speak the same things out loud. As quickly as she could Hannah turned the conversation back to Andrew, asking about his homecoming, his family, his business. He responded warmly, delighting her with his colorful accounts.

"It sounds like everything's going beautifully, Andrew, and I'm so glad."

There was a pause, and she could feel the change in the atmosphere.

"Well, actually, Nan, that isn't quite true. I'd hesitated even telling you about it and spoiling our conversation, for I've written the whole miserable thing out in a letter you ought to be receiving within the next few days."

"Andrew, please tell me. You've started—you must tell me now!"

He told her about Heber Shumway and the missing file, and she was so astonished that she forgot about the distance and the money, and she tenderly drew him out so that he told her of his deep and illogical disappointment. Her understanding was so complete, so sincere that it strengthened him, as he had known that it would.

"I won't go on at length, Nan, and upset you too much. It's all there in the letter. It helped me to write it out for you, though I don't really know why."

"I understand," she replied, and told him of the letter she had written the night before and kept for him to read someday. And then it became difficult, their desire for each other a tension that the thin line of communication could not diminish or disguise. She tried to tell him how much she loved him, but the only words she knew to use sounded worn and trite and thoroughly inadequate.

"I'm a writer," she told him finally. "When I have a pen in my hand the right words seem to come. But something happens when I try to speak."

"Then let me say them for you," he answered gently. And he did. In his warm and beautiful voice he said everything she had ever longed to hear, so that when she hung up the phone, alone at last, the thought came to her that it was almost worth the separation to be able to hear Andrew say those things to her; things he would never have said —perhaps never even felt—if he had always been near to nurture his love with his own presence.

She hurried into her room and, in spite of feeling ridiculously romantic, she wrote down all she could remember of what he had said, knowing in her heart that there would be many times in the years to come when she would take out the words and read them, reliving the beauty of those expressions of his love for her.

The next few days passed as though part of a lovely dream; the beauty and the wonder of her twenty-first birthday remained with Nan. It didn't seem to diminish or wear away. Everything she did, everything she touched or heard or saw seemed to bear a new beauty, a new purpose she had never been aware of before.

On Sunday she attended sacrament meeting at the brick chapel on the hill. The talks that were given touched her, but it was the songs which awakened her spirit. She asked Grant if she could borrow a copy of the hymnbook. He winked at her and asked her just where she was going to play those songs.

So she spent a Monday family home evening with Grant and, after they talked, she played on the piano a few of the hymns she had come to love: "The Spirit of God," "O, Ye Mountains High," "How Firm a Foundation," and "O My Father," the one she loved the best of all. The next morning she went down to the river early and sang the songs to herself, under the protection of the willow, until the music and words were her own, to take out and reexperience any time she wished. Tuesday she was busy with interviews most of the day, and when she came home late in the afternoon, the letter Andrew had told her about was there.

She read the long letter alone in her room, and Andrew was so vivid in describing his frustrations and woes that she felt angry and unhappy and frustrated again herself after she had read them through. Poor Andrew! He had given so much and cared so much, and now it would all be nothing but a waste.

The search had never been of as much importance to her, Nan admitted to herself, though she nurtured a soft spot in her heart for the old man, the original Buchanan who had lost his son and concocted his crazy will. Without that old man's preposterous demands, Andrew would never have set foot in Nauvoo, and Nan would never have known of his existence; she would have only dreamed and hoped and wondered if somewhere such a man really did exist.

She sighed. Everything had not been all happiness for Andrew, either. She wished she were able to help him somehow. He was so very far away! She picked up her Emily Dickinson and read about love and loss and bliss and pain, and felt somewhat comforted.

After that letter it was difficult for Nan to get Andrew off her mind. Usually she could push thoughts of him deep into the special little place where they belonged. But now, after his phone call and the letter, she felt so aware of his unhappiness and disappointment, and it seemed that everything she saw and did and thought about reminded her of him, and applied somehow.

"You really ought to go, Andrew. Now's a perfect time."

"Don't push the lad, don't push him. He's going to feel he's not wanted in his own home. Either that, or he'll detest the sight of me. Every time I come around, you start expecting Andrew to go off somewhere."

Edwin was in rare form. In fact, he had never been happier in his life. He was back at Bieldmor House, home to him, basking in the love and security around him, pleased with the outcome of his little enterprise in Salt Lake City. He had questioned Andrew casually about the progress of the work, and Andrew had been only too eager to tell him how the entire file on Charles Buchanan had been lost. So it *had* all been there. Edwin hadn't known at the time exactly how many of the research papers he had destroyed. He was in luck again, he decided with satisfaction!

To add to his luck, Jessie was happy again. Andrew had added that, though it was easy enough for Edwin to see the change in her himself. Janet seemed involved with concerns of her own, and even Andrew entertained little hope that anything could result from a renewed search at this late date. And now Jessie's proposal that Andrew take this little trip to Lancashire. Perfect. Keep him involved in the business, let the last few weeks slip quietly away. Then it would be time for Edwin to play his final hand.

"I know you're right, Mother," Andrew was saying. "Hastings is a capable man, but it's time I visited the mills myself. I haven't been there once since Father's death."

And so it was arranged. Edwin would take over again in Andrew's absence. But this time Andrew would be so much closer to home, and he would be gone for only a couple of weeks—less, perhaps.

Andrew spoke to Janet before he left. He couldn't quite bring himself to tell her of the experience he had had that night with the Doctrine and Covenants, but he did ask her forgiveness and assure her that he was thinking of possibilities, formulating a plan whereby he could approach his mother and secure her permission and support for Janet to be baptized.

Her eyes were shining as she kissed him goodbye. Andrew was still apprehensive of the results, but he had faced the fact that a devotion to Nan which sapped his courage, weakened his integrity, and glutted his selfishness was no devotion at all, and totally unworthy of Nan. He would have to trust—trust in what? Fate, the future, the hand of God?

The morning was cool, still wet with the touch of dew and wild with the music of a hundred birds singing their songs of innocence and joy. Andrew drove to the station wondering what it would be like to know exactly where you were going, and why you were going, and what it was all about. He knew there must be men today like Joseph Smith, who never walked alone, but who had the strength of some higher power always at hand. He drove to the station slowly, wondering what it would be like.

It was early in the morning still, clean and cool and fresh, when Nan headed out of town through the park, east on Parley, toward the old Mormon cemetery. She was on a special assignment, and she was excited about this one. She had only been to the cemetery once or twice before, and she watched the landmarks carefully.

Here was the narrow bridge; it wouldn't be much farther now. She slowed the Mustang and a meadowlark burst into melody in the tall grasses at the side of the road. There was the mailbox and the narrow lane leading off to the right. Grant had told her that Joseph Smith himself selected the ten acres for this cemetery outside the city limits of Nauvoo. It had fallen into disuse now, and was tangled and matted and overgrown.

Nan parked the car and began to follow the path down through the shady ravine, where a stagnant pond lay, choked and still; she then climbed the slope through the dense, wild-grown bushes and grasses, where the silence was as thick and impenetrable as the weeds at her feet.

She was here in search of the ginkgo, a rare, ancient tree, held sacred in China and planted within the royal gardens of the Chinese temples. The ginkgo was more uncommon here among the oak and elm and maple which were native to Illinois. She knew what it looked like and could identify its leaves: pale green and dainty, but leathery in texture and shaped much like a fan. They had told her at the newspaper office that there was a beautiful specimen right near the crest of the slope on the northeast side. Bill Johnson had offered to come and photograph the tree for her if she wanted him to, but Nan was eager for an excuse to explore the old cemetery herself.

She looked around, somewhat dismayed by the size and solitude of the place. It was as though she were lost in the midst of a dense forest with no sign of civilization, no trace of man, although she knew that she stood only a bare eighth of a mile from the farmhouse across the road. A fine mist rose from the earth forming little gray pools among the clustered flowers and dusty weeds. There were hundreds of trees here: elm and linden, mulberry and box elder, and dozens of sturdy oak. How was she ever to identify the one she needed?

Nan walked a few steps hesitantly, trying to pick out, by the shape of the leaves, something that looked different from the rest. Here was an apple tree, gnarled and dwarfed. And was that an elm? And there— there was the ginkgo tree! She came closer and took her camera out of her purse. The tree was beautiful. She took more pictures than she needed, but there were so many lovely angles, ways of photographing the tree with weeds or the broken stone fence or a leaning grave marker in view.

At last Nan put away the camera and began to wander among the old graves, scattered at wide intervals among the tall grasses and trees. She was saddened by the crumble and decay and neglect. Not a breath stirred; not a bird cried. But the deep silence held only a sense of peace for Nan.

There were so many children buried here! She brushed her hair back from her eyes. Three little markers in a row: Sarah, aged three months, William, aged two years, Lucy, aged five years. Nan shuddered involuntarily. How could a mother bear to lose three children, just like that? How could she stand the pain?

Nan wandered further and further into the cemetery. The stones seemed older here, more ruined, more difficult to read. Was that a ginkgo tree, off there to the left? If so, it was a wonderful specimen. Nan stumbled through the tall grasses, nearly tripping over a fallen log, but as she approached the tree more closely, she wasn't sure. The trunk looked the same, slender and straight, but she'd better examine the leaves. Even up close she wasn't certain; she'd better not take a picture of this one. If she was wrong the guys at the photo lab would never let her live it down.

There was a little group of headstones nearly at her feet. She bent down to examine them. It looked like ''Anderson'' on that stone, but part of the letters were gone. A child again, a boy. Ten years old—or twelve—she couldn't tell. What did the next one say? She bent closer and brushed away the crumbling fragments of stone and cement. Then she stopped in cold astonishment.

The stone at her feet was cracked and broken, one edge having disappeared entirely, and it leaned precariously to the right; but, somehow, it still bravely stood, and the letters on the stone read:

CHARLES BUCH   A

18   1844

Some of the lettering had been worn away and, where the corner had broken, some of the name was missing as well. It was only part of a name, really. Nan knelt in the dirt and leaves to examine it more closely. *Please let it be, please let it be*, she murmured to herself.

The date of birth was not discernible, but the date of death was definitely 1844. The rest of the name was no longer imprinted on the worn and tired stone. All that stood, mocking her eager gaze, were the beginning letters BUCH   A   —but it was *Charles* BUCH   A   ! It had to be him, it just had to be!

With a little gasp Hannah realized that another stone stood adjacent to the first one. The only letters she could make out read:

RA H L
BEL   D W F

She puzzled over this a moment, then realized suddenly that the name must be *Rachel*. And, of course, the inscription following must have read "Beloved Wife," a common enough tribute in that time. She rubbed the stone carefully, and pulled back the stubborn weeds, searching for dates, but she could discern only the faintest form of a "1" and an "8."

She dropped to the ground and sat there, hugging her knees, feeling ridiculously like crying. Was this, then, the end of the search? And was it to end in the decay of time and the mocking silence of the grave?

She realized there were tears gathering in her eyes. Wiping them quickly away she rose, brushed off her clothing, and recorded the information before her carefully in her notebook, marking, too, the exact spot, with landmarks, to help her find the place again. There were only two shots left in her camera, so Nan took an extreme closeup and then a medium view of the gravestones, hoping that the lettering would show up in the photographs.

With a mingling sense of excitement and sorrow she worked her way back to the car, planning what she would write to Andrew, knowing she must tell him in a letter, in spite of his strict injunction not to write, what she had discovered. What would he feel when he received her letter? What would he think of her strange discovery?

The throb of the Mustang's engine seemed an intrusion, a glaring inconsistency in the deathlike stillness around. She herself was an intrusion. She felt it inside. She looked back, but the pathetic little graves were hidden from view. Did they consider her an intrusion? Would they rather she leave them alone, to sleep on in peace? She turned the Mustang around, heading back along the narrow, grass-grown lane.

"Charles Buchanan," she said out loud, "have you any idea how much trouble you're causing after all these years?'' Only the silence answered her, and she seemed to carry it with her as she pulled out onto the highway and headed back toward Nauvoo.

16

Will Fortune never come
with both hands full,
But write her fair words
still in foulest letters?

2 HENRY IV

It was a good trip, much better than Andrew had hoped it would be. John Hastings had the three mills in Lancashire running like tops, but then Hastings was known for being able to accomplish the work of ten men.

Andrew remembered his father telling him that the smartest thing the old man, the original Buchanan, ever did while he was amassing his properties was to purchase these holdings in England. Years later when the bottom fell out of the cotton industry in Scotland and the First World War played havoc with profits, the steady trade in Lancashire just kept right on. Perhaps part of the problem with the Scots was that they had concentrated on fanciful items for show and taste, while the English produced strong, plain, unchanging articles for which there would consistently be a need and, therefore, a market as well.

Then, too, the original Andrew Buchanan had wisely invested his monies in other areas, totally separate from the mills, securing a fortune for his posterity which would never have existed if it rested on the mill trade alone.

There really wasn't much for Andrew to do here, he reflected, though there were two new managers to be hired, repairs in the Thistledown mill to be authorized, new machines to be purchased, and some crazy scheme Hastings was nurturing of expansion and consolidation and implementation, all mixed up together at once, and fired with the breath of genius, John was sure.

Andrew liked the man. Even when he was a little boy and accompanied his father occasionally on his Lancashire trips, Hastings had never "talked down" to him, but had always treated him with understanding and respect. Andrew had come to appreciate and trust Hastings, therefore, at an early age, and John Hastings had never let him down.

He watched the man walking toward him now, across the littered office. *If this were my office,* Andrew thought to himself, *I'd never be able to locate a thing.* But then he knew John could lay his hand on any item he wanted in a matter of seconds, and it seemed logical to him to know where everything was, though Andrew couldn't begin to discover any order or organization to the place.

"You're wearing the ring, I see. I hadn't noticed it before."

"What?" Andrew looked up, surprised. "Oh yes, the ring. I suppose you *would* recognize it after all this time."

"Absolutely. It's always fascinated me, you know. Pretty piece of workmanship, isn't it?"

"Yes, though I've always thought it was a rather flagrant thing for the old man to do. You know the story, don't you?"

"Indeed I do. The original Andrew had one made for each of his two sons. Gave them to the boys when they turned twenty-one, wasn't it? The rubies represented the sons, of course, but your father and I could never decide if the mammoth diamond in the center represented the old man, himself, or if it went deeper and represented the mills and the land and the fortune—all the things the old man was beginning to represent."

Andrew chuckled. "Probably the latter. At least it's more romantic that way."

His light manner was intentional, for the ring had always symbolized for Andrew his father. When he first slipped it on his finger after his father's death, Andrew felt as though he were usurping something not rightfully his. And yet, whenever he wore the ring since, it seemed a tangible link between himself and his father; a strength and a comfort, somehow.

A clerk came into the room with a question, and after he'd left they turned to business again. Andrew was glad. He'd just as soon not get too deep into the matter of the ring and his father. As comfortable as he was around Hastings, his feelings about the matter were too personal, too deep, and he didn't feel like sharing them with anyone just now.

Edwin was fitting back into things beautifully, Janet thought as she walked out to feed the collies, Tormud and Tybalt. Things were running smoothly, and she didn't have that awful feeling in the pit of her stomach that she'd had so often when Andrew was in America. It's different, she thought to herself. Andrew's different and I'm different. Even Mother seems to have changed.

She thought about Andrew's promise as she walked back to the house. For the hundredth time she offered a little prayer that, somehow, Andrew would find the miraculous formula to soften her mother's heart, to open her understanding just enough—just enough to give permission for Janet to be baptized.

She sat in the cool kitchen with a glass of chilled apple juice, enjoying the pale autumn sun spilling over the rough stone floor.

"Look at this, Janet." Her mother entered and handed her an envelope. "What do you think it is?"

Janet took the letter and examined it. It was addressed to Andrew. The foreign postmark wasn't from Salt Lake City as she had expected it to be. The name was unknown to her, as was the place: Hannah Martin, Nauvoo, Illinois. Janet could hear the concern in her mother's voice, so she spoke as lightly as possible.

"Must be something to do with the search, don't you think? I'll run it in to Edwin. He's working in Andrew's study this morning. He'll take care of it, Mother."

She gave her mother a brief smile and slipped past her and out of the room before Jessie had the opportunity to protest.

"I've just hired three new men, Janet," Edwin said as she knocked lightly, and then walked in. "I certainly hope Andrew approves. We don't always see eye to eye as to what qualifies a man, you know."

"Aye, I ken," she said, with a sparkle in her eye. "Andrew likes them sober and stable and you seem to think that a man who's popular with the lassies and can hold his whisky is much more likely to be happy and well-adjusted and willing to work."

148

"Janet!" He was surprised by her quite accurate appraisal of things, but she only laughed and handed him the letter.

"Do you recognize that name, Edwin? Did Andrew ever mention such a person to you?"

Edwin regarded the letter thoughtfully.

"I don't believe so, lass."

"Well, it must have something to do with the research. I can't imagine what else it would be. We'd best send it on to Andrew. He made me promise to forward all mail from America, you know. I think he's still hoping that something might turn up."

"I'll send it for you, if you'd like. I've some materials to mail off to Andrew myself this afternoon."

"Thank you, Edwin. Don't forget. I hope it says something that will please him, poor lad. I think he's more involved in this matter than we realize."

Edwin waited until Janet shut the door, then listened for her footsteps to die away down the long, hardwood hall. Off to the right of Andrew's study was a little narrow office, private, with a lock and key. Edwin took the letter with him and locked the door.

A sickening fear was growing somewhere inside him; he felt pale and a little shaky. He remembered now, vaguely, that Andrew had mentioned some girl he had met, but for the life of him Edwin couldn't remember the name or the place or any of the circumstances. *You're slipping, old man,* he said to himself, smiling grimly *It's a bad sign to forget anything concerning a lass.* But then, this one couldn't have been very important to Andrew, for Edwin would swear Andrew no more than mentioned the girl. Yet could she be involved in the research then as well?

Edwin sat in Andrew's burgundy leather chair and regarded the letter thoughtfully a moment, then tore it open and pulled out the sheets of paper, closely written in a delicate feminine hand. He read the lines hastily, and it didn't take him too long to discover that his fears, his worst possible fears, had been realized. He swore under his breath. This was the real thing, all right. No one, not even Andrew, had seriously believed that this dead ancestor could be found.

He drew out the pictures of the tombstones, choked with thick foliage and weeds. But the incriptions, or what was left of them, were easy enough to read. Edwin laughed. But the sound was harsh and cold, and entirely without mirth. How ironic that now, within hours of his own inheritance, this ignorant girl should stumble across the decaying evidence which would rob him of what was surely his—his by right, by birth, by blood! He, Edwin! who was alive and warm and real, robbed by the breath of death mocking him from some obscure little graveyard in Illinois!

Long minutes Edwin sat, clutching the letter, striving to control his senses and command his thoughts into some logical plan of action. At length he rose slowly from the chair. He copied the name and address from the envelope into the little black book he took from his lapel pocket, slipped the two glossy photographs carefully between the pages, then returned the book to its safe, private place. *There's more here than meets the eye*, he thought, and the premonition turned him cold.

Bless the builders of old houses for a fireplace in every room, Edwin thought, as he took matches and pulled open the firescreen, then placed the letter carefully on the grate. The orange flame teased the corner of the envelope, then suddenly caught hold with a clean, white blaze.

Edwin walked to the small, high window and opened it a crack to assure that the air in the room would filter out and the brisk autumn air pour in, leaving no trace of smoke or acrid odor. When he returned and stooped down beside the hearth, only a wispy heap of charred, blackened flakes remained. He poked the few ashes carefully, scattered them back into the dark recesses until, for all practical purposes, they had disappeared. He rose, pulled the screen snug across the opening, and brushed his hands together.

My time is short, he thought. *I must act quickly, and well. And a good excuse for leaving will be difficult to contrive.* Yet, even as he unlocked the door, walked into the main study, and gathered his materials from Andrew's desk, the plan was beginning to take shape and form within his mind.

He took the stairs two at a time, in his usual jaunty manner. Jessie was just coming from the kitchen, a tray of cakes and scones in her hands. Edwin grabbed a hot scone and winked at her as he passed.

"I'm off to town, Jessie. I've work to do and errands to run. Be back in time for dinner."

He whistled through the great hall, and down the curved brick stairs outside. Action! What a beautiful restorative it was. The sickening fear inside him was already beginning to subside.

Once in Paisley, Edwin made a few private calls from the safe sanctuary of Andrew's office at the mill. He made certain that he hailed Jock McCannon, Andrew's main plant manager, with a hearty "See you in the morning, then, Jock," before he left. Then he purchased his ticket, and drove the long, leisurely route back to Bieldmor House, enjoying the view of the great gray lake in the distance and the trees along the roadside, leaves deep red and warm yellow in the bright autumn air.

At the dinner table Edwin was as clever and complimentary as usual, though taking care not to overdo. About the time dessert was brought in, the phone from the library jangled insistently. Jessie asked Helen to answer it; she returned almost immediately.

"A call for you, sir. Long distance," she said.

Janet looked surprised; Edwin shrugged his shoulders and walked with practiced ease out of the dining room toward the library. Soon he was back in the doorway, his face looking drawn, his eyes pained.

"It's Ian MacDonald from Portree. Jamie's met with an accident. The lad's not too coherent, and I can't tell what's happened quite."

"Is he badly hurt?" Janet had pushed back her chair and was on her feet.

"Aye, lass. And the worst of it is that he's calling for me."

Jessie was already at the doorway and pushing Edwin aside.

"I'll talk to the boy myself," she said, and kept walking toward the phone.

This was a development Edwin hadn't anticipated! Janet hovered by the phone near her mother, but Edwin stood back a little, watching Jessie's face. She put down the receiver and turned to him.

"I told him you'd be there before morning."

It was the most difficult thing Edwin had ever done to control at that moment the fine lines of expression on his face.

"That's impossible, Jessie. Why ever did you tell the lad a thing like that?"

"No, Edwin, we can make it!" It was Janet. She was excited now and eager to help. "Helen can call Donald to bring 'round the car, and I'll help you pack. You can be ready in no time."

"Nay, lass, I canna leave, and you know it. Andrew has my word. He's counting on me."

"Don't be preposterous, Edwin." Jessie was beside him and placed her hand on his arm. "You know things can get by here these last few days before Andrew returns. He would expect you to go, when you're needed like this."

She looked up into his eyes, and her hand felt warm and light against his skin.

"When I really needed you, Edwin, you were there for me. I couldn't let you fail your friend when his need is now so much greater than mine."

For the first time since Edwin had set upon his course, a slight twinge of shame pricked a thousand sharp barbs into his soul. He looked into Jessie's eyes, and guilt, for a moment, bound his tongue, and he could not speak. She mistook the reasons for his silence. She pushed back the hair from his forehead and kissed him lightly on the cheek.

"Now hurry, Edwin. Let Janet help you. There may not be much time to lose."

So he had his way; more easily, more thoroughly than he had anticipated. Before he knew it his bags were packed. With kisses and fond farewells they sped him on his way. Once out of sight he followed the course of his already carefully laid plans. But the usual exhilaration of action was missing; he felt tired and heartless and strangely empty inside.

It was a cold day, even for October. The rain had poured steadily for hours and the air was so damp that its chill bit deep beneath the skin. The tall trees drooped and the sodden leaves, crumpled and torn, stuck to Nan's shoes as she walked. Her hair was wet, her shoes were wet; she felt as though she would never be warm again. She couldn't wait to get home, take off her drenched clothing, and curl up in a big chair with an apple and a good book!

She parked the Mustang back by the garage and made a beeline for the back door. As soon as she opened it, the aroma assailed her, surrounded her, bringing the first promise of warmth and comfort from within.

152

"Homemade bread!" she sighed, "and hot cinnamon rolls!" when she spied them laid out on the long wooden table, ready to be frosted. "Oh, Grandma, what a perfect thing to come home to!" She dumped her books on a chair and spread her dripping raincoat along the back. "Here, would you like me to frost these for you?"

"Heavens no, girl! You get those wet clothes off. They're too hot to touch yet, anyway. You've time for a warm shower if you hurry, Nan. These will just be ready to eat about the time you're done."

She kissed her grandma and hurried upstairs, the warmth of love and heat and good food dispelling the damp depression of the storm.

Nan had composed her letter to Andrew painstakingly, omitting everything of a personal or romantic nature, though she longed to be able to write as he did, pouring out the feelings of her heart. It seemed unfair. Yet when she thought of Andrew opening her letter and his mother standing over his shoulder reading—or if she imagined his mother finding the letter among Andrew's things and reading it—cold chills crawled up her back, and she knew this was the only possible way. Besides, she had given Andrew her solemn word.

So she had written a polite, impersonal letter, and had sent it with great care and not a little trepidation, counting carefully the number of days it ought to take for the letter to reach Scotland. She tried to calculate about how long it would take Andrew to read the letter, react to it, make some sort of a reply, then the days again for his letter to reach Nauvoo. So she had a date set in her mind before which she would just not allow herself to expect an answer.

She was bewildered, therefore, when Jonathan came into the living room that afternoon, as she sat curled up at last with her apple and a book, and dropped a letter into her lap. Certainly this couldn't be an answer from Andrew so soon! She tore open the envelope and read the short message inside.

"Oh, no!" she said out loud, so that Jonathan looked up from the model he was carefully gluing together in a corner of the room.

"Stop it, Nan," he chided her. "My hand jumped and I almost wrecked this whole section."

"I'm sorry, Jonathan." She rose, clutching her book and the letter, and walked upstairs to her room. A queer little feeling of apprehension began to rise in her stomach. She opened the letter and read the lines again:

. . . so I'll be in Lancashire a while, I'm not certain how long. Things at home are pretty quiet and I've left my cousin, Edwin, in charge again. He'll take care of business beautifully and keep Mother and Janet company while I'm gone. I wanted to tell you. . . .

Nan glanced at the postmark. Andrew had mailed the letter from England. How long had he already been there? Not long enough, she thought glumly. He won't be home when my letter comes. My letter will arrive and he won't be there! And this cousin will be in charge of the business. Will he open the letter, figuring it's some matter he should take care of while Andrew's gone? Or will his mother see it and notice the foreign address and the girl's name on the envelope?

Panic growing within her, Nan tried to remember exactly what she had written, grateful, so grateful, that she had decided to be wise and had not included any endearments, any feminine, romantic things which would embarrass her and thoroughly spoil things for Andrew. But still, she might have said something—some little slip which would reveal things she hadn't intended to make known. Oh, why had she written him at all? Why did he have to be gone—now, of all times? Why did it have to happen like this?

The day was destroyed for her now. The dark skies seemed to have intruded inside and darkened her own spirit. She couldn't go back and concentrate on her book. What should she do?

She took an old jacket from the closet; her raincoat wouldn't be dry before morning. In weather like this she had a pretty good chance of finding Grant at home.

She drank Grant's hot cider and explained to him about the letter, nearly begging him to tell her something to do.

"Well, seems to me, Nan, you've got to give the thing a little time. It could be no one will open the letter—could be nothing will go wrong."

"Do you think I ought to send him another letter? To Lancashire this time?"

"No, that might miss him, too, and cause more trouble than the first. Give it a little time, I said. But to keep yourself from going crazy in the meantime, I do have another suggestion or two."

So the next morning found Nan tremulously dialing a long-distance number in Salt Lake City! She had promised her grandma that she would pay for the call herself. She knew she couldn't stand the long wait of sending off a request by letter, then waiting for the information to return by mail.

The lady on the other end had a pleasant voice. Yes, the Historian's Office would be glad to release such information, she told Nan. Nan gave the woman her name and address and explained, as casually as she could, that it really was a case of some urgency, and the woman graciously promised to have the lists to her in a few days. Now all Nan could do was wait!

She took on an extra newspaper assignment the next day, and read ten chapters in the Book of Mormon before going to bed. She had begun recording her thoughts and feelings about the Mormon Church in her birthday journal and, as she wrote them, she wondered what Andrew would think if he were reading her words or hearing her thoughts.

What would he say when she told him she was becoming converted to the Mormon Church? Would he smile that comical way, taking it lightly, not realizing the import? Would he disapprove, thinking it was a wrong decision she was making? How might it affect their relationship? She remembered how he had mistaken her for a Mormon that first day they met, and smiled to herself. Andrew had seemed impressed with everything he learned about the Mormons—with Joseph Smith, especially, she knew. But that didn't mean he could understand her wanting to *become* one! What was he going to think?

The next day she had no appointments until two o'clock, so Nan wandered through the old city, down Kimball to Brigham Young's house and the open fields beyond. Autumn was her favorite time of year. The smells intoxicated her and it seemed her eyes could never get enough of the flagrant, burning colors autumn brought. Across the river the shades were barely discernible, blending masses of brown and yellow, russet and gold, with a bright spot of orange here and there.

Nan leaned against the tree beside her, threw back her head and gazed up into the network of branches. The little yellow leaves were flecked with a brownish-gold, and they danced above her head with the gracefulness of fairies, impish and light. How she wished she could understand what the breeze was whispering, and what the rustling leaves replied.

"Nan! Come back to the land of the living," someone said. There was a hand on her arm and she turned to look into Tom's face; close, much too close to her own. "Dreaming still, I see, as you always were."

"I'll never outgrow that, Tom, and you know it."

She made her voice sound light, but she was startled still, and uncomfortable. She moved out from under the tree and they began walking together.

"I've never thanked you for the birthday gifts, Tom. I tried to—I stopped by the shop three times, but you were always out."

"Yes, Ives has me driving the wrecker this month. Nelson's gone back east to visit his folks. I'll be back in the shop next week."

"Oh. Well, thank you anyway, Tom. It was very thoughtful of you. You didn't have to—well, I mean, I wasn't expecting anything from you."

"That's okay. I couldn't let you turn twenty-one without something."

She smiled at him, then was instantly sorry when she saw the effect it had. They walked for a moment or two in silence.

"Listen, Nan. Don't be angry. But I have to ask you one more time." He hesitated.

"Yes?" she encouraged him.

"Well, I don't know what kind of an arrangement you've got with this Buchanan fellow—or if you've got any kind of an arrangement at all. I just—well, I just want to know if you're okay, if things are all right with you . . . if you still feel the way you did that last night."

He was hoping still! He had watched Andrew come, and then go. He was aware only that she was alone, and Andrew was gone. Was he hoping that something had come between them? Was he hoping that perhaps she had changed her mind? *I don't deserve this kind of devotion*, she thought to herself. *And now I've got to hurt him again!*

"Nothing's changed since that evening, Tom. Except that I respect you much more than I did before. And . . . and—I suppose you have a right to know. Andrew told me he loved me. And I love him, Tom. I think I have from the very first."

156

He looked down a minute, and kicked at the leaves in his path.

"All right, Nan, as long as I know that's how it is. I had to be sure. You understand, don't you, that I had to be sure?"

"Sure I was taken care of? Sure that I wasn't hurt, like I hurt you? Oh, Tom—"

"No," he stopped her, and put a hand gently on her arm. "Don't say you're sorry again, Nan. I've been doing a lot of thinking these past weeks. I've always known you were different, Nan. And I'll admit I've never understood books and music and all the things that are important to you. I'd hate like heck to make you unhappy."

It was a new thought for Tom, and it had come slowly, Nan could tell.

"I guess you were right, Nan. You might not be happy with me. And if you weren't happy—well, I couldn't bear it if you weren't happy."

He looked up at her now and turned her face to him.

"So I won't be bothering you any more, Nan. Only, if you ever need me I'll—"

"I know, Tom," she whispered. "I know you'll always be there."

He cupped her chin in his hand and looked at her long, as though memorizing the features of her face. Then he drew her toward him until their lips met. She didn't try to stop him. His kiss was brief and gentle and sweet.

He walked away from her and she watched him, grateful for the acceptance, the understanding he had reached, yet knowing he would suffer still, and that his suffering and his solace were now and forever outside her reach.

They were here! While she was out on interviews, the mailman had brought a fat envelope with a Salt Lake City postmark. Nan tore at the paper impatiently. Copies of the lists of all the early wagon groups that left Nauvoo for the West! Every man, woman, and child listed according to groups and captains and companies.

She sat right down and began poring over the names. Her father finally had to demand that she come to dinner. But after clearing the table, Nan escaped upstairs and plopped on her bed, the lists spread around her. Page after page she scrutinized with care, until her eyes burned and the letters began to blur and run into one another. If she thought she was going too fast and might have missed a name, she would force herself to slow down and begin again at the top of the long, typed list.

She found one Buchanan, and her heart skipped a beat when she recognized the word printed there before her eyes. But it turned out to be an elderly gentleman, married to a woman named Jane, and they had come from England with a later group of Saints. Among the first companies of wagon trains that came from Nauvoo there were no Buchanans; no Charles Buchanan—not even an Andrew Buchanan, especially of a young and childish age. Her heart sank. She had hoped against hope that perhaps there had been children. Children who went west with the Saints, even though their parents had perished. Children who were recorded, who could leave some telltale trace of lives which seemed to exist only in that freakish frame of reality, the grave.

At last she rose, her neck stiff and her back aching, and gathered the papers together. She had never felt such a sense of defeat. She found herself dropping to her knees beside the bed. She closed her eyes and it seemed for the first time natural to be pouring out her heart, her hopes and dreams, sorrows and discouragements to someone who could understand.

She didn't worry about the right words to use, but prayed much as she would have talked to Grant if he were there. There was an intensity, a desire in her prayer which Nan had never experienced before, and which seemed to waft her words upward, past the dark barriers which usually seemed to block her prayers. A peace began to spread over her spirit, and a soaring feeling which must be faith. For when she rose from her knees she felt, for the first time since discovering the tombstones, that something good would work out, even though she couldn't see or anticipate what it would be.

Things continued to go smoothly in Lancashire; too smoothly, really, for Andrew had anticipated having to spend twice, maybe three times what it was taking to conclude his business there. So, as the days fitted into each other, firm and full and organized, Andrew became almost obsessed with the idea he had been carrying with him for weeks. And time and circumstances seemed to be playing beautifully right into his hands.

Why not make hasty arrangements and fly to the States? Only for a few days. Only long enough to see Nan, to tell her that he was sure of some important things, things he had never known nor understood before.

So Andrew made arrangements, feeling much like a little boy with an unexpected vacation from school. Then he called home, determined to offer some good excuse for staying in Lancashire another week. Janet answered. He asked her how things were going, and her answer spelled instant doom to his eager plans.

"Edwin gone? Whatever do you mean? What's going on there, Janet?"

She explained the emergency departure. Explained, too, how eagerly his mother was planning for Andrew's return. As he listened, Andrew realized that he could never delay his homecoming under such circumstances.

"Well, I'll be home in a day or two, Janet, so just hold on until then. And tell Mother I want a big pot of barley soup and hot scones waiting when I arrive!"

He held the dead receiver limp in his hands, trying to fight the hollow, aching feeling inside. Then he replaced the phone and looked up the number of the airport, knowing he must call now and cancel his plans—his innocent, ridiculous, unrealistic little plans. He had never dreamed that he could ever feel so dismal at the prospect of returning home.

17

He was fascinated with this place. Never before had he seen such wide expanses of rich, cultivated land. And the soil was as black as the rocks in the pass of Bealach-nam-bo in the highlands above Loch Katrine. It was October and the cornstalks, standing higher than a man, were withered and dry. They stretched on sometimes for miles, tall stately figures, golden against the sky, bowing and sighing beneath the fingers of the wind. Edwin liked the large prosperous farms, and was thrilled by the massive red barns so many seemed to boast.

He found a room in Keokuk on the other side of the river in Iowa—close, but even more anonymous than an Illinois town would be—and checked in under his faithful standby of John MacKenzie. Then he rented as old and unobtrusive a car as he could and drove the short distance to Nauvoo. He pondered as he drove how much more at ease he was "this time around." In Salt Lake City his nerves had been drawn as tight as an overstrung fiddle; his one obsession had seemed to consume all his energies and thought, so that he looked and moved and existed only through it. Was he becoming so inured to a life of avarice already? He smiled at the thought. Or had the astounding ease of the thing begun to influence his mind?

His plans for the girl in Nauvoo were very vague and general. Do something to slow her up, frighten her away. If she proved difficult to frighten? Well, he would have to face things as they developed, one at a time.

160

He drove into the little town, continuing on Highway 96 until it ran into Durphy Street and brought him closer to the old, restored parts of the city. It looked like they were mainly off to one side, so he turned down Kimball and drove slowly through the narrow streets, still busy at spots with groups of eager tourists, their cars, trailers, and buses parked in every conceivable position along the road.

Edwin didn't want to risk being recognized by anyone who might have known Andrew, or even remembered seeing the Scotsman. So he asked no questions and made no stops, but after a few times around the circuit he had a pretty good idea of the lay of things.

It was a bit more difficult to find the street in the new section of the city where Hannah lived. When at last he located it, he stopped along the parkway behind the sheltering protection of a huge, spreading maple that was flaming with color. He turned off the engine and studied the house. Two cars were parked in the driveway: an old, beat-up estate wagon back by the garage, and a sleek, rather sporty model closer by the house. *I'd bet my kilt and sporran that the yellow car is the girl's,* he thought. It was a warm, creamy color, meticulously clean, almost with an air of femininity about it.

Just as he was trying to decide what to do—whether to wait right now or come back later—a movement caught his eye. The girl had come out of the house and was walking to her car. Even from this distance, mottled behind the maple leaves, Edwin could see how gracefully she walked. She had on a skirt and a tailored white blouse and her long chestnut hair swung against her back.

She got into the car, backed out of the driveway, and passed on the street within inches, it seemed, of Edwin's car. She was looking for something on the seat beside her, and Edwin was afforded one long look as she went past. *She's a beauty, then,* he said to himself. She was an "Andrew girl," all right. Long hair, delicate features, lithe and feminine. And he wondered, for the first time, just what kind of a relationship did exist between the two.

The yellow car was easy to follow, no matter how winding the road or how heavy the traffic, but it led Edwin a merry chase. After half a dozen stops in Nauvoo, she headed down the highway toward Warsaw, stopping briefly in Hamilton and ending up at a long, sprawling old folks' home somewhere between Hamilton and Warsaw. As she pulled into the avenue, Edwin drove on in disgust. A retirement home!

161

Whatever could the girl be doing there? He'd wait a safe distance away.

It was nearly two hours before Nan reappeared and the yellow car moved up the gravel road, spurting clouds of white dust behind it, and pulled out on the highway at last. Edwin started up his car, shifted it into gear, and moved into place behind her. And so it was for the next two days, so that Edwin resigned himself to the fact that there would be no easy, scheduled pattern to follow as far as Hannah Martin was concerned.

Hannah finished the entry in her journal and put away her pen. How many days had it been now since she received Andrew's letter from Lancashire? Six days—eight perhaps. Was he home yet? Had he—or had anyone else—opened and read her letter? Sometimes she felt a sense of urgency for Andrew to read her letter, for him to know what was going on! She stared at the journal in front of her, wondering what to do. Should she write to him again? Soon? Right this minute? Should she call him—could she ever gather the courage to call him?

The next morning Nan walked to the library, still puzzling over what to do, still thinking of Andrew and the letter and the tombstones in the silent old graveyard outside Nauvoo. Two doors north of the library was the Hotel Nauvoo, and the smells of breakfast cooking made her realize how hungry she was, since she had left home after only a glass of orange juice. She looked up wistfully as she opened the library door, then paused. There was a man walking out of the Hotel Nauvoo, and he looked amazingly like Andrew. He was large, he moved with graceful ease, and he had the same dark hair and jutting forehead, the finely penciled brow. The man turned and walked off in the opposite direction and the impression began to fade.

She walked into the library and let the door swing shut behind her. *I'm jumpy*, she said to herself. *And I've got Andrew on my mind. If I'd been closer to the man, I'd have noticed the differences. I was thinking about Andrew and saw him. That's all.* But it left her with a strange, tight feeling inside.

That evening at the dinner table Jonathan looked up from his ear of corn, butter dripping down his chin, and said, "I saw a man in the park today, Nan, who looked just like Andrew. Ronnie and I were on our bikes, and I called to him, but he didn't look up. He just stuck his head forward and started walking as fast as he could."

"That was a dumb thing to do!" she snapped at him.

"What was a dumb thing to do?" He looked up, offended, the butter smeared on his chin.

"To call out to a stranger like that. He probably thought you were up to some mischief."

Jonathan started to answer in defense of himself, but Julie stuffed a napkin into his hand.

"Wipe your mouth, Jonathan, and be quiet. You didn't see Andrew this afternoon and you know it."

"Well, if it wasn't Andrew, I'd like to know who it was," Jonathan sputtered. Julie kicked him under the table.

"Be quiet, I said, and leave Nan alone. I don't think she's feeling well and you're getting her all upset. Nan, are you all right?"

"I'm not sure." *Does it show that much?* Nan thought in panic. "I think I'll go up to my room and lie down."

But escape to her room wasn't the answer. She felt stifled, with a strange sense of foreboding that seemed to crowd just inside her skin, and after ten minutes she found herself pacing the floor like a caged animal. I've got to get out of here, she thought.

It was growing dark much earlier now, and by the time she reached the end of Parley Street, shut off the Mustang, and began walking toward the river, long shadows were beginning to cast their searching fingers around her. But the river shore in the darkness held no fears for Nan. She had walked there alone since she was a girl and had never met anything to frighten her. She knew her grandmother would be distraught with worry and her father would forbid her if they knew she ever came here alone at night. But she liked the patterns the shadows painted beneath the trees, and she felt safe and comfortable among the lonely sounds of birds and water insects and the shifting tones of the river she had come to know so well.

Nan loved the soft crinkling crunch of the leaves underfoot as she walked. Somewhere nearby leaves were burning. She closed her eyes and let the full, pungent smell course through her. Along with freshly cut pumpkins and the sharp smell of tomatoes warm on the vine, the fragrance of burning leaves was her favorite smell.

A cool breeze lifted her hair with tentative fingers and sifted the brittle edges of the leaves, and the bittersweet sensation of being alive surged through her. Nan flung back her head and let the wind tangle her hair at its will. The chill on her face felt good. She stuck her hands into the pockets of her trenchcoat and took longer, faster strides.

Edwin kept far behind her and not so close to the shore. The darkness had closed around now, and her graceful form had become a mere shadow moving on ahead.

His patience had rewarded him, and he knew at last a few things concerning the girl called Hannah. He knew, for instance, that in less than three days' time she had spent four hours sitting on the front porch reading; six hours wandering, what appeared to be randomly, through the quiet, deserted streets of the old Nauvoo; three and a half hours at a certain house on Mulholland Street, where the only other person Edwin had seen was a quiet old man—Edwin guessed not a day less than eighty. He had learned, too, that she ran all over the countryside in her little yellow car, ending up at the strangest, most out-of-the-way places. And, at last, he had also learned why!

Yesterday, late in the afternoon, he had followed her to a tall building in downtown Warsaw. She went inside and he craned his neck to see the lettering on the broad stone front: *Hancock County Herald.* She was a newspaper woman!

That certainly explained a lot. Could she possibly be doing this research for Andrew out of the sheer challenge of the thing, out of professional curiosity or whatever? He had wondered then. But he had also discovered that she was never seen with a young man her own age. That was odd for a girl as pretty and interesting as she. And now, walking lonely along the river—it was easy for Edwin to surmise. Aye, something must have happened between Andrew and the lass. She was missing him now, walking the quiet stretches they perhaps had walked together.

Edwin cursed, for perhaps the first time in his life, his extreme likeness to Andrew. It was becoming a great nuisance to him. But it was more than that. He had a feeling about this girl. He would have liked to just happen upon the river walk himself and approach Hannah. He wanted to see her close, very close. What was her voice like and how did she smile? No one held better than Edwin those gentle powers to soothe a lass and at the same time bring her out of herself. And he itched to try his hand with this one. If he didn't look so much like Andrew, what fun he could have!

Nan had retraced her footsteps and was wandering back in the direction of the car. It was getting cold now and the wind was stronger. She sat for a moment on the log at the base of two tall elms where Parley spread into a wide oval space of gravel and stopped. The log was partially covered with a mound of leaves. They made a soft, though moist, spot to rest.

Perhaps it was the wakening influence of the wind, or the fragrance in the night air. But Nan was no longer as concerned about her situation as she had been, as hesitant about what to do. She had come to a decision. She would write to Andrew again; it would be a registered letter this time, sent direct to him. Tomorrow morning early, before anything else, she would go to the old Mormon graveyard and photograph the headstones again. Surely this time Andrew would see her letter and have the proof before his eyes so he could decide for himself.

She heard a sound behind her that could have been someone walking in the leaves. Or it could have been a gust of wind in one of the little leaf-filled hollows, or the stiff, splintery pieces of driftwood colliding in the dark waters along the shore. Hannah wasn't afraid. She set her face to the wind and walked the few yards remaining to the car. Her hands and her face were tingling with the cold, but it felt good. Once inside the Mustang she didn't turn on the car heater, but rolled her window down and drove home that way, savoring the feel of the night for as long as she could.

Early next morning Hannah opened her eyes and checked the alarm clock beside her bed. Five-thirty. Much too early! The morning sky was still hazy and gray. She turned over on her side. The alarm clock would awaken her again in an hour and a half. But she couldn't get back to sleep. She pulled the covers around her and changed position. But the minutes passed and sleep would not return. With a sigh she got out of bed, turned off the silent and unneeded alarm clock, and pulled on a pair of old jeans and a sweatshirt.

No one else in the house was awake. She cut a thick slice of zucchini bread in the kitchen and munched on it as she gathered her materials and found her old jacket, which had slipped off a hanger in the hall closet. The air outside was nippy. She zipped her jacket and hurried to the car.

By the time she reached the highway, Nan had decided that only fools stay in bed in the mornings. Six o'clock was a lovely time to be awake! The world was her own. She hadn't passed another car nor seen another soul. The cozy houses along the road lay wrapped in a lethargy of warmth and peace, not even blinking as she passed.

Near the mailbox she pulled off into the narrow lane. She turned off the motor and everything seemed still until she opened the car door. Then she realized that the morning was filled with sound. The birds, of course, were awake! Although she couldn't see them, their voices surrounded her, lilting, lifting her along as she went.

The cemetery ground was still wet, and the tall weeds clung to the legs of her pants. She stepped into a sticky spider web spread across her path, and pulled back quickly with a little shriek. After that she picked her way more carefully. Beside a stand of scraggly lilac bushes Nan paused and checked the directions in her notebook, just to be sure. Everything looked different in the pale, filtered morning light.

She looked up suddenly, with the strangest feeling that she was being watched! It had crept along the back of her neck as she bent her head over her notes, the crawling sensation of eyes upon her, steady and intent. She shivered once and looked carefully around. Nothing. She continued on, but the birds seemed suddenly still, and the feeling persisted so that she found herself stopping every few steps to look around. She had felt so safe and peaceful here before.

She was approaching the second gingko now, with the graves beside it. They were only a few feet ahead, behind the tall forsythia to her left. She caught a sudden movement out of the corner of her eye, and whirled around to see a man standing off a little distance. He heard her, too, and turned, and she saw his face. She didn't stop to think, to reason out why or how he would be here. She ran a few steps toward him, wildly calling out his name—"Andrew, Andrew!" But he turned and ran quickly away from her, not stopping nor looking back.

Nan hesitated then, and leaned shakily against the trunk of a tree. Unshed tears were burning in her eyes and throat. She felt betrayed, confused, humiliated. The man looked like Andrew, he dressed like Andrew, he even moved like Andrew. But the feeling she always had when she was near Andrew—surely this cold new feeling could not be coming from the same man!

Wearily she turned and worked her way back again toward the

graves. Her pulse was beating against her throat and head and she was trembling violently inside. Once or twice she paused and looked behind her; but, of course, the man was no longer there. He had fled from her, his face angry and startled, his eyes wild. She pushed aside the spreading branches of the forsythia and approached the gingko tree, then dropped to her knees with a cry of despair. The stones were gone! There was nothing beside her but a scar on the earth, clumsily covered with leaves and mulch. No other trace of their existence remained.

A cold fear gripped Nan's heart. Something was going on, in dead earnest, and she was right in the middle of it. Where was Andrew? She refused to believe that the sinister stranger, who kept appearing and disappearing, could be him. Yet the evidence of sight and circumstance were so overwhelming. *Andrew! Andrew!* her heart cried.

She felt so utterly deserted and alone. She wouldn't dream of telling her father, or anyone else in the family. There was always Tom, but her pride would never allow her to run crying to him. Should she go to Grant? For the first time since she could remember, she didn't want to turn to Grant for strength. Why? Was she afraid of what advice he might give her? Afraid of what his older, more sensitive wisdom might discern? She tried to think of her mother, but it didn't help. Nothing, nothing! She was entirely alone!

She knelt in the moist black earth, her knees aching, her hands cold and covered with dirt. Her mind seemed a seething mass of anger, bewilderment, and pain. Then through the swirling confusion came the lines of one of the hymns she had memorized. First the ribbon of tune began to run through her mind, then the words materialized and took form:

> When through the deep waters I call thee to go,
> The rivers of sorrow shall not thee o'erflow,
> For I will be with thee, thy troubles to bless,
> And sanctify to thee thy deepest distress.

Nan sang the words out loud, very softly under her breath, and they brought an unexpected strength. Why hadn't she even thought of Him? She closed her eyes, but no words would come. She didn't know what to pray for, really, but she knew she had to try. The sun was warm now. She could feel it on the back of her head. She knelt there in the stillness, the warmth seeping into her, until at last the words began to come.

18

He was home again, but it disturbed him how little pleasure he took in it. There had really been no need for the rush. Edwin had left things in beautiful order, organized and controlled. His mother was happy, and so was Janet. Andrew kept himself busy, being agreeable to anything and everything that meant activity, that would keep him going and working and never at rest.

He had been home three days when Ian MacDonald called. Janet happened to answer the phone, and she happily reported that Jamie was out of the woods, but he would take time to mend, and she had assured Ian that Edwin must feel free to stay there, certainly, now that Andrew was home, for as long as he was needed.

Andrew stirred the fire. The last two evenings had been very cold; he had recognized the smell of snow in the air earlier tonight. It would be November soon. The end of everything, and the beginning of what? Janet curled up on the floor beside him, watching the flames. She yawned and turned to him.

"By the way, Andrew, what was in that letter that came from America? You know, the one from a girl, from a different address somewhere. Was it anything important?"

"What letter? Whatever are you talking about?"

"The letter from America. It came while you were in Lancashire and Edwin sent it along to you with some other things."

Andrew was staring at her strangely, and his voice when he spoke sounded ominous and low.

169

"I never received any such letter. I tell you, Edwin never sent me a letter like that!"

"Well, perhaps he forgot to put it in. Have you noticed it among the things on your desk?"

"Of course I haven't 'noticed it'! Janet, this is very important. You must tell me about it at once."

She told him what she remembered, which really wasn't much. But before she was through he was pacing the room, his eyes excited, his mannerisms distressed.

"All right, Andrew. Now *you* tell me. What is this all about?"

"I'm not certain, Janet. I don't know! But even if I did, I couldn't tell you."

She opened her mouth to protest, but he went on.

"I've got to think about this, Janet. I've got to figure out what to do. Oh, I wish you'd have opened that letter!"

"I'm sorry, Andrew. I never dreamed of opening it. You told us in no uncertain terms to send everything from America on to you."

"If Edwin failed to send it, do you think it could still be somewhere about the house?"

She went up with him to his study and they searched every corner, the little private office as well. Then they searched Edwin's empty room, and Andrew's room. Janet couldn't believe her brother's driving intensity. At last she refused to go on.

"I'm exhausted, Andrew. It seems as if we've searched everywhere a dozen times. It can't be here. It must have been lost in the mails. You know how undependable they can be."

"I'm sorry, Janet. Go along to bed."

"You should go to bed, too, Andrew. It's late, and—"

"Don't worry about me. I've got a lot of thinking ahead of me tonight."

She left him at last, realizing that her protests were of no avail. She had never in her life seen him like this before.

Andrew had forgotten Janet before she had even left the room. His thoughts were consumed with concern for Nan. He knew instinctively that she would never write unless for some important reason. But what could it be?

He came up with a dozen possibilities, but discarded them all.

One, however, kept coming back, ugly and foreboding: What if her father was trying to force her to marry that local boy she had rejected? Andrew could see her, striving to stand firm, bearing their ridicule and disdain—disdain of *him* for leaving her with no apparent assurances or security. He couldn't bear the picture his mind created.

The thought came to him that he might call Edwin, just to be sure. Or he could even call Nan, herself. But Andrew didn't want to call. Desperately he wanted a reason, an excuse to go to her! If he called he might discover that it was really nothing drastic after all. Or Nan might dissuade him from coming on her account, and he would have no reason for his wild journey of thousands of miles. *If it is, indeed, pressure to marry another man,* he thought vehemently, *then Nan will need me there!* So he struggled within himself, knowing all the while, deep inside, what the outcome was going to be.

In the morning Andrew sent word through Helen that he would like to see his mother for a time alone. He had suffered much agony contemplating what to do about Jessie—to best preserve her dignity as well as her faith in him, and yet safeguard not only her interest but his and Nan's as well. He had even considered not telling her the truth at all. Perhaps it would be enough to urge upon her how short the time was growing, to express his need to check up on the American research—to wind things up, so to say, before letting them go. He could bluff it through and win a grudging acceptance, at least. But he entertained the tempting possibility only briefly. He knew in his heart what had to be done.

His mother came into his study with a tentative walk, looking slightly perplexed.

"You wanted to see me, Andrew?" she asked.

"Yes, Mother, it's important. Would you like to sit down?"

He indicated his most comfortable chair, but she didn't move.

"Really, Andrew, I hope this won't take too long. I've an appointment in town later this morning and so much to do to get ready. Cultural and Heritage Committee, you know. And then this afternoon—"

"Mother, I said it was important. And it might take a little while, I'm afraid."

"Oh, dear. Well, couldn't we discuss it later, Andrew?"

"No, Mother, no. I'm afraid we could not."

She sat down then, the premonition which had fluttered, inconsequential and vague, settling upon her with cold reality.

She was difficult to talk to, purposefully misconstruing and misunderstanding the things he said, until Andrew had to request her to be silent and to merely listen to him.

He began at the beginning—when he had arrived in Nauvoo and why, and what he had thought and had felt when he first met Nan.

"Now really, Andrew. If you think you're going to try and tell me that you've formed some ridiculous attachment—"

"Mother! I know that you're frightened, but you mustn't refuse to listen to me like this. I shan't keep trying to tell you much longer. I've reservations on a flight to America this evening, Mother. I would like to talk to you before I leave. But if you'd prefer that I did not—"

"Continue, Andrew. Go ahead." Her face was stony and set now, but there was no other way.

Andrew continued, carefully and colorfully depicting his days in Nauvoo with Nan. He wanted his mother to see things through his eyes; he wanted Nan to come alive, with all her beauty and gracefulness, her sensitivity and warmth. He wanted desperately to break through the stony barrier and touch his mother's heart.

As she listened a thousand thoughts and feelings and remembrances crowded into Jessie's mind. Flashes of her own courtship with Alexander, when he had been so like Andrew was now; handsome and impassioned and idealistic. How clearly she remembered Andrew's birth; the sharp, ecstatic, almost painful joy it had brought to both her and Alexander. Moments would flicker into her mind of the days when Andrew was a little boy, loving and trusting, and hers alone. Part of her seemed to stand apart now and look down upon the scene and say, *This isn't happening to me! In all my darkest fears and phantoms I never glimpsed the shape and outline of this day.*

The depth of Andrew's sincerity she did not doubt; his voice betrayed all the surging emotions he was striving to hold in check. Jessie wanted to believe that Andrew's feelings could change, that he could bring himself to forget this girl, recognize the awkwardness and implausibility of such an association, learn somehow to forget.

But she knew Andrew well. She knew that he had never yet been in love. And she had always known that, with Andrew, love would come only once and, when it came, it would be deep and lasting and real.

He was on a chair beside her now, turning her gently to face him, and she trembled as she looked into the depths of his powerful eyes and read the pain and love mirrored there.

"Mother," he said, taking her hands in his own, "I love you. It is one of the deepest desires of my heart to bring you happiness and peace. But I cannot do so at the price of betraying my own self!

"It is because of my love for you that I am being this honest with you, in spite of the pain it brings to us both. And I want you to know, for whatever joy or compensation it might bring you, that the love I offer Nan is something you can be proud of, Mother. I've kept my love untainted, Mother. Can't that and the life I've lived serve to vindicate me in your eyes?"

It was a beautiful speech, innocent and exalted, as only Andrew could give. How painfully she wanted to take him into her arms and hold him!

I must not cry before him, she thought, *or all is lost.* But the tears were dangerously close, and it took all her energies and determination to fight them back. Andrew had never seen her cry. He must not see her—like a woman, weak and hurting. He must not see her weeping now!

"Leave me," she said, and it was little more than a whisper. He leaned closer, for he had not heard her words.

"Leave me, Andrew, please. I can bear it no longer."

He rose heavily and silently left the room. Only then did Jessie allow the tears to come—the weak, yearning, womanly tears she had been too proud to show her departing son.

Two slow days passed for Nan and nothing more happened—nothing at all that was unusual or strange. Nan mailed her second letter to Andrew, with the peculiar, wild tale it had to tell, and tried to relax, reminding herself that things would be all right. Andrew would answer this time. There would be some natural, plausible explanation for things which had only appeared to be strange at the time.

She had even gone into the Hotel Nauvoo and asked Philip, the desk clerk, if a young stranger answering the description she gave had registered there during the past few days. He assured her that no one even mildly fitting Nan's description was staying there. So she tried to calm her fears and be patient. Patient, for just a few more days. She might have been able to talk herself into it except for one thing: the gaping scar by the gingko tree in the graveyard where the two faded headstones, wasting and decayed, had stood in quiet dignity together.

It was the middle of the week now and things were slow, and she had promised Julie and Jonathan that she would drive them to a movie in Warsaw tonight. It was a good film, one she had been looking forward to seeing. At least it would prove a diversion, a way to submerge, if only momentarily, the tormented sick feeling inside.

It *was* a good film, and while it was before her, Nan found herself totally involved in what was happening on the screen. They walked out of the theatre into a night brilliant with starlight. The moon rode high, with no trace of cloud, and the sky seemed to go on forever, farther and deeper than the eye could see, living and throbbing above her.

Nan was the first to reach the car, her key ready to unlock the door. There was a folded sheet of paper secured behind the wiper blade. She pulled it out and opened it. By the mellow glow of the parking lot lights it was difficult to distinguish the words. She turned a little pale as she read them, but no one was there to see. Jonathan came up behind her and she slipped the paper as casually as she could into her open purse.

"What was that?" he asked.

She turned the key in the lock and the little door button came up noiselessly.

"Just a flyer—an advertisement," she answered, and by that time she was inside the car, and Julie was there, chattering about the show.

"Why are you taking the shortcut, Nan?" Jonathan complained. "I'm not in any hurry to get home."

"I like this way. It's much prettier."

"Well, you can't see anything in the dark," he grumbled.

Nan realized that she was driving too fast, and she forced herself to relax. The road stretched black and empty ahead.

Nan looked in her rear-view mirror and saw the lights of another car approaching, and a faint fear began to flutter inside her. The lights were gaining on her much too quickly. They were close enough now that the sharp, yellow brightness flooded her mirror and blinded her. With a sickening feeling Nan realized that the car behind her wasn't going to stop.

"What's that idiot doing?" Jonathan was on his knees on the back seat, shouting insults at the driver.

Nan accelerated, but still he was right behind her, hugging her bumper. She was a good driver and she knew this road well, but she couldn't lose him. Recklessly he closed on her again, and she moved over to the shoulder of the road as far as she dared, hoping he might pass.

"Nan, be careful!" Julie shouted.

Hannah ignored her and kept her eyes on the other car. The driver pulled out from behind her, and it looked for a moment as if he might go around. He was flush with her now, and Nan realized suddenly that the driver was creeping over next to her car, closer and closer. She began to honk wildly and edge even closer to the dangerous drop at the shoulder of the road.

Around a touchy curve they sped, rocking dangerously, spitting gravel; the car beside her rumbled and swerved, and the driver had difficulty straightening the car around. Nan prayed inwardly that someone else would come along, or that somehow she could hold out until she reached the lights and safety of Nauvoo.

Around the next bend Nan spotted the lights of an approaching car. She leaned on the horn to draw attention and clutched the wheel, carefully maintaining the balance of the Mustang. As the approaching car drew closer, the man in the car beside her began to fall back. For the first time Nan stole a real glance at the driver. In the lights of the approaching car she saw him quite clearly, for only a second or two. Involuntarily she drew in her breath. Then the moment passed and the car beside her dropped, miraculously, back and fell in behind her as the oncoming car streaked by on the other side of the road.

Taking advantage of the opportunity, Nan accelerated and began to pull away from the menacing car behind her. But for some reason the man did not pursue the chase but fell further and further behind. Jonathan, still kneeling on the back seat and watching out the window, reported that the car turned off onto one of the narrow side roads, and its lights were swallowed by the darkness.

Nan realized that she was shaking and gripping the wheel so

tightly that her hands, and even her arms were beginning to ache. The silence in the car was palpable. At last Julie attempted a faint, scornful little laugh. "The dumb drunk! I was scared to death for a while there, Nan."

There was silence again, until Jonathan cut into her thoughts, saying evenly, "The man driving that car looked exactly like Andrew."

Something went haywire inside Nan's head. "You're crazy, Jonathan! What kind of nonsense are you dreaming up? First you think you see Andrew walking in the park, and now this. How dare you?"

"Jonathan always did have an overly active imagination," Julie quipped.

"Shut up!" Jonathan demanded. He leaned over the back of the seat so that his face was right next to Nan's and Julie couldn't hear. He said quietly, to her alone, "I'm sorry, Nan. I promise I won't mention it again. But it did look like Andrew. And you know it. I saw your eyes when you looked at him."

Stupidly, silently, Nan began to cry, her tears making the road a crazy myriad of streaks and sparkles of light. It was true. She had read the note. The typed message, short and terse, was totally understandable to Nan:

In Life . . . or in Death . . . stay away from that which is not your own.

And she had seen the man—the man who had tried to kill her. And he had Andrew's face.

19

Nan didn't know how Julie felt—perhaps Julie had really convinced herself that the driver last night was only a crazy drunk, met by chance and quickly forgotten. But it wasn't so with Jonathan. Nan realized that he was still deeply concerned when Ronnie came over that morning and Jonathan didn't even mention what had happened the night before. Normally an experience of that kind would be considered high adventure, something to talk over and exclaim about for weeks to come. But Jonathan hadn't said a word.

Nan didn't know what to think. Or, rather, she didn't let herself think at all. Even in the sanity of daylight she couldn't talk herself out of what had happened and the fears that now gnawed inside her.

It was impossible for her to concentrate on anything. So she threw together a sandwich, grabbed an apple and a thermos of milk, and headed for the river. She needed to be alone; entirely alone, where she could look scared if she wanted to and sit staring into space without someone watching her every move, her every expression.

She ate her lunch and tried to read, and it helped a little, though sometimes she would have to go back and read an entire paragraph over again because she had come to the end of a page and didn't know what was going on.

At last she leaned back against the log and closed her eyes, listening to the gentle slap of the water, smelling the river and the dusty leaves she had crushed underfoot. Suddenly she felt an arm laid across her shoulder and a hand placed over her own. She jumped and drew back with a little shriek, opening her eyes to look into Andrew's face close to her own!

Nan rose quickly to her feet and stood back from him, trembling, stifling an urge to cry out, afraid her leaden feet would not take her away quickly enough if she needed them.

Andrew's face registered his surprise.

"Nan, whatever is the matter? You look as if you've just seen a ghost."

He moved toward her and she stepped back.

"Nan, you look—you look as though you're afraid of me!"

They stood gazing at each other across the little space. She looked into his warm, troubled eyes and knew that this was Andrew. He couldn't possibly be the man who had seemed so like him, yet oppressive and dark. This was Andrew—tender and kind and safe as he had ever been. Her need for him swallowed up her caution, and she flung herself into his arms, burying her head against his shoulder, crying at last, as she had wanted to for so long.

After a while they sat on the log together and she told him her story—everything from the discovery in the cemetery to her frightening experience of the evening before. It was impossible for Andrew to take it all in. He stopped her a dozen times, making her go back over some point, incredulous at the things she was describing and relating. *What a fortunate impulse,* he thought, *has brought me to her now! I wanted to be with her, I feared she might need me, but I never dreamed how real, how awesome that need really was!*

When she related the story of the appearance of the mysterious stranger whose resemblance to Andrew was so uncanny, Andrew thought immediately of Edwin; his blood turned cold. It was a natural reaction, he told himself, nothing more. He had lived with Edwin looking like him, being mistaken for him, ever since he was a lad. But what an insane idea—totally ridiculous and insane!

Telling Andrew of the stranger in the car last night, saying the words out loud, made it somehow appear less evil to Nan than it had before. Perhaps he hadn't really meant to harm her, only to frighten her. But whichever of the two were his motives, the question that taunted both of them was, Why? Neither Andrew nor Nan could begin to imagine a reason why.

Andrew took the note that had been stuck beneath the windshield blade of Nan's car and studied it carefully. A plain white sheet, the words typewritten, no identifying marks—but it sounded like Edwin. Just the kind of high-flung, ambiguous language he would tend to use.

The thought was insupportable, but once it had entered Andrew's mind it lodged itself there with a life and power he could not ignore. He was more deeply disturbed than he wanted Nan to see. What she needed now was strength and support and tenderness.

She was lovelier than he had remembered her during the weeks apart. Now, as she talked, her cheeks were flushed, her eyes dancing. *In spite of all her gentleness and sensitivity, she's a courageous little thing,* Andrew thought.

He couldn't rest until he had seen the cemetery, so they locked the rented car and drove out in the Mustang, Hannah directing the way. The afternoon sun had silenced the birds, but the insects kept up a lazy, persistent drone, weaving almost hypnotically beneath the surface sounds that moved and shifted above.

It was an Indian summer afternoon, the warmth from the sun dissipating the cool air, sprinkling itself across the splendid autumn colors until the bright red maples sparkled and the yellow leaves on the slender elm trees trembled and glowed.

They worked their way back until they stood beside the gingko and the chopped and furrowed earth where bits of stone and upturned rocks were scattered.

"Does it look any different since the last time you were here, Nan?" Andrew poked around a little, curiously.

"No, it looks exactly the same."

"Perhaps he figured it wasn't safe to come back now that you had discovered him." Andrew picked up a clod of black dirt and crushed it, the pieces crumbling unheeded through his fingers as he thought. "If this was indeed Charles Buchanan, then what was he doing here?"

The possibility of Charles having been a Mormon excited Andrew, drew him toward the man with a new sympathy and interest. He sat beneath the gingko and pulled Nan down beside him, and she thought of the last time she was here, kneeling frightened and alone; Andrew thought of Charles Buchanan, who seemed more a link to himself than he had been only yesterday.

"It is conceivable, then, that Charles joined the Mormon Church and settled here. But is that why he came? I mean, had he learned of the Mormons in Scotland and came here to join with them? Or did he discover them only after he had already come to this country?''

"I don't know, Andrew! But if he'd joined the Church somehow in Scotland, that could have been the reason he was afraid to tell his father where he was going and why."

There were so many questions, so many possibilities. They talked until it was too painful to tease their curiosity any further. The one question that haunted Nan kept throbbing through her mind: Did Charles die here uselessly, his life wasted and forgotten, leaving nothing behind?

Andrew was developing a fierce desire to know the truth. She could hear it in his voice when he talked; she could see it in his eyes. She longed to be able to grant him his wish, to uncover the illusive secrets that seemed locked as surely as the grave.

"Well, lass, I've a lot of work ahead of me, so we'd best be going." Andrew stood up regretfully, and helped Nan to her feet.

"What do you mean, Andrew?"

"It looks to me as though there are some matters here that need to be taken care of."

"But how? It seems like there's nothing we can do about anything. It seems—"

"You leave that to me, Nan. I'm here now. It's not all on your shoulders any more."

"You mean the stranger, don't you? The man who looked like you."

They had reached the Mustang now. He turned to face her, leaning back against the door of the car.

"Yes, that's something I can take care of, I think. Though I can't help hoping—"

He stopped. Nan was too sensitive to his feelings. He didn't want her sensing his concern and cajoling it out of him.

"There is one thing more important than finding your mysterious stranger, I'm afraid."

His eyes were teasing her. What he could do with his eyes! Nan blushed, and looked away, not wanting him to read the depths of her own desire for him.

"Now Andrew," she said, as he drew her closer, "I seem to remember down by the river—"

"Yes," he interrupted, "I remember, too. I kissed you once, while you were crying in my arms. One salty, comforting kiss. This is for more than comfort, Nan."

He took her into his arms then, and for one blissful moment there was no mystery, no fear; no strangers, dead or alive, making demands. There was nothing but the two of them together.

"I was afraid to tell you, Grant! It seems I've told you everything I've thought or felt or done since I was a little girl. Why was I afraid to tell you?"

Grant looked across the room at her tenderly. It was a long, strange story she had just spun for him. He had wondered at her absence the last little while, when he had been used to seeing her almost daily. Perhaps he *was* getting old. He should have sensed that Nan was in some kind of trouble; he shouldn't have let the days slip by without contacting her.

"Now, Nan," he answered her gently, "don't torment yourself about it. There are too many factors involved for you to pinpoint exactly why; find some newspaper woman's clear, logical explanation for it all."

He smiled at her, for her face was still so drawn and intent.

"Look at it this way, honey. I'm nearly eighty years old and I'm just beginning to figure myself out. If I had to come up with some clear, logical explanation for everything I do, I'd be hard-pressed, believe me."

She laughed then and ran across the room to hug him, only to gaze up at him with those serious eyes again.

"Grant, whatever would I do without you? You know, I've figured out part of it, at least. I think I was afraid you wouldn't understand, that you'd see something much more evil and awful than I could see. And once you had seen it and pointed it out to me, then I'd be bound by it as well. And what if you really implicated Andrew? You don't know Andrew like I do, you could easily have thought him capable. . . ."

The old man let her ramble on, enjoying the sound of her voice.

Nan's always been like this, he thought. *She's got to talk it out. Thank heaven I've been here to listen. And,* he thought, with a little stab of pain, *thank heaven there will be someone now to take my place.*

Nan left him at last. It was nearly noon and she *did* have a lot to do, though she didn't know how she was going to be able to concentrate on anything! This talk with Grant helped immensely, though; it had been such a burden pressing down on her spirit.

She hadn't seen Andrew at all today. He had told her last night that he didn't know how long it would take him. *It.* Nan assumed he meant finding the stranger, though he wouldn't breathe a word about what he had in mind. She didn't know what he could possibly do and she was afraid for him, besides. When she told him so he smiled, but in such a sad and wistful way that it did nothing to allay her fears.

"No, lass, there's no fear of that. There's nothing to fear at all."

There may not be anything to fear, she thought after he had spoken, *but there's something else. I can hear it in your voice and see it in your eyes.* She longed to question him but sensed, somehow, that it would only make things more difficult for him if she did.

So here it was, nearly noon. She backed out of Grant's driveway and pulled into the street. *Where is Andrew right now?* she thought. *And what is he doing?* He had said he would call her tonight if he could. But if he didn't, she was not to worry. No matter what, he would phone her first thing in the morning.

It didn't sound good to Nan. And the prospect of any sort of a day ahead of her without him seemed dismal indeed. She drove without looking or thinking, and she was two streets past her own before she realized she had gone too far. She turned the Mustang back in the right direction. She had been seeing Andrew's face at the cemetery when he told her not to worry, wondering what it was that had been bothering him enough to bring that kind of pain into his eyes.

Andrew started with Carthage. He had already eliminated any possibilities in Nauvoo itself, and the little towns nearby; Hamilton, Kinderhook, even Warsaw. Motels and guest accommodations were so scanty that a few phone calls assured him he must look elsewhere. He had a hunch, anyway, that his cousin wouldn't risk staying anywhere too close.

It took a while to cover the city of Carthage thoroughly. By the time he had satisfied himself that Edwin wasn't there, he had at least worked out a smooth, acceptable approach.

He checked over the map and considered. There was Quincy to the south, but it was a good distance down the road—a two-hour drive, he would guess. Just across the river on the Iowa side sat Keokuk; closer, more accessible, with the added attraction of being in a different state altogether. He turned west along Highway 136; he would try Keokuk first.

After a while Andrew lost track and the sprawling motels— brightly colored and sporting gaudy, tasteless advertisements—began to blend into each other until he couldn't have distinguished one from another. Most of the people he talked with were friendly and polite, many curiously interested by his accent and his questions, but their answers were always the same, and so he continued on.

He worked his way into the center of town where there was a cluster of older, more conservative hotels available. With a feeling of relief Andrew began trying these. At least they each had a personality of their own, and often a touch of warmth and taste, so different from the string of look-alike motels.

There were two on the right. He crossed the street and decided to try the further one first. It was taller than the other, dark gray stone with lovely carved doors and a stately look about it.

He pushed open the doors and strode in. There were a few people in the lobby, but no one seemed to notice his entrance, and he continued walking toward the desk. At his approach the clerk looked up, then rose to his feet.

"I've got the newspapers you asked for, sir. Right here behind the desk."

He ducked out of sight for a moment and then reappeared with several papers in his arms. The lad held them out toward him, so Andrew took them, grateful for the brief pause in which to gather his wits.

"Thank you," Andrew said with a smile. Edwin would add something clever, but Andrew couldn't begin to think of anything clever right now. He hesitated. Should he tip the boy? Had Edwin always tipped him before?

He took from his pocket a five-dollar bill, which would amply cover any cost or inconvenience to the clerk, and placed it as casually as he could by the boy's elbow. The lad saw it and grinned, then pocketed it with a brief, acknowledging nod of the head. *There is a pattern between them, then,* Andrew thought. The boy began to turn away.

"Excuse me, but could I bother you for another key to my room? I seem to have misplaced mine somewhere."

The boy grinned again. "Sure thing." He turned and began scanning the board on the back wall where the keys hung in tidy rows.

"Let's see . . . it is 337, isn't it? Yep—here it is."

He turned and handed the key to Andrew, who managed a crooked smile at the corner of his mouth and a wink that he hoped looked a little rakish or conspiratorial or something that would do, and walked as casually as he could toward the elevator at the end of the hall. In this he felt relatively certain; Edwin would never take the stairs, not when the elevator offered the possibility of an encounter with a pretty girl. The machine shuddered and the doors slid open. Andrew stepped inside, pushed the button for the third floor, and sighed in relief as the doors closed noiselessly again, shutting him away from view.

He opened the door to Edwin's room with caution, not able to even begin to define the feelings throbbing inside him. He looked quickly around; Edwin himself was not in the room, but it spoke Edwin clearly in everything about it.

In spite of his casual manner, Edwin was fastidious when it came to order and cleanliness. His clothes were organized neatly on the rack by the door, his shoes lined in order underneath. Andrew recognized Edwin's favorite after-shave lotion on the dresser, the shaving kit his own father had given Edwin years ago. And tucked away in a corner was a small oval photograph of Morag, taken only months before on the moors above Bieldmor House. Andrew felt suddenly sick. He crossed to a chair in the corner and sat down, leaned back his head, and closed his eyes.

When Edwin came into the hotel an hour later he walked straight through to the elevator. The clerk, having already dispatched his errand, was gone from the desk for a few moments. Edwin whistled as he hit the elevator button. He had pushed as far as he dared, but he felt he had done sufficient to secure his interests. He would keep watch on

Hannah Martin for a while; just how long, he wasn't yet certain. But the headstones were disposed of, and without proof Hannah wouldn't have much of a case to go on. And today was the second of November. Time was on his side. Soon it would run out altogether, and he would have won.

He turned the key in the door and entered the room. As soon as he looked up he saw Andrew, facing him from the opposite corner. He took care to turn away as he closed the door behind him, knowing that the few seconds it gave him were all the time he would have to compose himself. What the devil was Andrew doing here? How did he find him, and how much did he know? A sharp feeling of panic drew his muscles tight; but his fighting instinct, his total confidence in his own cleverness, and his keen, consuming desire crushed the fear as he turned again to face his cousin. He caught sight of the pile of newspapers on the table beside his bed. He cocked his head and nodded, "The lad gave you the papers, then, I see. Well, at least you had an easy time getting in. I hope I haven't kept you waiting long."

The same smooth coverup, the flippant ease. *He will make it as difficult for me to actually accuse him of anything as he can,* Andrew thought. He might as well follow Edwin's line. He lifted an eyebrow.

"The papers—what are they for?"

"A mere precaution, really. I wanted to make certain no reporting of the cemetery incident had slipped into one of them somehow."

"Oh, yes, and Nan being a newspaper woman would increase that risk, I'd imagine."

"It's Nan, then, is it?"

Andrew ignored that; he didn't want to get off the subject just yet.

"Where are the gravestones, Edwin?"

"Safe, Andrew. Sunk somewhere in the mud in the middle of the Mississippi."

"Of course. You would dispose of them. I should have thought of that."

Edwin crossed the room and sat on the corner of the bed, removing his suit jacket and loosening his tie with maddening calm.

"It was an easy business, that. Even digging them out wasn't much of a job, actually. You've been to the cemetery, I assume, and seen that awful mess I left? I intended to take care of it, you know.

185

Cover up the digging and smooth over it all. But Hannah surprised me, and there wasn't much I could do then but get out of there.''

"And you were afraid to return for fear some watch may have been laid to catch the culprit if he hazarded coming again."

"Yes, you might say that. I didn't think it would be worth the risk.''

What an insane game we are playing, Andrew thought! *He expects me to break first, play into his hands, so he can act the role of defender, mistreated and maligned.*

"She's a lovely girl, Hannah.'' Edwin grinned; the same lopsided, endearing grin which Andrew had never been able to resist. "You've aye had an eye for the beauties, Andrew. The real ladies, you know. But Hannah, I'm afraid, outdoes them all.''

"It's a strange thing to be saying, that, after you've just tried to kill her.''

Edwin rose to his feet, his eyes bright.

"Don't be insane, Andrew. I'd never dream of actually hurting the lass. What gave you that idea?''

"Nan told me, herself. She's convinced that's what you had in mind the other night.''

"I only meant to scare her away. Purchase a little more time, Andrew. I didn't realize I had frightened the lass that badly. And whether or no you believe me, it was I who was nearly killed. I had a deuce of a time keeping that blasted machine on four wheels driving on the wrong side of the road, from the wrong side of the car, as you're forced to do in this reasonless country.''

"Bit off a little more than you could handle that time, did you? And what of the note? That ridiculous note you left on Nan's windshield? Really, Edwin. Don't you think it's time you came up with some sort of an explanation?''

Andrew kept his voice light and even, with the barest tinge of sarcasm, but his heart was pounding inside him. Edwin began to speak, then stopped suddenly and considered Andrew a moment.

"You really don't know, then. I can see it in your face. If you don't know, Andrew, what in creation did you come all the way out here for?''

Andrew considered his cousin in return and decided to tell the

186

truth. He sketched for him the circumstances of his own discovery of the existence of Nan's letter and his concern over what it might contain. He played down the extent of his worry about Nan and the intensity of his desire to see her, but Edwin possessed more than enough romantic insight to read between the lines and supply very credibly what was missing. As Andrew spoke, Edwin's features became dark and disturbed, his eyes angry.

"I am undone, then, by your love of the lass and nothing greater. Poetic justice, you might say, but I find it difficult to swallow after all I've been through."

Andrew was on his feet now, the threads of his closely held patience tattered.

"After all *you've* been through! That *would* be your first consideration. What of Nan? What of—"

"All right, Andrew, all right. I think you'd better sit down again and let me give you that explanation you've been chafing for."

As Edwin unfolded the story of that day in Jessie's room—his happenstance finding of the will and his innocent discovery of the new will which had been drawn by Andrew's grandfather in 1927—Andrew felt as though his senses were spinning. The entire pattern of things for the past months had been shifted and broken into scattered, disjointed fragments of chaos and deception. He marveled at all the things which had been happening around him, deep and often dreadful, while he had gone about his life, trusting and placid and unknowing.

The many implications crowded into his mind with devastating force. Edwin stopped talking, but Andrew couldn't speak. His cousin sat quietly watching him, though Andrew noticed that his eyes were alive and probing and he knew that the keen mind wasn't missing a thing.

"So that explains what happened to Nan's letter," he said at last, softly, with almost a reflective air, and he was relieved at how strong and natural his own voice sounded. "How did you talk Jamie and Ian into lying for you?"

Edwin smiled slowly. "You ought to know better than to ask such a question, Andrew. They've been up to greater mischief than this many a time before." Poor Andrew, Edwin thought. For all his strength and dependability, the lad's led rather a sheltered life.

Things were falling into place for Andrew now; slowly, incredibly, piece by piece.

"Well then, the first time, Edwin—the other time you left to supposedly visit Jamie—" Andrew's eyes grew wide as the idea began to materialize within his mind. "No, Edwin, you couldn't have, you didn't—"

"Salt Lake City and the missing papers? Of course it was me, Andrew." He shrugged slightly, as if to dismiss the matter. "Sorry, Andrew, but you must admit that I had to be thorough."

He grinned suddenly, mischievously. "You taught me well, cousin. All those lofty lectures about being conscientious and hard-working and applying myself."

"Edwin!" Andrew felt sick inside. "Can't you see what you've done?"

"Aye, I can see well enough. I've protected what is mine and nothing more. And let me ask *you* something, cousin. Have you wondered yet, in that great, noble mind of yours, just why I had to do it?"

"What do you mean?" Edwin sounded vehement and Andrew was becoming uncomfortable.

"Haven't you wondered why I didn't come to you in the first place, after I had found the will? No? Well, let me enlighten you. You came home from America literally glowing with righteous purpose. You were thoroughly taken, lad, with the nobility of your role; Andrew, the mighty miracle worker who would achieve where past generations had failed, who would unlock all the secrets that no one else had been able to tap."

"Why didn't you come to me, Edwin, talk to me—"

"Don't deceive yourself, Andrew! If I had come to you then and ruined your grand opportunity? You were enjoying playing the part of God all too much to have been bothered by my petty demands."

The bitterness in Edwin's voice cut Andrew and probed his conscience like the fine-honed edge of a blade.

"It's not too late, you know." The control was already returning to Edwin's voice. Andrew looked at his cousin sadly.

"To abandon the search? Just barely. Yesterday I would have agreed with you, Edwin. Before I knew what I know now about Charles Buchanan."

"Charles Buchanan!" There was almost hatred in the way Edwin spit out the words. "You've lost your reason, Andrew. You still don't know for certain that this *is* your Charles Buchanan. And if it is—he's dead, lad! Dead and buried with his wife beside him and nothing left behind!"

"You don't know that, Edwin. You can't surmise—"

"The past has buried its dead, Andrew. But that isn't enough for you. And you would rather some asinine American upstart receive the old man's legacy than—"

"Stop it, Edwin, stop it! You know that isn't true. I owe it to the old man's memory. I owe it to my father. It's a matter of—"

"Pride!" Edwin came close and hurled the word at him like a challenge. "Don't mistake the emotion, Andrew, and call it honor. With you it has always been a point of pride."

Andrew didn't protest. He sat silent, and Edwin continued.

"That's all right, Andrew. I've never counted on any help from you. Continue on. I'm going home now to wait out the contest, but by all means, Andrew, carry on."

"You're going home now? You think you can go home now, just like that?"

"Don't be archaic, Andrew. Would you feel better if I turned myself in to the police? Or would a full confession, neatly written and signed in blood, do the job?"

"You can't go home to Bieldmor House now, Edwin. Perhaps you can't see it, but the things you've done have changed you. You're a different person than you were before. It's not that I don't want you, that I don't care—"

"Save your pretty speeches, Andrew! They always were wasted on me."

"All right then, Edwin. I'll try to state it plainly. I don't think I can ever trust you again; I don't think I can work with you and live with you. What existed between us—"

"I've sullied your precious honor, your grand name!"

"That's not it, Edwin, that's not it, and you know it! You've destroyed what existed between us! *You* have destroyed it, not I. And I think it's too late to pick up the pieces."

"You're on your moral high horse, Andrew, and you can't see the ground. You'll come down eventually and feel awfully foolish."

"No, I don't think so. Not this time. You'll have to leave, Edwin."

"Leave? What in the devil are you talking about?"

"Leave . . . disappear. You're good at disappearing. You'll have to find something to do. Jamie's been after you to buy into his fishing business."

"That's far enough away for you, is it? I haven't the capital now, and I don't relish the idea of catering to a bunch of blithering tourists."

"I'd be happy to set you up, Edwin, and help you get established."

"I'm not interested in your charity, Andrew!"

"You seem interested enough when I have to pay your gambling debts! Be realistic, Edwin. You'd never need anyone's charity, as you call it, if you'd once decide to settle down and apply your native abilities to getting something done."

"So that's it. You're banishing me. Playing God again. To what purpose, Andrew? I'll only be back again in January to collect my inheritance. You're not going to find your miserable descendant, and you know it."

"We'll have to see. But I don't want to find you here in the morning. And I don't want to find you at Bieldmor House when I return."

Edwin bowed mockingly.

"You've spoken. Do I dare disobey? Haven't you always pretty well managed to get what you've wanted?"

Andrew rose slowly. He had never felt so shaken, so thoroughly hurt and miserable inside.

"Not at all, Edwin, not at all."

He walked to the door, then paused and turned back. For a moment their eyes met and held, but it was too painful.

"If you think I'm getting what I want in this, Edwin, you're wrong again. What I really want is impossible now. But I'd gladly give half a lifetime to gain it back again."

Edwin didn't reply. Andrew turned and left, closing the door behind him.

20

W here's my outfit, Nan? I can't
find it. Didn't you put it in my room?"

Nan looked up from her typewriter and scowled unconsciously.

"What in the world are you talking about, Julie?"

"My costume. For the dance. I asked you this morning if you'd
go up in the attic and get it for me."

"You did no such thing! What's the matter with you going up to
look for it yourself? I'm rather busy, as you can see, Julie."

"I have to be ready in half an hour, Nan, and I've still got my hair
to curl and my makeup to apply. And besides, you said you'd go because you know what to look for. I don't know what they wore in the
Gay Nineties! You said you loaned the stuff to Michelle last year."

"Okay, okay. Get your hair curled. I'll go look for the clothes."

For all Nan knew Julie might have asked her that morning, before
she left for Grant's. She was so concerned about Andrew and what
could be happening that she may very probably have forgotten.

Julie shot her a brilliant smile and disappeared out the door. Nan
walked to the end of the hall and around the corner where the narrow
attic staircase rose, nearly hidden from view. She climbed the steep
stairs, then pushed at the heavy doors above her until they parted,
spreading open. Nan walked up the remaining few steps into the dim,
musty room.

She pulled the string on the light, but the one weak bulb shed only a pale, wan glow, leaving the corners in shadow. She looked around her. Everything seemed grimy and stale, piteously camouflaged by layers of fine dust on top. And yet the place held for her a certain compelling appeal.

She remembered trying to play in the attic as a child, her romantic young soul hungering for the nostalgia of past times. But in the summer the breathless heat stifled her, and in the winter the damp cold ate through to her bones and drove her back to the warmth and comfort below. There had been a few perfect autumn afternoons, mild still, before the cold seeped in, when she would pull on a heavy sweater and cuddle by the window with an apple and a book, staring out through the rain-streaked glass, dusty and blurred, at the wild, torn landscape below.

Over there stood the little pile of things that were her mother's. How many times, when she was thirteen and fourteen, did she storm up here, lonely and afraid, and cry over her mother's possessions, holding them fiercely, possessively, as if their presence might somehow fill up her aching need!

She had better start looking; but she didn't know where to begin. She tried to remember just where it was she had tucked those things away last winter. Probably in that enormous mound of boxes stacked hodge-podge over there. Gingerly Nan began shifting and opening and rummaging through. Where stiff, dead spiders, frozen in grotesque shapes, guarded the cardboard-flap entrance, Nan didn't venture inside. She may not be afraid of the river in the darkness, but spiders of all kinds—dead or alive—made her skin crawl.

Where were the miserable clothes anyway? Nan could see them in her mind as she had stuffed them into the box months earlier. She should have marked which box it was then! She was running out of patience. The next two boxes were big and tall and heavy, barely budging as she tried to tug or push them around. *I ought to have Jonathan up here to help me,* she thought. She gave the top box one last angry shove, pushing her weight against it with both hands. It slid, rocked precariously, then fell, taking three other boxes and a hamper along with it. The hamper, stuffed with discarded baby clothes, rolled onto its side, spreading a profusion of little dresses, booties, and nightgowns over the floor. The boxes emptied most of their contents, too, so that Nan stood in the midst of the mess, looking around her helplessly.

In spite of the dim light, Nan's eyes focused on a trunk, off in the corner which had been hidden from view by the pile of boxes. It looked very old. Could it have been her mother's, and might it hold treasures Nan had never seen?

She picked her way back to the trunk and bent down beside it in appreciation. The wood appeared to be in good shape still. She began to blow off the dust, but thought better of it. Instead she found a Kleenex in her pocket and was able to wipe away some of the dust and grime. A line of fine carving appeared along the edge of the lid. Totally interested now, Nan pried open the rusty latch and carefully lifted the heavy, rounded lid.

Inside were stacks of old papers, newspapers, and books. She felt a twinge of disappointment. But perhaps they were her mother's. And maybe there were other things underneath. She lifted one of the books up to examine it when she heard Julie's voice calling her; faint, but anxious and irritated—then footsteps pounding up the stairs.

"Nan! Where are you? Where are my clothes? Jeff will be here in less than ten minutes and he's never late! Can't you find them?"

"Oh, be still, Julie. You'll yell yourself hoarse. They're right over here, I think. Grab that piece of red satin and pull."

Nan had skipped away from the corner at the sound of Julie's voice, and she spied the tattered edge of a gaudy feather, buried somewhere amid the confusion on the floor. These were the goods, all right. A little faded and crumpled, but Nan could make them do.

"That's cutting it down to the wire, isn't it? Come on downstairs, and I'll help you get into these."

Nan started down the stairs, Julie behind her.

"Pull the light, Nan. Aren't you going to close the doors?"

"We're in a hurry, remember? I'll come back and take care of it after I see you safely gone."

Julie looked adorable. That carefree, vibrant era was a natural for her. Nan had never seen her appear more sparkling and alive. She heard the car door close and Jeff's muffler-shy Chevy rumble away down the street. Her father was off to a meeting, Jonathan safe in front of the television. Her grandma was in the kitchen cutting quilt pieces at the big table with Mrs. Yater from down the street. Andrew hadn't called yet. Nan hesitated. Should she ask someone to listen for the phone? She decided against it. Jonathan was too engrossed to hear, anyway, and her grandma would make sure that someone found her if the call was from Andrew.

She slipped back into the attic, spread out a blanket, and sat down beside the trunk. She switched on the flashlight she had brought with her and carefully lifted out some of the crumbling newspapers near the top. Under the scrutinizing beam of light the pages looked terribly yellowed and old. She examined the brittle sheets cautiously, amazed by the dates the papers bore—1887, 1863, 1846—that was getting back to the time of the Mormons, back to the time when *her* Nauvoo was alive!

Eagerly Hannah sorted through the materials, setting aside in a special pile all those with the very earliest dates. These, of course, were the first ones she would read. As she dug deeper into the musty depths of the trunk her hand touched something cold and smooth; a leather covering. She lifted out the narrow volume. There was a name engraved on the cover, the letters faded and faint: Daniel Martin. Daniel Martin—that was her great-great-grandfather!

With trembling hands she opened the cover of the volume and played her light over the first entry, written in the delicate, sweeping style of that day, so beautiful, and yet difficult to read. She held the page close, the light full upon it. The dates were easier to discern, and they seemed to leap out to meet her. February 1842; she flipped carefully through the pages. April 1843, July 17, 1844—this *did* take place in the old Nauvoo, while the Mormons still lived in their city! Her own great-great-grandfather! What part did he play in those exciting times? Nan turned back to the beginning of the journal and began to read.

After a few pages she could discern that this was mainly a record of Daniel's romance with a certain young woman, Rachel Miller. As Nan read on she became caught up in the story and in the sensitive relationship which seemed to have existed between these two: the things they did, the places they went, their customs and manners, so different from her own.

Then she came to one entry, written in bolder, darker ink, as though the hand that penned it had been angry and curt. And the date was underlined in thick gashes.

September 29, 1842—Rachel was baptized a Mormon today. I

know how she's always felt about the Mormons; haven't we argued over it often enough? But she'd never have had the courage to go against her kin if it wasn't for Charles Buchanan. God curse the day he came here! A Mormon and a foreigner besides, though Rachel is mighty taken with his fancy accent. Her folks turned her out like I told her they would. She's living with Mr. and Mrs. Richards on Parley Street. God knows what will happen to her now.

Nan realized that she was clutching the book so tightly that her fingers hurt. She tried to relax her hold. She read again the entry for September 29, and a third time, unable to believe what was stated before her. She couldn't begin to trace her emotions, but the need to go on, to know more, swept over her.

She read the next entry; it said nothing about Rachel. Before her eyes were wheat prices and the cost of flour, and something about a new horse he had bought from Mr. Simpson over in Ramus.

Then in November of that same year, Daniel recorded that Rachel and Charles were married. November—this month, this *very* month, over a hundred and thirty years ago! Daniel's bitter hurt came clearly through the pages and, in spite of herself, Nan's heart ached for this proud and wounded man.

There were spaces then where months would pass with no entry, or perhaps only a phrase or two:

I saw Rachel today. She looks well.

And again,

Rachel came into the blacksmith shop today. I don't know why she has to look so happy.

Then, in January 1844,

I took a joint of beef to Richards house today. She promised to get it to Rachel. Charles isn't getting any better, and when I saw Rachel in town yesterday she looked awful weak and pale. Don't know when her child is expected. I can't understand why he doesn't take better care of her, coming from some great, wealthy family like he's supposed to. You'd think at least he'd make sure that Rachel doesn't go hungry this way.

Vividly Nan saw in her mind the struggling young people. Charles, sick? Unable to care for his new wife and their unborn child? What of all his plans, his dreams? Was Rachel sick, too, and afraid, and hungry? Had the happy light Daniel wrote about gone out of her eyes? And there was Daniel—swallowing that fierce pride of his, unable to stop himself from helping the woman he loved.

Under the date of February 17, 1844, there was a rather lengthy entry:

> Charles Buchanan died two days ago. They buried him today. Temperature is six below and there's three feet of snow on the ground. I didn't even go near. I know Rachel wouldn't want me to see her now, and I couldn't bear to lay eyes on her. How could he do it? Die and leave her alone like that? Rachel—if you'd only listened to me! If you'd married me you'd be happy now. You'd always be happy. I'd take care of you, Rachel. Why did you marry a Mormon?

Nan realized that the tears were blinding her eyes, and she wiped them impatiently away. These three tragic people seemed so real to her; their pain and sufferings so vivid, so overwhelming. Unable to control her anguished curiosity, she turned the pages. The next entry was dated March 9, 1844:

> Rachel's child came today. A son. She named him after Charles and his father—Charles Andrew Buchanan. The child came early, but Mrs. Richards said he's healthy and fine. Rachel isn't well—she can't seem to recover from Charles' death.

Nan could picture the delicate young woman, bearing her child alone, longing for the tender husband who was no longer at her side to soothe and strengthen her. But now there was his son. Surely Rachel would be able to rally, to live for her child! The next entry came on July 12, 1844:

196

Rachel is in bed again. Mrs. Richards said if I was going to go, I'd best go now. She looked like just a shadow of herself, but beautiful still. I told her so and she smiled the old way at me, and I nearly had to turn and leave the room. She's heartbroken about Joe Smith's death. Doesn't she understand yet it's him caused her all this suffering? I say, good riddance. Maybe these Mormons will come to their senses now.

July 17, 1844, followed:

I spent two hours with Rachel today. She says she's dying. I asked her what she thought it was all for now. She just smiled the old way. Said Mrs. Richards would take her child and raise him a Mormon, and her blood and Charles' would go on through him. She said she had nothing to regret but my unhappiness. I held her in my arms. She felt lighter than a child. I held her and held her—

Sunday, July 19, stated simply:

Rachel is dead.

Nan sat there a long time, crying silently, yearning over these people who had come to life before her and acted out their loves and sufferings and deaths with such painful reality. At last she turned the pages of the journal which now seemed sadly neglected, with only a scattered entry here and there, as though Daniel Martin, too, had died with Rachel's death. As she flipped the pages to close the cover, some writing near the back caught her eye. Turning to it she read:

July 19, 1846—Rachel has been dead two years. This morning early I went to the graves and put new markers there, for her and Charles. Nice stones. I think Rachel would be pleased.

So it was Daniel, out of the depths of his sore heart, who had engraved "Beloved Wife" to please the woman he loved. Nan was struck, suddenly, with Daniel's likeness to her own father: the pride, the same lonely pride which caused him to hug his pain to himself, private and deep. And the gentle sensitivity, always hungering for expression.

Hannah closed the volume, flicked off the flashlight, and sat alone in the dusty dimness, and her thoughts were of Charles and Rachel, and the joy and purpose which were about to be brought forth out of their sacrifice. And of Daniel, who had left her a heritage of ignorance and bitterness. If he could see her now, now—after all that had passed —would he be angry with her, as he had been with Rachel, if she deserted her own and joined with the Mormons? Or now, at last, wherever he was, would he understand?

Edwin left Keokuk that very night, glad to be going back to Scotland. He flew not for the north highlands, however, but for home. Andrew's visit, their conversation, his cousin's horror and pain had touched Edwin more deeply than he had wanted it to, more deeply than he would ever have let Andrew see. And it took longer to recover himself than it ever had before. But by the time he was on square footing again, he had decided to try one last ploy.

He would throw himself upon Jessie's mercies. His aunt and his cousin adored him. Surely their more tender sensitivities would be aroused in his favor. Surely, with Andrew gone, he could talk himself back into their good graces, make some more agreeable arrangements with his aunt. And then, when Andrew returned, things would already be established and Andrew would have cooled down some, and be able to look at the situation less emotionally. So Edwin convinced himself, and he formulated his plans as the plane, swift and silent, carried him home.

21

When Andrew left Edwin's room he hurried to his car and drove straight back to Nauvoo. It was late when he arrived, though not too late to call Nan. But he knew he couldn't call her; even Nan stood outside and apart from him right now.

He went up to his room, but he couldn't sleep. His thoughts were too muddled, too seething to sort into any kind of sense; peace was impossible, and inaction was pain. He dressed again and drove through the old city. After a few minutes he decided to park the car and walk a while.

The silence of night was thick, as if there were too many memories crowded into it and only now, unseen by the eyes of the living, could the spirits of the dead walk free. Andrew moved down Kimball Street, then turned onto Main, coming at length to Joseph Smith's mansion house and the old homestead, only across the street, where Smith's family had lived when they first came to settle Nauvoo. He walked over to the homestead and stood staring at the graves where Joseph Smith and his brother Hyrum were buried.

Here the silence seemed deeper, impossible to penetrate, and Andrew felt overwhelmingly alone. Losing Edwin in this way was much like seeing a part of himself decay and rot away, leaving a dull ache and a handicap which would be difficult to compensate for. He thought of his mother, who had relented enough before he left to kiss his cheek and tell him to take care, but who had offered no word of understanding, acceptance, or love. He felt as if everyone's problems, everyone's pain rested upon his shoulders. He searched the depths of his soul, struggling to understand.

Andrew had never tried to really pray. But here, on the cold November ground, he knelt. The profusion of his thoughts and feelings began to spill out, and he found himself able to express some of the vague doubts and desires which had moved uneasily within him for so long. He prayed for all the people whose lives seemed bound to him— bound *by* him, by what he decided, by what action he took. And in the agony of his concern for others he began to find himself. He needed strength desperately, and in the cold silence he found it, and knew for the first time what it was like to turn to a power greater than himself, and be filled.

That night it rained with a fury, lashing the long, trailing arms of the trees, which bent and arched in intricate grace and timing, moving with patience and skill in measure with the haughty power of the storm.

Andrew woke to the sound of the rain and realized that it was late, much later than he was ever accustomed to rising. He got out of bed, feeling neither tired nor depressed, but aware that this day was in many ways a beginning, and that some things had passed out of his life, forever gone and changed.

The phone on the desk jangled into sound, startling him. He picked up the receiver and heard Nan's voice. It seemed an elixir of joy, his first contact with the beauty and promise of the sane world which he had stepped out of so inadvertently only the day before—or had it been a year before? or a lifetime before?—when measured in the pain and emotion and experience it had held.

"Nan, Nan darling, I—"

"That's all right, Andrew. You don't need to explain anything. I'm not calling because I'm angry or upset. I'm calling only because I can't wait any longer. It's nine-thirty, Andrew."

"I know. And I'm sorry, Nan. I don't think I've ever slept this late in the morning in my life."

Nan laughed, a ripple of sheer joy that spread through him like a warmth.

"You don't understand, Andrew! You don't know what I'm talking about. Because of this awful rain we can't walk by the river. You could come here, but I know we'd be interrupted. What about the Seventies Hall? It's fairly certain to be deserted this time of year, especially in weather like this. Besides, it would be fitting, I think, since that's where we first met, Andrew—where all of this began.''

"Nan, whatever are you—"

"Shhh! Don't ask me, Andrew, or I'll tell you right now over the phone and spoil it all! How soon can you meet me there?"

He hesitated, trying to take in what she was talking about.

"Are you afraid to venture out in the storm, Andrew?" Her voice was light and teasing.

He smiled. "Lass, such weather is our daily fare in Scotland; something we don't even think about. For your future sake, I'm glad it doesn't bother *you*. I'll be there in twenty minutes. Can you wait that long?"

"I'll try. I'll be ready. Please hurry, Andrew!"

There was no one else in the Seventies Hall. It even took Andrew a moment to locate Nan, scrunched down in the very front pew, her coat and raincoat, purse and umbrella, books and papers and plastic bags stacked neatly beside her.

"Nan, have you come for a picnic? Or will we be camping here for a couple of days?"

She smiled at him and pulled him down beside her.

"You're all right, then! I didn't even ask you on the phone if you were all right."

He touched her cheek gently and smiled.

"You found the stranger, didn't you? And you're not really all right. I can see it in your eyes. Oh, Andrew, what is it? Please tell me."

"I will, Nan. But can you be patient just a little while longer?"

"But, Andrew, I—"

"Please, Nan. You don't have to worry. Things are taken care of now. I just need a little more time."

She sighed. "I'd go crazy not knowing, if it wasn't for this."

"For what?"

She turned to him, her eyes eager.

"I want you to know I took every precaution this time, Andrew. I wrapped it in three layers of plastic bags so no rain would get it, and I even copied the pages before coming, and had Mr. Schaeffer, a notary public two streets down from us, notarize them all.''

''Lass, what in the world—''

''This, Andrew.''

She handed him the slim, worn volume. He read the faint lettering—Daniel Martin—on the cover, then looked up at Nan questioningly.

''Daniel Martin was my great-great-grandfather,'' Hannah explained. ''He was a young man in Nauvoo during the 1840s, when the Mormons were here.''

Andrew raised an eyebrow, interested now. ''And this is his journal?''

''Yes.'' Nan's eyes sparkled with suppressed excitement. She opened the cover gently.

''Begin reading here,'' she told Andrew. ''Go ahead. I'll follow along.''

He looked a little doubtful. ''Would you like me to read it out loud?''

''Yes,'' Nan answered. ''Yes, why don't you.''

He began. Nan closed her eyes and listened to his voice, loving the masculine beauty of it; soft, yet deep; warm, yet strong. He came to the entry on September 29, 1842. Nan opened her eyes and leaned forward, waiting for him to read the words.

He didn't get through it. He just sat there, holding the little volume and staring at it in shocked amazement.

''Go on, Nan. Read it, will you? I can't.''

She took the book and continued through to the end, not spoiling Daniel's story nor Andrew's feelings by any of the enthusiastic interruptions she longed to make. It was difficult to finish, for the tears were choking her throat and causing the thin, elaborate lettering to weave in front of her eyes. Andrew was too deeply touched to speak. A miracle had unfolded before him, and he felt a great surging happiness building inside.

He saw before his eyes for a moment Edwin's angry face, heard again the lonely arrogance of his voice: *You're not going to find your miserable descendant, and you know it.* But he pushed the unhappy remembrance aside.

The images Daniel's words had called forth were real, possessing Andrew with a strength which was almost frightening. He said out loud, half to himself and half to Nan, "The Mormon Church was the answer, of course. Charles must have discovered the Church in Scotland. That would explain his strange disappearances, his preoccupation."

"But when his father confronted him and accused him of all kinds of awful things, why didn't he tell him about the Church then?"

Andrew smiled at the intense look on Nan's sensitive face.

"He knew his father well, Nan. Old Andrew Buchanan was not only a pillar in the community, but a pillar in the Presbyterian Church as well. And Mormonism wasn't exactly a popular sect at that time. In fact, it was very much detested and despised. He felt pretty certain about how his father would react, I'm sure."

"And the argument—the argument that always haunted the old man only substantiated what Charles already felt?"

"That's right. And so he must have decided to join the Church—throw in his lot with the Mormons, go where they were prosperous and strong, and prove himself somehow—"

"And make his father proud of him again!" Nan's eyes were shining.

"I suppose. After proving himself, perhaps he felt he could be free to approach his father with the truth."

"But it didn't work out the way he wanted it to, did it?" Nan's voice was quiet and her eyes deep and sad. "Do you suppose he tried to write?"

Andrew ran his hand through his hair, restlessly. "He might have. There's no way to ever know. But if he did write and his letter was lost, he would have thought that the old man refused to answer, that he was angry still—"

"And so perhaps he gave up trying, working all the harder to make it on his own, feeling sad and rejected and homesick—both of them suffering without knowing what the other was going through." Nan reached for his hand and held it tight. "Oh, Andrew, I can't bear to even think of it!"

Andrew put his arm around her and held her gently against him, both of them filled with their own thoughts.

After a moment he turned to her and spoke softly, a sense of wonder in his voice.

"Do you feel it, Nan?"

"Yes. It's almost as if their spirits are near, somehow, as if we can feel their gratitude and joy. They've waited so long, Andrew, so long!"

He felt the urgency, too. Here were people calling from the grave, needing his attention, his help. He felt strength surge through him, warm and sure, and knew it had been given him, somehow. This was his work. Once he put his hand to it, the miracles would increase, and the purpose and the joy. It was all bound up together; their joy and his own, and some kind of fulfillment that he didn't yet understand, but which he hungered for, eager and unsatisfied.

22

I've been expecting you, Edwin. Come in here."

Edwin had decided to make his arrival one of surprise, all the more to assure his having the upper hand. He had just entered the door and set his bags down in the hall when Jessie discovered him. He followed his aunt now into the library, madly trying to figure what had happened to warn her of his arrival. Did she know something? And how much? Surely Andrew wouldn't have called and burdened his mother with that kind of news long-distance.

Janet was curled beside the fireplace reading. Her eyes lit up when she saw Edwin, but she didn't have a chance to speak.

"Your cousin and I will have to be alone for a few minutes, Janet. Will you please excuse us, dear?"

Janet rose, beginning to protest. Then she saw her mother's face and thought better of it. She gave Edwin one brief smile as she left the room.

Jessie was a little frightened. She knew the magnetism of Edwin's personality and the strength of his will. Could she do what had to be done? And how should she begin?

Edwin wasn't going to help her. He needed time to determine what she knew. Jessie hesitated and then decided that if she tried playing games she would lose for certain. She could never match Edwin on those grounds. It would have to be honest and up front; a display of authority, and of strength, somehow.

"Did you find America enchanting, Edwin? Or were you too busy to take notice?"

She watched the color drain from his face and knew that she could proceed. All her doubts were settled now; he had assured her that the awful circumstances she had pieced together were true.

"Has Andrew called you?"

"No, but I assume, then, that you've seen him. We'll get to that later. I love you, Edwin, and I won't prolong your agony unnecessarily. If you've talked to Andrew I assume you know what called him to America?"

Edwin nodded briefly and she went on.

"After Andrew left, a second letter from Hannah—or Nan, as Andrew calls her—arrived. Janet and I didn't know what to do, but at last we hazarded opening it, in case it contained something important which Andrew should know about. She was concerned about her first letter and why it had never been answered. Then she told some incredible story about missing gravestones and a stranger who looked like Andrew.

"Janet was worried and amazed. She couldn't understand what was happening. But I suspected instantly. I phoned Jamie's asking for you—half a dozen times, Edwin. But you were never available. Out on the boat, perhaps, or drinking in town, but never able to come to the phone."

Edwin was intrigued, in spite of himself. "Why did you suspect something instantly, Jessie?" he asked.

"Because *I* know the provisions of the new will. I am the only living member of this family who even knows of its existence. That is, until you somehow discovered it. How did you happen to read the will, Edwin? That is the only thing I haven't been able to figure out."

He smiled, but a small knot of fear was beginning to grow inside him.

"In your room that day after Andrew's telegram arrived. Remember? You were totally distraught at the prospect of him staying on in America. You slept in the boudoir and wanted me near, so I worked at your desk—."

"That's right," she interrupted. "The wills were still on my desk. I hadn't returned the envelope yet." The realization seemed to disturb her.

206

"Why did you have it out?" Edwin asked.

She paused and looked at him, her pain so piteously evident that he almost forgot his own.

"I wasn't myself in those days," she said, "as I'm sure you remember. I was so angry, so deeply resentful. There was nothing I could do to control things, to prevent Andrew from going, and I hated it! In my bitterness one day I took out the wills, entertaining the idea of showing them to Andrew, confronting him with the entire thing."

"And that, you hoped, might dissuade him from going, make him realize the futility of it all."

Edwin could understand perfectly. "Why didn't you show him, then?"

"Pride, Edwin. And a certain amount of loyalty, I suppose. I had promised Alexander not to break faith, to carry the wretched thing through to the end, knowing that, after Andrew, there would be peace."

"You promised him? Just before his death?"

"No. There would have been no time then. Years before. I would rant and rail against it insanely, even then. I think he knew that, unless I gave my word, I would never have the strength to keep my knowledge from Andrew when the time came.

"So all I have suffered," she continued, and her voice dropped lower, deep with emotion, "I have suffered with the knowledge that deliverance lay within the power of my own hand—"

"If you chose to betray Alexander and lose your integrity!" Edwin couldn't bear the pain in her voice.

"As you have done, Edwin." It was half a statement, half a question, and she spoke it softly, but with horrible impact.

"It's different with me!" Edwin cried out. "Surely you can see that, Jessie!"

"Different, Edwin? Integrity is integrity and falsehood, falsehood. You've created a shaded area of gray for yourself that feels comfortable and safe. But it's an illusion, Edwin. I know."

He tried to explain, panic rising within him, realizing that if he didn't make her understand now, he never would. She let him talk. When he paused she asked him,

"What did Andrew tell you? What did he say?"

"You know the lad, Jessie. He's always had such exaggerated

ideas of morality. He doesn't believe he can ever trust me or work with me again. He thinks—"

"Did he send you away, Edwin?"

How did she guess that, even about Andrew? he wondered.

"He didn't know what he was saying, Jessie!"

Jessie began to protest, and panic rose in Edwin again, like a bitter bile.

"What did you expect me to do, Jessie? What would you have done? Stand by and see your future—all that is rightfully yours—snatched out of your hands by some unknown person who doesn't give a hang—someone who may not even exist?"

Jessie didn't answer him. She rose and opened the grate, stirring the remaining fire until it began to spark and glow deeply again. She turned to face him with a sigh.

"I don't know, Edwin. I don't really know what I would do in your place. I only know what I have done in my own. I only know that, despite my personal feelings and prejudices, there are certain things I would never stoop to and never countenance."

"Implying that you've taken it like a man, and I have not! You may have imagined that you had a lot to lose, Jessie. But you didn't. Andrew came home to you safe and sound. You had two loving children and the memory of a husband who adored you. Wealth, security, luxury, beauty, influence—shall I go on?"

"And what did you have to lose, Edwin? Money. A little money, and nothing more. And I might have lost Andrew. Life is never certain, and I knew that well. Death, disease, evil—any of them might have claimed him from me. He might not have come home to me at all." She paused and looked down at the pattern her foot was tracing on the thick oriental rug.

"I've lost him in some measure, as it is. He'll be bringing Hannah Martin home with him, you must know." She looked up and met Edwin's eyes. "Which is one good reason why you must do as he said and go away, Edwin. After what you have done to frighten and harass the girl, you could never expect her to accept you as—"

"Accept! It's a grand thing, Jessie, to hear you talking so sweetly about acceptance. I take it *you've* accepted the idea of Hannah—a stranger, an *American*—coming home to be Andrew's wife."

She winced beneath his words, but he went on.

"Whence this great strength, Jessie? This sudden rallying to the cause? You who have always hidden behind your anger and raving, your weak and ridiculous fears!"

She looked up at him slowly; when he began to speak again, she shook her head and moved her hand in the air, as though waving aside his rudeness and his cruelty.

"You accuse me justly, Edwin. I've allowed things to be very much as you've described them for too long. You see—" She hesitated, struggling with the pride which had ruled her all these years.

"You see, after that first devastating time when I failed so miserably, I've never needed to be strong. Alexander was always there, and then Andrew. They were strong for me. I've now come to see that it was easy, much too easy to hide."

She had never looked more noble, more fair. Edwin's admiration rose in his throat, and he choked back the emotion. It was dangerous and much too painful to feel this way. He had always known that behind that beautiful exterior, somewhere within the fine spirit and mind, this kind of soaring quality existed.

"My strength," she said, and her voice was low and sad, "has come at a price, Edwin. An exquisite price. But it has come at last."

He looked at her, not knowing what to answer. She moved closer to him, and he saw that her eyes were wet, swimming in tears.

"Too late for you," she said, so low he barely heard her. "I have indulged my weakness too long, and now you are the one who suffers because of me."

She thought of many things as she spoke, many times when she might have swayed the course of his life. Even the will, the malignant will that had corrupted him, would never have been seen by Edwin's eyes if it were not for her own weakness and pride.

"Don't, Jessie! Please don't!" She was crying now, and he couldn't bear the sight of it.

"It will be better for you, Edwin, as well as for Andrew—this enforced separation, this facing of reality. Perhaps one day he will come to understand and forgive you, as I hope you may come to understand—or at least to forgive—me."

He started toward her, but she raised her hand and moved silently to the door. She opened it, then stood aside. Edwin paused when he reached her, but she didn't look up. He passed through the doorway, and she listened as he gathered his luggage in the hall.

Jessie had thought there was nothing left in her heart to break. She stood and cried, heedless, anguished tears. *I have always wanted to cry for myself,* she thought, *and have hidden the weakness of tears behind my pride. Have I never cared enough to cry over the pain and suffering of someone else?* She marveled at her former pathetic and tragic egocentrism and self-love. The bitter tears fell, in themselves some sort of a balm, a cleansing of the deep wound inside.

23

Go thy ways; the field is won;—
Well, forward, forward!

THE TAMING OF THE SHREW

The Illinois air was cold, but the morning sky was clear and the sun was just beginning to light upon the brittle, ravaged fields, revealing briefly their subtle splendor; gold and bronze and rustling brown, shining silver beneath the dazzle of the white sun. The air was wild with birds and a dozen fragrances, tangy, mellow and bittersweet, so that Andrew, walking alone in the deserted streets, trembled with the tension of life and beauty which only the last bold defiance of autumn can produce.

In an hour he would drive over and pick up Nan. At noon he would phone Salt Lake to see what Heber Shumway had to report. He smiled to himself as he remembered the elation in Heber's voice on the phone yesterday when he heard the news of Nan's discovery. Andrew and Nan had gone over the lists of wagon trains again and found the Richards family, whose children included an infant, Charles Andrew. Armed with this information, Heber ought to be able to turn up something. . . .

Andrew had wanted to call his mother then, too, but had decided to send only a telegram now, assuring her that things were all right and that he would call in a day or two with more details. Things were happening quickly, and it gave him a heady feeling.

He rounded the corner onto Munson Street and thought he heard someone call his name. He looked back to see Grant waving his arms, so Andrew retraced his steps and joined him.

"What are you doing out so early, young man, and where's Hannah?"

"Nan's asleep still, I hope. She had a big day yesterday."

"And yourself?"

Andrew smiled. "I've got a lot of thinking to do."

"I'm sure you do; I'm sure you do."

They walked together and talked of the discovery in Daniel's journal, of Heber's possibilities for coming up with some missing descendants, of Nan's harrowing experiences of the past few weeks.

The old man was so easy to talk to, so easy to trust, that Andrew found himself telling Grant Morgan about Edwin. Not everything, but enough that the burden wasn't so difficult to bear. Grant listened attentively, and when he spoke he didn't say much, but it was what Andrew needed, and by the time they reached Grant's house the companionship between them was deeper than before.

They reached Grant's door and the old man asked him to please come inside for a moment. Andrew agreed and followed him through the door. Grant sat heavily in a worn chair and indicated another for Andrew.

"I'm too old to be giving lectures," he said, "and I suppose you'd consider yourself too old to have to listen." Grant's eyes twinkled, though his voice had grown serious. "I promised myself if I ever got you alone, Andrew, I'd at least give you some pretty strong instructions on the kind of care I expect you to take of Nan. But I don't think that's really necessary any more."

He looked into the young man's eyes, glad again of what he was able to read there.

"But there is one thing I'm still concerned about."

"Yes?" Andrew knew how much the old man liked him and trusted him, but he could feel the real concern in Grant's voice.

"Well, I don't know just how much Hannah's told you, Andrew. But these last few months have marked quite a change in her life." He paused. "Maybe I'd better tell you from the beginning." At least this might gain a little more understanding from the boy. And Nan was going to need as much understanding and cooperation from Andrew as she could get.

So Grant told the story of Nan's childhood, including kindly but honestly Abraham's stipulations concerning his daughter, including his and Ellen's desires to teach her of their Mormon faith. Andrew listened, wide-eyed, and by the end of the tale his eyes were wet; he leaned forward and grasped the old man's hands tightly in his.

"I was right," he said, his eyes shining. "The feeling I had in the Seventies Hall yesterday. The miracles aren't over yet, are they?"

"I don't quite follow you, Andrew."

"Why hasn't she told me, though? I wonder why she hasn't said a word about it? But then, I haven't said anything to her. So much has been happening, so many unbelievable things to talk about and marvel over. And perhaps the lass was afraid, not certain what my reaction would be—"

"Andrew, for mercy's sake, I'm an old man! Will you please hold up and start back somewhere where I can follow?"

Andrew laughed, patted Grant's hands once, then let them drop, and settled back into his chair.

"You're going to like this story, Grant Morgan. I can assure you of that."

"Still asleep! Well, wake her up, Julie." Julie started up a few steps, then paused and looked back at Andrew uncertainly.

"Hurry, lass, hurry."

He had come here straight from Grant's house, and he couldn't wait much longer. How he had enjoyed watching the old man's face as he told him of Janet and his father and his own conversion to the principles of Mormonism. What had Grant said? Something about the salt of the earth and the sons of Abraham coming into their own? Andrew loved the old man, and realized that the time they had just shared was the closest thing to a substitute for his relationship with his father that he could ever have hoped for. How he wished he could talk to his own father now!

Julie's head appeared at the top of the stairs. "Five more minutes, Andrew."

"And not a second longer," he called out. "I've already started timing."

At last Nan was there, coming down the stairs toward him.

"I'll forgive you for sleeping so long, if you're going to look this beautiful when you wake up." He was teasing her, talking lightly, but her beauty and his love for her were overwhelming.

"Is anything the matter, Andrew?"

He loved the deep, intense look on her features when she was concerned for him.

"The matter is this, Hannah Martin. You've turned into a Mormon girl, right under my nose, and I didn't know a thing about it."

She was staring at him and her face was white. He cupped his hand under her elbow and began leading her through the kitchen toward the back door.

"What could you possibly find attractive about Mormonism?" He screwed his face up into a concentrated scowl. "Of course—it would be their marriage in the temple you'd be liking. I should have thought of that."

They were at the door and he turned her to face him. She squirmed and the little white face turned to a lovely, rosy shade.

"For the life of me I can't imagine what anyone could find attractive in the idea of being married to one person forever and ever."

He pulled her into his arms and kissed her. She started to pull back, flustered, embarrassed at his open attentions with her grandmother in the next room and Jonathan whistling just outside the window. But he drew her close again and whispered against her hair. "Though, to tell the truth, lass, one more kiss like that and you might begin to convince me."

She drew away from him then, and saw that his eyes were spilling over with mischief.

"Andrew! How dare you? You're awful! You're teasing me!"

"I'm in love with you, Hannah." He drew her close again, and this time she did not draw away. "A hundred times more in love with you this morning than I was last night." He took her arm and led her through the door and into the big backyard. "And you and I have a lot to talk about."

"Wait just a minute, Heber. I didn't get that last name. Go over it again, will you?"

214

Andrew couldn't believe that he was so nervous and excited.

"That's okay, Andrew. This is what—only the third time you've dropped your pen?" Heber was delighted. "You ready now? We'll start again. Charles Richards. The infant son of Charles and Rachel Buchanan, whom Thomas and Emma Richards took in when Rachel died."

"Heber," Andrew interrupted. "Why wasn't his name preserved? Why didn't Emma Richards keep some record of his parents? You'd think she would have, especially if she was as devoted to Rachel as Daniel Martin's diary indicates."

"Perhaps she did. You may be interested to know that Emma Richards didn't survive the trip across the plains. She was buried somewhere near South Pass in Wyoming. Thomas married again, shortly after they arrived in the valley. And records, you must remember, Andrew, were much more haphazard back then."

"Yes, I suppose you're right. And they could have been easily lost, I would imagine. And the second wife might not have even been aware—I mean, she—"

"Andrew! Do you want these names, or don't you? When you get here Lucille will make us a double banana split and we can talk about the could have beens and the possibilities to your heart's content."

"All right, Heber, all right. Who did you say was excited?"

Heber read off the names and Andrew copied them carefully, along with addresses. There were two great-grandsons and a great granddaughter living in the Salt Lake area, and another in California: Bradley, James, Sheila, and Mary Ann. Bradley William was the oldest. Andrew hung up the phone and turned to Nan, his eyes shining.

"Two great-grandsons, two great-granddaughters. Names, addresses, and phone numbers!"

"Andrew! Doesn't it seem strange? Just knowing their names makes them seem more real."

"Bradley W. is the oldest. We'll begin with him."

They were both eager now to get going—to leave for Salt Lake City and find these people who were the last link in the chain, the triumph, the culmination—not only for themselves, but for those forces which had silently worked toward this end for over one hundred years.

But there were still many details to take care of, things to tie together and arrange. And perhaps the happiest of these was their baptism. Through the quiet park they walked, down Locust Lane where the giant elm had split and spread full across the path. Here Andrew read Nan's letter, which expressed more beautifully than she could speak the feelings and desires of her heart. There was too much to talk about, too much to comprehend all at once. But as soon as they spoke them out loud to one another, their convictions took on a glow and a power which startled them both.

They met with Grant and some of the local missionaries, anxious to begin the discussions, anxious to have every question answered, every beautiful principle drawn out and explained.

Later, after the missionaries had left, they stood before Grant together and asked if he could arrange to be the one to baptize them into the Church. This had been the pinnacle, the wildest reach of his and Ellen's dreams when they had prayed about Nan together through all the long years. This perfect fulfillment of his desires was nearly too much for the old man. He took each of them by the hand and asked if they would kneel with him in prayer. And, perhaps unwittingly, he gave them one precious gift which they both were in need of: an example.

In simple, yet beautiful language—flowing, natural, and sincere —Grant spoke to his Father in heaven. The two young people listened as he poured out the feelings of his heart: his gratitude, his joy, his faith. Then, with wonder in their own hearts, they heard him pray over them. His familiarity with the personage he was addressing was easy to recognize, but his own power, his confidence as he pleaded for them and their future, was something Nan and Andrew had never experienced before. They rose, their ecstasy shining in their eyes, marveling that this kind of joy and culmination could ever come to pass. But Grant knew that this was only the beginning.

The next morning, with an anxious heart, Andrew called his mother, longing to be able to really share with her the things that had been happening and the feelings he now was experiencing inside. Instead, he gave her a scanty outline of the events which had taken place, skimming over anything he felt might upset her too much. To his surprise she interrupted him.

216

"You're not really telling me anything, Andrew. You sound as though you're reciting a long and distasteful lesson at school, anxious to reach the end and be done with it."

Andrew couldn't help laughing, in spite of his shocked reaction to what she had said.

"Yes, I suppose that's exactly what I sound like. I'm sorry, I—I'm—"

She ignored his attempt at apology, wondering what she could say that wouldn't be maudlin or melodramatic but would help him understand that she had changed, that things would be different now.

"I'm interested, Andrew," she told him. "More than you realize. Now start again, please, and tell me everything this time."

He hesitated, unable to believe what was happening, not knowing how to react. But his mother was warm and attentive, asking questions, responding with sensitivity and delight, urging him on. It was easier this way, Jessie decided. Less humbling than confronting him face to face. Andrew, warmed by her attitude and responses, decided to try once more, and opened his heart to her in ways he had never anticipated doing again. She was there. She had never been there before. He could tell by the tone of her voice, by the words she spoke, that something new had come to life within her.

"There's so much still to tell, Mother," he said at last, "some things I really don't want to talk about until I get home."

He thought of Edwin as he spoke, and of his own baptism, which would be one of the most difficult things for her to accept. There were too many changes at once, most of them things he would have expected would appall his mother. How, just because of this difference he had detected in her, could he expect her to accept them all? He hesitated.

"Some of them, I'm afraid, you're not going to like in the least."

Jessie knew, and sensed, much more than he realized.

"I know that, Andrew," she replied. "And I'm going to try to be prepared. I can't promise that everything will be smooth and happy and easy, but I don't want you to worry about it. I've let you worry about everything in the past. I don't want it to be like that any more."

She talked of the wedding then, urging him to set a date, to make definite arrangements and plans, until he said they were leaving for Salt Lake in a day or so, and promised that he would call as soon as they

217

returned to Nauvoo. She could talk to Nan then, and they could plan the wedding together.

Jessie wondered what Andrew would do if he knew how terrified she was at the idea of talking to this girl, of meeting her long-distance that way. Nan, of course, would be frightened and uncertain, too. It was difficult—nearly impossible—for Jessie to think of herself as a mother-in-law; she knew that she mustn't look too far ahead, but take one small step at a time, else her strength would fail her and she wouldn't be able to make it at all.

So she forced herself to think only of this moment; what to say to Andrew right now. And she discovered that she loved it, the feeling of strength and power it gave her. After Andrew hung up she walked in the gardens alone and thought it through, and perceived that this was a very different kind of power, this power to make people happy. There were too many counterfeits in the world, she decided, and the realization nearly overwhelmed her. She had thought she possessed power before—power based on self-indulgence, unkindness, and fear. And she had been terrified at the prospect of giving it up, never dreaming that this other power—beautiful and dignified—was waiting for her.

Andrew and Hannah wandered Nauvoo, a city now chill and wind-swept; swept, too, of tourists and noise and confusion, so that their spirits walked the quiet places in harmony with the spirits that had come and gone before. They talked and talked, for the future was a bright gem before them, with so many gleaming points and shimmering possibilities to look forward to and explore.

There was one dark part of the past that still needed to be put to rest. So with pain in his heart Andrew told Nan about Edwin, the stranger who had looked like him, but had seemed ominous and evil, not gentle and full of love. It was easier after having talked with Grant, but it was still one of the most difficult things Andrew would ever have to do in his life.

"You would have loved him, Nan. You may not believe it, but if it wasn't for all this, you would have loved him as I do."

She took him into her arms and held him, aching for him, but feeling at the same time motherly and warm and strong. "I love you," she whispered against his hair. "I love you, Andrew, I love you." And she thought to herself, *This is a part of being a woman that I've never even dreamed about before.* And her mind was filled with the wonder and beauty that she was only beginning to understand. And when his lips touched hers at last, she kissed him eagerly, from the depths of an inner response to him which was too encompassing, too total to deny.

Walking hand in hand through the cemetery, standing together at the gravesite, they decided to order new headstones for Charles and Rachel, choosing an inscription carefully, and resolving, out of respect to Daniel, to include the original inscription as well. It was Nan's idea, really, and when Andrew protested, saying that the right lay now with Brad and James and Sheila and Mary Ann, she disagreed.

"The right is ours, Andrew. Without us Charles and Rachel wouldn't even exist for those great-grandchildren in Salt Lake City and California. We can tell them that the old stones were destroyed, but we need not tell them why and how."

"In deference to Edwin?"

"Yes, in deference to Edwin. And to you—and to many things that are too hard to express."

In the afternoon they parted. Andrew still had some things to take care of, he said, and Nan wanted to say goodbye to Grant alone.

She walked the familiar path to his door, exquisitely aware of the countless times she had walked there since the days of her childhood. She had grown and changed with the years, but always it had been the same person: Hannah—a little older, a little altered, but Hannah still. Today was different. Today she was a new person, with new goals, new desires, and a totally changed outlook on life.

It frightened her. For even though the future shone with the brightness of a dream come true, nothing it contained would be familiar and known: her home, her station, her way of life—even her name—everything would be alien and new.

Grant held her and let her talk out her fears as he always had done.

"The unknown is bound to be frightening," he assured her, "and this much change heaped up at once is a little overwhelming. But it's the only path to happiness and fulfillment that I know—and you're prepared to walk it, Nan."

"Do you really think so?" she asked him, with the innocent tone of a child, as though his judgment, his faith would make a difference.

"I know so. And no one can know better than I. And besides, you'll have a lot of help, remember? The Lord will take care of you, Nan."

She nodded and smiled up at him through gathering tears.

"He's already proven that he can do a pretty good job, don't you think? And once you step into the waters of baptism, you're going to open up so many new ways for him to enter your life and bless you, Nan."

They sat together in silence—Hannah wondering how she was going to live without Grant's care and strength, and Grant, guessing her thoughts, wondering how long it would take her to discover the love and support behind his simple assurance that the Lord would take care of her. He smiled to himself, knowing what kind of power he was trusting her to.

It was late when Nan at last returned home. She only hoped that it wasn't too late, for there was one very important thing she still had to do.

The door to her father's study was closed. She knocked hesitantly, hoping he was inside.

He came to the door himself and invited her in. She perched on the edge of a chair uncomfortably. He looked over at her, and there seemed nothing but awkwardness between them.

"You all ready for your big adventure tomorrow?" he asked, his voice almost expressionless.

"I think so. Though there have been so many things to organize and remember that I'm afraid I've forgotten something."

He smiled slightly. "I doubt it, Nan. You've always been too well organized for that."

She smiled back. "I suppose so," she admitted.

"Andrew says you'll both be baptized as soon as you complete the missionary discussions after you return from Salt Lake. Are you ready for that, Nan?"

"Father! I didn't think you knew! I was going to try and tell you—I mean—" She was embarrassed now, and confused. "When did you talk to Andrew?"

"This afternoon. He had a deuce of a time finding me. We had a nice long visit." He paused, struggling with himself.

"He's quite a boy, Hannah. You see, he came to ask me for your hand." Abraham chuckled a little, on the verge of embarrassment himself.

"You didn't know, I can see, or you wouldn't sit there so dumbfounded. Perhaps that's still the way in Scotland. I don't know—I didn't ask him. But it's a very proper, very old custom which has been neglected here for a long time."

"You must have been so surprised, Father."

"Yes, I certainly was." He paused, then looked directly into her eyes. "And very pleased, Nan. Very pleased."

"Oh, Father, I'm so glad!"

Suddenly she was beside him and his arm was around her.

"I know you love me now," she said, without looking up. "I didn't see it before. I didn't realize—"

She could never actually tell him what she knew, what Grant had revealed to Andrew, and how grateful she was for knowing at last how much both he and Grant had cared for her—even though their ways had been so different, so entirely incompatible. Nor could she express how much she had come to understand him because of Daniel, who had the same fierce pride and noble sensitivity, which can sour a man and break his spirit when he is forced to suffer almost more than he can bear.

She couldn't tell him any of that, but they did talk. And the longer they talked the easier it became. And when at last the light disappeared from the little square window at the back of the house, Abraham Martin had found his daughter. And because he had found her, he was able to let her go.

It was an early-morning flight. The day was blue and clear, and warm for November. Nan sat by the window watching the thin line of clouds and the blue expanse above. There was no sense of substance or proportion here! A small plane passed, blown along, tossed, it seemed, by some power which held it in tumultuous, capricious control. What are we sitting on, she thought suddenly? What's holding us up?

She glanced over at Andrew and saw that he was watching her, amused by her reactions. He looked over her shoulder and leaned forward suddenly.

"We're approaching the Colorado Rockies! Look, Nan!"

Nan pressed her face against the little spot of glass, straining to catch her first glimpse of a mountain. The clouds thinned and disappeared, and below her, carved against the outline of land and sky, spread range after range of mountain. Jagged lines of snow crisscrossed the gray expanses, which sprawled in mammoth curves, or rose in lofty pinnacles, proud and defiant and rugged against the sky. It was a splendor such as Nan had never seen; cloud and sky and rock, merging together in beauty and power too magnificent to comprehend! She turned to Andrew, her eyes alight with wonder.

"Immensity made manifold," she said, with awe in her voice. "Those are the only words I know to describe it."

"They do quite well. Whose are they?"

"Edna St. Vincent Millay's, from her *Renascence*. Oh, Andrew, I didn't know this kind of beauty existed!"

As they drew closer to Salt Lake City their anticipation rose.

"I'll point out the temple when we get close enough, Nan. We ought to be able to spot it quite easily."

He took her hand, smoothing it idly with his fingers. "It ought to be the very first thing you see."

"When you saw it, what did you think, Andrew?"

"Do you really want to know?"

She nodded.

"I stood gazing up the length of that solid gray mass, crowned by graceful spires, and I was overcome by the strength and nobility of the building itself. You can feel a certain power just looking at it, Nan. But, of course, I didn't know then that the real power comes from within; from what takes place inside the walls. Rachel knew. She understood that this power could unite her with Charles forever, past doubt, past death—as I plan for it to unite me, Nan, with you."

Nan leaned back against his shoulder and closed her eyes, almost fearful at the sweeping happiness which had been granted her so suddenly. She thought of the people whose lives she and Andrew were about to enter, to change and alter so dramatically. How altered her

222

own life was! Love and truth—united. She was beginning to believe that there was nothing these two powers could not achieve together.

In Salt Lake City the time was eight o'clock, and Brad Richards was running late. After a hasty breakfast he knotted his tie, pulled on his watch, then carefully lifted his ring out of the velvet-lined box that held it. Tonight was their anniversary, his and Jenny's. A good reason to remove the ring from its dark haven for a while. Its beauty would be an asset to the beauty of the day.

Brad took a few seconds to study the ring, as he usually did—this ring he had admired as far back as his memory would go. The one link with his real ancestry, passed to him as the eldest son of an unknown line.

Would he ever know? That was a question he couldn't answer. He had come to believe that, if it was meant for him to know, then, somehow, he would. So he had not given up his private quest. For the time being he had decided to keep praying and waiting and believing.

One day at a time. For one more day, at least.